J.B. DANE

RAVEN'S
MOON

Burns and Lea Books

LOUISVILLE   NEW YORK

Burns and Lea Books
7919 Niemann Drive
Louisville, Kentucky 40291
www.burnsandleabooks.com

Layout by www.formatting4U.com

Publisher's Note: This is a work of fiction. Names, characters, places, and incidents are a product of the author's imagination. Locales and public names are sometimes used for atmospheric purposes. Any resemblance to actual people, living or dead, or to businesses, companies, events, institutions, or locales is completely coincidental.

Raven's Moon: The Raven Tales Book One/ J.B. Dane -- 1st ed.
Ebook ISBN: 978-0-9995083-9-8
Paperback ISBN: 978-1-7339806-0-9

Dedicated to
my dachshundric nieces
Gizelle and Gretta Mae

Oh, and to the rest
of the family, too!

Prelude

Bram Farrell, the man who doesn't exist. That's my handle. I'm only a figment of Calista Amberson's imagination. A figment that's resulted in millions of rabid fans descending on bookstores to find out what Otherworld baddy she's cast me against in The Raven Tales.

Don't pity me. Pity poor Detroit. Well, *fictionalized* Detroit. I'm guessing *real* Detroit lacks witches, faeries, and other legendary types with murderous intent. The clients who show up at Raven Investigations never have a problem as simple as a cheating spouse.

Things in my world had been quiet lately, which made me nervous. You'd think that after twenty volumes' worth of situations, enough to leave any bird plucked clean, I'd welcome a break.

Yeah, right. Like that would happen.

Calie puts me through hell—frequently. I retaliate with writer's block, refusing to do what I know will get me flayed, gutted, possessed, crippled, or close to giving those proverbial daisies a push from the wrong side of *terra firma*. At least on paper.

I'd been idle much longer than usual, which is why I'd stopped by Calie's muse's office hoping to wheedle information about the twenty-first book. He and I both live in the same world, fortunately.

The muse was leaning back in his chair, his feet on his desk, the mockup of the first Raven Tales graphic novel propped on his chest.

"Look for yourself," he offered, waving me toward the door that connected to Calie's place. I hadn't known for long about the portal's existence, and I'd been fighting the urge to visit it again. There was no crossing the threshold between my world and the real world, but I'd considered an attempt.

A fella can dream.

Even if he's only alive when the ink hits the page.

Tonight, my glimpse wasn't of Calie's office but of a different room. Cushy place. No expense spared. Lots of windows, and beyond

1

them one hell of a nasty storm raging. It was past midnight, and though I couldn't see it, I knew the moon had risen. I could feel that it was gibbous and waxing, coming in at around 78 percent illumination.

How'd I know? Picture me shrugging.

Calista stood at what was obviously center stage, poised for act one. The way the torrent battered the landscape and rattled against the windows, the act would be a dramatic one.

I took the position she frequently wrote me into, shoulder propped against the doorjamb, arms crossed over my chest. Total stakeout mode, *sans* munchies.

The scene inched toward high drama. The sky cloaked in cloud, the wind drenched with rain, and Calie framed against the violence of it all within the archway that led to the wide patio beyond. She appeared to be transfixed by the scene, which usually meant she was imagining how to use the setting in the next book.

Then inertia turned to motion. Though I'd been expecting something to occur, it still took me by surprise when her hands fell to the lever door handles, pressed down and pulled them inward, throwing the room open to the storm.

The storm took the welcoming gesture to heart, roaring into the house, swirling around her with violent results. The long, silken folds of her robe lifted and snapped in the onrush of wind. The white streaks Mother Nature had artistically placed in Calie's dark tresses flew in unruly tendrils. Within a nanominute she was soaked to the skin, every line of her wizened body outlined by the clinging black gown beneath her robe. The robe, which should have been hanging in sodden folds around her as well, leapt with life, streaming with angel-wing grace behind her.

In the sky, a smoky roll of transparent cloud flashed briefly with the reflected glare of lightning, followed shortly by an ominous growl of thunder.

Calie lifted her arms to the storm, then turned her hands from palm up to the sides and brushed her long fingers through the air as if to push the clouds apart.

And, like the Red Sea obeying Moses, the damned things moved aside, curtains drawn on a stage to display the waxing moon front and center, bathed in cool, calm, pure white light while the night roiled around it.

"Sister!" Calista cried in welcome.

Now that was new.

She'd written similar scenes in some of the tomes I starred in, but in all the years she'd kept me on a leash in her mind, I'd thought only her pen took those rubbishy steps into prose.

Now she was cosplaying it. Story-wise, magic would follow.

Still, Calie's done enough research into the various lunar cults to know that a moon several days shy of being full was a lousy power source. Any wizard worth a bag of philosopher's stones knows that. Combine this with a genuinely lousy night for conjuring, and she was writing this volume's villain into the sort of trap Merlin stumbled into.

Apparently, the old girl cared not for such considerations, for her arms stayed raised in supplication to the storm. Or the moon. Whatever.

"Sister, have you heard my plea?" Calie's voice was pitched to a normal tone now, as if she were conversing with someone nearby. As far as I was aware, there was no one else around but me, the figment of her imagination.

"Shall you grant this wish?" Calie asked. "All that I do, I do in your name."

Who the hell was she talking to? A disembodied spirit? Someone who was equally nuts enough to be out in the storm? Hell, gusts were whipping the landscaping into a frenzy!

Was it a hitherto unknown sister? I lived in Calie's mind, and I'd never run into a stray memory of a sister. A heck of a lot of discarded lovers, but no sister.

Extremely uncivilized to invite one over on such a night. Unless she'd passed beyond the physical state and wasn't the type of spirit for whom one dropped the drawbridge down over the moat.

Calie closed her eyes and stepped further out into the storm, her miraculously alive cloak flying, snapping, and soaring around her as the rain pelted down.

Insanity reigned. Pneumonia would no doubt frolic in its shadow. Calie was blind to the possibility of either. If anything, she moved farther from the woman I thought I knew. As though she'd been reenergized, her arms lifted higher, were spread wider.

"Sister!" she cried once more, voice rising in volume as though she needed to be heard over the storm. "I call on Menily, on Huitaca, Chia, and Ka-Ata-Killa of the council of goddesses."

3

Was it my imagination, or had Calie's voice caressed the syllables of each name before they were caught up by the wind?

I knew those names. They were all moon goddesses, though not the ones commonly heard by modern ears. They belonged to the long-dead tribal wilderness of America.

This wasn't Calista's normal mode of plotting a story. She'd never enacted a scene physically before, much less keep secrets from me that involved research into beings I'd be facing down in an adventure. What was my creator up to?

Beyond her, the moonlight wavered as though disturbed by unseen, vaguely human figures, forms that were mist-like and yet not part of the storm.

Calie was firmly in chant mode now, for more names dripped free into the night. The goddesses of not exactly kindly religions. What might any of these deities attempt to do to me in Book 21? I was going to get totally screwed in the next volume, and not in a good way.

Names rilled as Calie plucked deities from more ancient pantheons, her voice as strong as it had been at the start. There wasn't a hint of the cough that had plagued her these past months. As she added to her tally, the silhouettes of more moonlight beings joined those already formed. They were separate yet joined, pinned by Luna's spotlight. None moved. They waited as my creator requested that they guide her words, weave a spell.

I'd mentally been ticking off the names—she'd tallied up thirty-five already—charting the course Calie was taking through godlings' halls around the world, but that one word shredded my concentration. A spell? Calie was working a spell?

Holy hell spawn! This had nothing to do with the plot line of a book. This was serious shit!

Or else it was one seriously dangerous way to research the old ones.

While I dealt with this mental machete strike, Calista swayed slightly, as though each additional manifestation drew energy from her. Yet she continued, adding more obscure and nearly forgotten goddesses, until she had forty-three deities seeming to hover just beyond the open doors.

"I petition you, sisters, to make the wish flesh."

Her plea was barely voiced when a jag of lightning struck a hapless tree somewhere in the woods that bracketed the house beyond the well-manicured swath of lawn. The crack of the tree's cry added punctuation to her prayer. The thunderous boom that followed seconds later appeared to be an answer from the skies. Considering she'd called back nearly every lunar goddess the planet had known since mankind took a chance on walking upright, it could be nothing else.

Calie had pitted me against paranormals, demons, and the more vicious beings and creatures of legend in The Raven Tales. Could she be about to throw me into the already-bubbling cauldron of an ancient god in the next book? Or perhaps that of more than one manifestation of a goddess?

The wraiths gathered in that moonbeam had seemed centered on Calista, but now their attention appeared to shift to where I stood in the doorway. Creepy. Really creepy, considering I was the guy Calie merely *pictured* propping up the doorjamb. How could they know I was there?

"Sister!" Calie shouted again into the wind.

Which of the horde of gathered goddesses had she addressed? Not that they were really separate, considering all names were aspects of the glowing lunar orb above. Well, partial orb. She was one-fifth shy of being full. Yet the building power behind the light, behind those gathered goddesses, was palpable. Even a non-magical human would have felt the weight of it.

The light crept into the room, covering Calie and casting a long shadow behind her. The shadow touched the floor at my feet. Then Calista shifted slightly to the side, and moonlight struck me as the wisps of the gathered goddesses rushed forward.

Whether it was the power of the chanted words, the assault by the spirits of nearly forgotten deities, or the stunning effect of the heightened candle-power of that lunar glow, something unseen hit me. It swirled around, dived through me, leaving an unnatural chill working its way through my arms, legs, chest, mind. Felled to my knees, I gripped the doorjamb to keep from falling flat on the faded fibers of Calie's favorite antique Oushak rug.

The tips of my fingers tingled. I felt the way the cut of my jacket pulled across my shoulders, the way my toes flexed within my boots as I knelt, determined not to be forced into the prostrate pose of a supplicant worshipper in the onslaught. *Fixate on something, moron,* I snarled. Fictional experience had to count for something. I knew better than to let any Otherworld type get control of my body or gain a hold on my mind.

But it wasn't the goddesses or the moonlight that was the problem. As I stared at the protection symbols the Turkish weaver had incorporated into the design of the rug, the colors mesmerized me. Startling shades and variations that contrasted, complemented, and blended into new hues, colors I had not realized were missing from my monochromatic visual repertoire. They were there now, blazing in the moonlight. As the goddesses dissipated into the night, I saw deep, rich reds, glowing golds, midnight blues, and lush greens mixing with the familiar whites, blacks, and thousands of shades of gray that were all my fictional eyes had ever seen, even though Calie delighted in running through a universe of shades in her descriptions. They'd been words, not colors, to me before. Now they were sensuously real, and they seared my sight with their beauty.

My sight wasn't the only sense to suffer turmoil. I'd also suddenly been cursed with a sense of touch, or so it seemed, considering the way the fluted edge of the doorjamb bit into my fingers. My shoulder ached from leaning on that same doorjamb earlier. Feelings of hunger and thirst prodded, lusts I'd never experienced, though on the page I knew I favored mushrooms and peppers on pizza, drank aged Kentucky bourbon, and shared with E.T. a weakness for Reese's Pieces.

I could even feel the beat of my heart.

And I could hear a rush of blood through my veins as my hearing also intensified. The storm I'd watched so casually cranked its volume to a deafening roar. I could hear the rain lash the windows on either side of the open doors, could identify the rattle of drops hurled at the plantings near the house. The wind was a scream and the lightning a veritable front line explosion when it flashed.

I confess I cowered before these new sensations, arms over my head, trying to protect both eyes and ears but failing miserably. Each bolt Zeus loosed flared with blinding brightness. I could taste the rain in the air, although I was at least twenty feet back from where it invaded the room. Astonishingly, I heard an agonized groan and realized it had originated in my throat.

Calista stayed silhouetted in the archway, though her back was turned partly away from the storm. In the moonlight, I could see her aging face break into a smile of nearly childish delight.

"Bram." She breathed my name in a rather reverent way.

Only then did it truly strike me.

A character born on a computer screen, brought to life only in a million print runs in over forty languages, a character who had a Wikipedia entry of his own, did not feel physical discomfort, could neither hear a sound nor identify a scent or taste, and could not be blinded, much less speak and be heard.

I pushed to my feet. Took a step forward—my first step—stumbled and caught my balance on the back of a chair. The texture of the polished wood, the softness of the cloth and the scent of beeswax polish were nearly enough to unman me. *Me!* The guy who faced down demons in book after book and limped away only partially the worse for such wear.

"What...?"

But Calie had already turned back to the night and lifted her chin to gaze at the still-visible moon.

"Thank you, sister," she whispered, drawing her hands together to assume a worshipful stance.

In the sky beyond, the clouds closed over the lunar face once more. Only the storm remained, and it was moving away. This act of the play had firmly closed.

But not for me. My story was at Chapter One, and there was a lot of unknown world to cover in a life that might still last for the span of ninety thousand words but not much longer.

I was her boon, the reason she'd cast a spell. To give me a physical presence in the real world her wish, and it had been granted. Why she'd made the request, how she'd contrived the spell and gathered the power, I had a feeling would be up to me to discover.

But apparently, when a congress of forty-three goddesses and one insane author put their heads together, a moon registering 78 percent luminescence can work some powerful shit.

Who'da guessed?

7

Day One, October 27

Was I human now? I doubted it, though what did *human* feel like? I'd been a creation on paper, just a string of words to describe my actions, my thoughts. Every word credited to me had come from the clatter of a keyboard.

I was more than that but less than—well, whatever—yet. There was a path that needed to be discovered, a sense of self that was absent. There were too many distractions, too many questions to ask.

And Calie was in no condition to answer them.

Once the storm passed and the night quieted, Calie collapsed on the sofa, apparently lacking the strength to make it to her bed. Careless of her drenched state and tangled hair, she simply murmured, "Not tonight, Bram," and passed out, but not before the plague-like cough made its reappearance.

When I grabbed the fringed length of fabric tossed decoratively over the back of Calie's reading chair, the pure softness of the thing against my newly gifted sense of touch was enough to make me forget what I'd grabbed it for. Once I shook free of the mesmerizing experience and draped the cloth over Calista's unconscious form, I checked the lock on the now-closed patio doors and drew the heavy drapes across every window in the room and in the study next door.

Security chores seen to, I settled behind Calie's desk with a bottle of bourbon and a cut crystal tumbler. My hand shook a bit while handling the unaccustomed weight, but once bottle and tumbler kissed and two fingers of Evan Williams bourbon sloshed into readiness, I was girded for still more sensory battering.

The scent of the bourbon wasn't familiar, and while between the covers of a book I might have been able to discern the effect that twenty-three years in an oak barrel might have contributed to the finished product, right then I was more interested in the numbing effect it might have.

It took two drinks to accomplish that numbing, accompanied by a burn in my throat and stomach that hurt and satisfied at the same time. Perhaps I should have found some pizza to accompany the whiskey down my gullet.

I didn't sleep that night. Couldn't remember that sleep had ever been written into my script in the past. With hours to fill before my creator (in more ways than one, now) stirred, I rifled through her desk, looking for any notes she might have ferreted away about the next book. The search came up empty. I cranked up her laptop.

Luck was with me. She hadn't changed any passwords. Not a bit of treasure came to light, though. Not even a tentative title or newly created file. Defeat was difficult to admit, but as the sun cast aside the swaddling clouds and pushed a determined path through a gap in the drapes, I gave up and headed for the kitchen. It was time to test-drive those bright and shiny new senses again.

The number one item on Calie's "must have" list was a chef. A status thing, I presumed. The current chef was female. The music spilling from the room indicated she had a weakness for Michael Bublé. Mike's voice was already stroking the cook's soul, courtesy of a portable CD player, insisting she should call him irresponsible.

I knocked on the cabinet nearest the door to get the chef's attention. Being irresponsible might have resulted in her spilling hot, spitting oil from the skillet she had in hand.

"Morning," I called.

The appearance of a strange man in the kitchen, hours before the mistress ever chose to rise, didn't faze her a bit. A smile lit her classically molded face as she slid the pan back onto the burner.

"Oh, you must be the nephew," she greeted, her accent claiming that she hailed from somewhere in the middle of New England. "The one Ms. Amberson named that character in her books after."

Hmm. Seemed Calie had paved the way for my arrival.

"Yup, that's me. Bram Farrell," I said.

"You must have been little more than a toddler when she started writing," she declared. "I'll bet there are even people who think you're lying when you tell them your name."

"You got it. They think I'm fictional." Which, up until a few hours ago, I had been. Perhaps I still was.

"I'm P. T. Kosmas." A hastily wiped hand was extended my way.

9

I shook it. "P. T. as in Cruiser?"

"As in Philomena Theora," she said. "You can see why I decided to shorten it."

"But not to Phil."

"Too butch for me. You're probably looking for a cuppa coffee," she said, grabbing a serviceable mug from the nearest cupboard. "You take it black like your fictional namesake or with cream and sugar?"

"Sugar." Considering my fictional self preferred thick Turkish coffee, which when delivered was already an overly sweet sludge, I'd probably need the two-pronged kick of caffeine and sugar high to survive the day. Dealing with my new senses was not going to be... well, *easy* hardly described it.

P. T. motioned me to take a seat at the kitchen island and reached for the already freshly brewed coffee. "You an early bird, then? Ms. Amberson is never up until noon."

"Night owl," I said. The Raven—the moniker nasties knew me best as in the series—stalked night creatures. "Just dealing with a major case of time zone confusion today."

Okay, I lied. That also went with The Raven's territory.

She slid the mug across to me. It was a promotional product for *Raven Takes Rook*, the most recent of my fictional adventures. A reproduction of Calie's scrawled signature was on one side, the book's cover on the other, featuring a Hunter's Moon and an artist's rendition of me. I'd have to find a mirror to see if I looked anything like the guy featured. Somehow, I doubted I did.

"Then this will be the only breakfast you'll be needing?" P. T. asked, placing a spoon and sugar bowl next to the mug.

"I could always adjust my sleep priorities if you're offering food—or anything else—at the crack of dawn," I offered, adding a generous scoop of sugar to my coffee.

That wasn't a total fib. She was a nicely shaped woman, round in all the right places. Her fair curls clustered at her nape and ears and tumbled over her brow. Her eyes were blue, I suppose, for the shade was a near reflection of the now cloudless sky beyond the broad kitchen window. The come-hither grin curving her lips wasn't bad, either.

P. T. chuckled. "Oh, you've as wicked a tongue as Ms. Amberson writes for the other Bram, but yes, I am offering breakfast today. It's closing in on nine, though, which is not exactly the crack of dawn."

"Feels like it to me. What are we having?"

"A nice Mediterranean omelet."

"With a side of bacon?"

She frowned at me, then turned to the ingredients. "You don't understand what a Mediterranean diet consists of, do you?"

Considering she'd laid out a selection of fresh vegetables and herbs to be chopped up, I had a pretty good idea.

"Oh, I'm fine with it, as long as there are three to five pieces of bacon on the plate as well. Carnivores have their needs." Plus, I was curious to know what bacon really tasted like. With such a bad rep, it had to be a food fit for the gods. Those of Asgard rather than Olympus, of course.

P. T. blew a stray curl out of her face with a disgusted sound and reached for a chef's knife. Her wrist action was fast, accurate, and impressive as hell.

"Bacon isn't something I keep on hand."

"Prejudiced against pig products, huh?" I asked, taking shelter temporarily behind the mug.

"All I'm saying is that this household gets healthy meals. A bit of chicken, often fish, but in terms of meat, that's it. Tonight, Ms. Amberson is hosting her lady friends at dinner and requested we have octopus because the doctor told her to increase her iron intake," P. T. said, totally destroying any desire I might have had for dinner that evening. I'd had to deal with a kraken in the third book in the series, and I didn't fancy having anything with tentacles anywhere near me.

That Calie had been to the doctor's office was news, though. Had she gone about that nagging cough that had bothered her the past few years? I had little practical medical knowledge, but a dearth of iron didn't seem like something that would be connected with a chronic cough. Had Calie endured more than just a bloodletting for tests?

"Thanks for the warning." I raised my mug to P.T. in a salute. "Here's to finding a steak joint to amscray to this evening."

If Calista let me off the leash, that is. She certainly hadn't gone to the effort required to call me from the shadows to the solid world without a good reason. Would she give me a fond grin and wave me off to find my feet, so to speak, or turn despot and insist I be homebound?

"There's a place only a mile away," P. T. surprised me by saying as she put down her knife and scraped a neat pile of julienned vegetables and shredded herbs into the warming skillet. "The assistant manager went to culinary school with me. I'll call and make a reservation for you."

"Great! My metabolism thanks you."

She looked away from cracking eggs into a bowl to study me, one corner of her lower lip caught between her teeth, her head tilted to the side, her eyes slightly narrowed.

"Now, the question is, are you a toasted bread man or a whole grain muffin man?"

"A large cinnamon roll with thick cream cheese icing man."

"In other words, a culinary philistine and a future heart attack. You should take a note from your aunt's book," she suggested.

Which book? There were twenty of the damn things, and considering that I had eaten, though not tasted, the heaven of a soft, warm-from-the-oven cinnamon roll in more than one adventure, I was pretty sure Calie had a thing for them too. Or perhaps she *had* had a thing for them. That mysterious doctor's visit nagged at me.

"She never used to watch what she ate," I said. "When did this begin?"

I was serious. *When* had Calie begun to develop health problems? It was difficult to remember that while I'd only aged a little more than a year during the progression of the series, she had aged over twenty. Calie hadn't been young when she began writing me to very profitable life, either.

P. T. shrugged as she beat the eggs into submission. "No idea. I only took over the kitchen three months ago, but I'm under the impression she'd been trimming a lot of foods from her diet for a while before that."

I gulped down a mouthful of coffee. Whatever it was supposed to taste like, I decided this batch was nowhere close to Nirvana.

"Damn," I muttered.

Miss Efficiency was adding the eggs to the mix in her skillet, but she spared me a glance back over her shoulder. "Coffee not to your liking? We do have a variety of juices. I make them myself."

I pushed the mug aside. "What's in them? They're not those noxious things that look like fresh cement, are they?"

"Pure juice. Nothing added, and any seeds removed. Right now, all I've got made up is orange or carrot, though."

"Opting for orange, please," I requested. "It wasn't the coffee I was commenting on but why Calie didn't tell me she was worried about her health. I knew about the cough, but she spent years lighting one cigarette from the embers of another. Seemed a logical progression that she'd have throat problems as a result."

It was certainly why, in the series, I frequently fumbled for a cigarette or got possessive over any shaman's proffered pipe. Okay, so the pipes were loaded with damn powerful hallucinogenic shit. Sue me. Maybe I was in one of those dreams and only thought I was real.

"Your aunt doesn't seem to be close with family members," P. T. commented. "I didn't even know you existed until she told me you'd be coming to stay for a while."

A while. That didn't sound like I had a permanent gig in the real world. Wasn't sure how I felt about that. Yet.

"She's close to her female friends, though," P. T. continued as she headed to the refrigerator at the end of the long counter. It had two doors and looked capable of housing an abominable snowman. "They get together frequently. When the weather is nice, it's a picnic in the woods Ms. Amberson orders. There's a very pleasant, natural clearing there. As I'm heading for home, they troop off with baskets, blankets, and lanterns."

"You don't live on the estate?"

P. T. returned to the counter with a large carafe of liquid that I suppose was orange in color. There was so much to learn!

"Oh, now you're disappointed," she cooed, setting down the juice and a dinky little glass, gesturing for me to help myself while she turned back to the stove. "No sneaking from the guest room to some servant's attic room to tempt me into some lurid mischief."

I laughed. "Can't picture you in a dinky attic room, sweet."

"But you can see me getting up to mischief?"

"You said *lurid* mischief. Was that just to get my hopes up?"

She turned off the stove burner and whisked the omelet from the skillet, dividing it neatly onto two waiting plates.

"Perhaps," she admitted. "I'm not sure I should take anything a confessed carnivore tells me as gospel."

"I do have a reputation to live up to," I said. "Bram Farrell *is* the—"

13

"The Raven," she said, shaking her head.

My fictional self was more than merely a carnivore, a scavenger. He was a hunter.

So, I realized, was I.

I was rifling through Calie's financial papers in search of clues to who her doctor was, and whether he specialized in anything, when the doorbell pealed. A second later, P. T.'s voice blasted at me from the intercom on the desk. "I'm in the middle of kneading bread. Could you get that, Bram?"

Having no idea whether there was a button I should push to answer, I simply yelled, "Got it!" at the top of my lungs and pushed out of the comfy office chair. I'd only reached the study's open door, though, when I heard voices in the entryway.

"Don't you dare ask me what I'm doing here, Calista Amberson," a woman's voice growled. "You knew I wouldn't be able to wait until tonight to find out how things went. *If*, that is, you had the strength to do it yourself. I told you a group effort was needed."

"You could have called," Calie said at her most arrogant.

This would be interesting. I assumed the same stance I'd had when the moonlight whammied life into my fictional self the evening before. The sensation of the sharp edges of the doorjamb stabbing into flesh nearly made me reconsider. The stance was natural, though. Calie painted me thus poised, while on stakeout somewhere, in nearly every volume of The Raven Tales.

The unknown woman snorted inelegantly at the very suggestion of picking up the phone and brushed past Calista. "Patience might be my middle name, but it isn't a virtue I've ever nurtured, dearest, as you know quite well."

"Patience has never been your middle name, but judge for yourself, Delia," Calie invited, and gestured dramatically to where I stood. How she'd known I'd be in that spot, I've no clue. Probably just expected that I'd materialize where she wanted me. "Bram, meet your... hmm... distant cousin Delia Maddox."

The *distant cousin* swept down on me in a wave of perfume.

"Oh, my!" she gushed.

I straightened and stepped away from my convenient prop, hand extended to do things properly. The woman ignored my mitt and circled around me, taking an inventory of everything else in sight. I feared for a moment she'd decide a fondle would clarify what her eyes told her. Rather than a grope, she settled for poking one well-manicured, bloodred, lacquered claw into the center of my chest.

"Oh, he *is* real!" she exclaimed, whirling to face Calie.

"You doubted me?" My creator sounded honestly surprised. "After all the things we've done over the years, I'd—"

"We did those things *together*, sister. But this... *this*..." She waved distractedly in my direction.

"*This*," I pointed out, "is standing right here, you know. Sight, sound, touch: all came with the package deal."

In fact, to prove it, I was rubbing the aching spot where she'd nearly impaled me with her fingernail.

Delia cocked her head to observe me further. "I don't remember that he was this touchy in the books, Calista."

"He was," Calie said. "You don't remember because it wasn't directed at you personally."

"Still standing here," I reminded.

"Yes." Delia sighed, this time in wonder, as she turned to me. "Isn't Calista marvelous? I never would have believed it was possible, but Calie always planned to make you flesh. I don't know what took her so long."

"It would only work when I required him here," Calie explained.

"I was forgetting that," Delia admitted.

"Required me for what?" I demanded. Knew a pound of flesh would be due for my arrival in the physical world. Just hoped it wasn't a *literal* cut of personal beef.

"You'll find out in time, dear," Calista soothed.

Didn't soothe me in the least. In fact, I felt a chill run up my spine. This did not bode well for continued existence.

"You need to learn *this* world first," she said. "In fact, I was about to send you out to explore."

That didn't sound too bad. In fact, I was anxious to venture out.

"Beelzie!" Calie called.

On the floor above, I heard a hinge creak, then a scrambling of clawed feet and a thundering on the hardwood floor. The tip of a dark

15

snout appeared. Then the rest of the creature trundled into view as it lumbered down the stairs.

"A dog?" Seemed incredible that she had one.

"More than merely a dog," Delia said.

The pooch had traversed the staircase now and stood in a threatening stance, four paws planted on the rug, a growl emanating from deep in its chest. The creature was a deep-space sort of black, his coat glistening with a sheen very like the moonlight of the evening before. His lower jaw was burnt caramel colored, but it was the eyes that weren't right in the face of any dog that really drew attention. They were bloodred. Floppy black ears and a long, curving, non-feathered tail completed the picture.

The beast would have been intimidating even without the low growl had the dog not been less than a foot tall, though far longer in length.

"A dachshund? You want me to take a doxie for walkies?" I demanded. A man had his reputation to maintain. Well, at least the reputation he'd gained at the bookstore.

"Beelzebub is not a dachshund," the ladies insisted in unison.

"He's a hellhound," Delia said.

"A *modern* hellhound," Calie added. "Did you think they all looked like rottweilers?"

I'd met a few hellhounds in my years adventuring as The Raven, and every single one Calie's pen had described looked more demon than any sort of dog, therefore the answer was simple.

"I've never run up against one like this, as you very well know."

I stared at Beelzebub, and he showed me even more teeth. "Has he been fed lately?"

"Beelzie has a special diet. He doesn't eat snarling fictional heroes," Calie said. It sounded a lot like a snarl when she said it, too.

"Does *he* know that?" I demanded.

"Beelzie. Leash," she ordered.

And like the good dog I doubted he was, the short-legged hellhound trotted off to the kitchen. I heard P. T. greet him with pleasure, giving the beast a gushing welcome that no doubt involved a tummy rub. "Who's a good boy?" she cooed, and the damn pooch's answering yip sounded anything but demon bred.

Of course, the fact that there was a demon on this plane sorta answered something I'd been wondering about: Were there Otherworld beings in the *real* world? If the hot dog from Hell was any indication, the answer was, yup.

"I'm sending Beelzebub with you to ensure that you come to no harm," Calista said.

Me? Ah, Raven, remember?

"This isn't your world," she continued.

Damn right, it wasn't. This one should be a hell of a lot tamer! Even if there were Otherworlders in it.

"And if anyone asks if those eyes mean he has a contagious disease?" I essayed.

"Birth defect," she said. "He's missing some DNA link or something. Babble anything that sounds like science. Most people will tune you out."

Not rabid doxie owners, but the rest of the world? Yeah, she was right.

"And how long should we be gone?"

"As long as the dog thinks you should be," she said.

Well, I knew where I ranked on this scale.

"Before you leave, is there anything you need?" Calie asked.

Oh, so tempting to say "My head examined?" or something equally glib and clichéd, but I had given this some thought.

"Cash."

"Of course."

Calie had changed from the fluttery silk robe and gown of the evening before into sensible slacks and a sweater that on a younger woman I'd have taken a chance and stroked; it looked that soft. Textures were calling to me. Naw, that's too tame. Everything around me was yelling to be touched, felt, tasted. The sheen of a tabletop, the petals of the flowers in a vase on the sideboard.

And, because whether I was human or not, I was male, P. T. was on the list as well. Even if she was more inclined at the moment to rub hellhound tummies than mine.

As though he knew I was sending decidedly unfriendly thoughts his way, the beast returned with a leash in his mouth. Practiced little monster that he was, he didn't even trip on the dragging ends of the thing.

Calie had turned to a cabinet. Unlocking a drawer with a whispered word, she extricated several greenbacks. Another soft murmur relocked the drawer.

"Here. Five hundred should take care of any desires you develop along the way this afternoon. If you need more in the future, help yourself from the drawer," she offered.

"No security protocol?"

"Of course there is, dearest. Whisper your name to the lock."

"My name," I repeated. "*Which* name?"

Calie smiled, though she was the only one who found anything amusing about the situation. "Whichever you feel is most likely to do the trick."

And if I picked the wrong one, would I go up in an impressive plume of smoke?

But I knew Calie. Knew how she thought. How she thought about me. What she always called to me when she was ready to begin writing.

Raven it was, then. Still, I did wonder what happened to anyone who hadn't been programmed into the system. And what security firm used spell technology rather than depend on things shot from Silicon Valley schematics. How long had Calie been using spells, not merely writing about them? Spells were a part of my fictional world, though I didn't personally use them. I'm not a wizard, just an adept, you see. If I thought I could manifest something, it usually happened. One of the wonders of the fictional world, no doubt. But I hadn't associated spells with *her* world until she'd turned me into a corporeal being.

She handed me the greenbacks then stooped to attach the leash to Beelzebub's collar. I shoved the bills into my pocket. The idea of a dog protecting me grated. *I* was supposed to be a predator. The predator who preyed on predators, as a pseudo glib reviewer once remarked. Not today, though. Unsure of whether I had arrived with the regular arsenal of power at hand, I was the man being taken for a walk by an animated sausage.

Beelzebub cranked up his low-pitched growl again. Great! The hell-cast mutt could read minds. Just my luck.

"Be back before dark," Calie said.

"Yes, Mom," I snarled.

"I was talking to the dog, Bram," she said. "Both of you keep a sharp eye out, though."

Nice hierarchy we had in the "family." I really was royally screwed.

My new pseudo cousin Delia waved me off from the porch. She was a predator, too, though I figured *cougar* applied to her brand, since she gave me another thorough once-over with sultry eyes before the hound tugged at my leash. He was supposed to be walking me, after all.

Considering the pace Beelzebub set, the beast had an itinerary in mind. We were soon out of the lush, open grounds of Calie's ample estate and headed for the bright lights of the city. I recognized this when the dog barked at a taxi parked curbside. The driver got out, opened the back door, and the hellhound hopped in like he owned the banquette seat. In fact, the pampered little demon lolled with royal grace across the entire seat, ensuring that there was no place for me.

"Interesting," I murmured.

The driver grinned. "Yeah, there aren't many mutts with the ability to cadge a ride, but Beelzie here has the power."

"Calista keeps you on retainer, I take it?"

"You got it. You're new on the job, though. Usually it's the cute blonde who takes him to the groomer," the cabby said as he circled around the rear of his vehicle. Left to my own devices, I pulled open the door and slid into the shotgun position, merely grateful that there would be no tussle with the cur of Hades in the back seat for it.

"In some circles, I'd be considered the wiener's cousin," I told the driver as he swung his own door closed.

The Mighty Mutt, lolling in comfort, took exception to my term and amped up his sinister growl, tossing in an extra portion of teeth baring.

"Get over it," I told the beast. "You are what you are."

"Ms. Amberson's nephew, then?" the human behind the wheel queried as the cab leapt forward.

"Yup. Arrived last night."

"Nice lady," the man said.

"She has her moments, and she has her moments," I replied.

The fellow chuckled. "While His Majesty is with the groomer, is there anywhere I can drop you? Ms. Kosmas usually heads for the organic market."

Of course she does. I needed something different.

"Is there a part of town where... hmm, how shall I put this... companionship can be acquired?"

"You mean like hookers?" He didn't seem in the least fazed.

"Something like that."

"Yeah, I know a few corners, but it might be a bit early for the girls to be working."

Not the kind I had in mind. They usually didn't take time off from hunting food. Of course, perhaps the beings I was looking for didn't exist beyond the pages of a book. This was a research trip, nothing more.

In the back seat, the hellhound's growl dissipated. When I twisted in my seat to glance back at him, he met me eye to eye in a silent stare. Then I swear the damned creature gave me a nod.

Twenty minutes later, when the cab pulled up before the door of Damian's Sublime Pet Spa, rather than exit the vehicle as the door was held invitingly open, Beelzebub raised a regal snout and looked the other way rather than bound forth.

"Really?" I said. "You're going to turn down a sublime pet experience?"

I got what I was beginning to consider *the look* for my trouble.

"Apparently, the pompous pooch is with me," I told the driver. "Can't blame him. The sublime spa doesn't sound all that butch. Onward to the vice district, then?"

The dog agreed with a quick yip, the cabby with a chuckle. It was barely another twenty-minute drive as we crossed from posh to pulverized neighborhood.

I spotted the ladies in question easily and will admit it was a relief to recognize their true nature.

"You can stop here," I told the driver when we were a block away.

"And you can give me a call at this number when you're ready to be picked up," he said, handing me a business card. "Not many fares in this neighborhood."

"But plenty of prospective carjackers who wouldn't care if you were in current possession or not," I added.

"You got it," he agreed.

Beelzebub and I were barely on the pavement before the cabby peeled off. This time the hound didn't strain at the leash, eager to be on his way. If the beast could be said to have a mind capable of the action, his mind was sizing up the situation before making a move.

"Know what they are?" I asked in an undertone.

Beelzie gave that odd imitation of a nod again.

"Let's get to it, then. Time's a-wastin'."

In unison, the hound and I went into motion. Was rather like having a partner to back me up. Whether the Mighty Hot Dog would truly watch my back was still debatable, though.

The Detroit of the real world was even more of a city of contrasts than the city painted by Calie in The Raven Tales. In Calie's neighborhood, folks had money. Here, they were slipping ever closer to the icy waters of poverty or were already submerged in them.

The boarded-up buildings were few but had failed the test of history: no one famous had built them, lived in them, or died in them. Plenty of nobodies had, but that wasn't going to pass muster with a preservation committee. Those buildings that weren't boarded up catered to whatever clientele was brave enough to set foot through the sagging portals.

The businesses taking their chances in such quarters tended to be hole-in-the-wall bars, tattoo parlors, pawnshops, and a few places featuring scanty female attire and sexual enhancements for sale.

The people out making hasty trips to deceptively safe destinations looked as worked over as the buildings. They probably thought the apocalypse was near. Or had already arrived. No one would have been surprised if the Four Horsemen had roared up on vintage 1524cc Harley Davidson Shovelheads.

The only bright spots in the neighborhood were the bits of brightly colored plumage twittering together on the corner I ambled toward. Whether by choice or by instinct, the locals altered their steps, circling the startlingly made-up femmes. To those cruising for a good time—and there were still some unlucky fools doing so even this early in the day—no margin of safety was in place.

Up ahead, one of the Sukis—succubus, if you want to be formal—leaned toward the open window of a Lexus pulled up curbside.

Thanks to some quality internet time with color swatches at a paint company's website, I was up to speed when it came to identifying the vividness of the world I now inhabited. Streaks of pink and yellow were painted through the strands of this particular Suki's cropped midnight locks. A bodice of silver lamé hugged a boyishly slim body. A short skirt flared over a host of stiff net petticoats, their shades as variegated as a color wheel. When she moved, the whole getup sparkled and shivered, drawing attention to her and to the long stretch of leg on display above tall, white doeskin boots. The tall wedge heels of her footwear were a clever concealment for her hooved feet.

Calie had never painted Deer Woman to look quite so fetching in print.

Her sisters were as cleverly made up, one enhancing the catlike features of her face, another boldly incorporating her long, bushy red tails into part of a pseudo bustle of fur that swayed when she moved.

The Sukis were shopping for their next meal and doing it in broad daylight.

Even legends have to evolve. No longer could these ladies find a lone warrior, shepherd, charcoal burner, or lost traveler in the woods to snack on. The woods had been converted into paper products, and in place of trunks and branches that reached for the sky, buildings now attempted to scrape the underbellies of clouds. Demons had changed in The Raven Tales. It was comforting to find they were evolving in the outside world as well.

Right now, discovering what sort of Otherworld community existed in *this* world sat at the top of my mental to-do list.

On the corner, Deer Woman ran a teasing finger along the jaw of the man straining against his seatbelt as he leaned toward the passenger window.

And five tough guys stepped out of the alley ahead of me, blocking the way.

"You da Raven?" the lead guy said.

"You talking to me or the pooch?" I asked. Beelzie flipped his growl switch into the on position again. At least this time the teeth were bared for the benefit of the muscle-bound barricade.

"He don't look like his picture," one of the muscles behind the point man said. Incredibly, the dude had a book in his hand. A paperback, well thumbed. He didn't look like a reader to me.

"That you?" the head honcho asked, gesturing to the cover.

"That's an artist's rendition of a fictional character. Do I look fictional to you?"

"It's him," a third guy announced. "I read the book and he's the guy."

His friends were startled enough to forget both Beelzebub and my unworthy self. They stared at the man.

"You read the book?"

The Mensa candidate frowned at them. "How the hell else were we going to get a decent description of him?"

"Yeah," I agreed. Let's face it, I'm used to being the center of attention. I'm the hero in the series, if you recall. "What's it say? This Raven guy is so handsome women melt at his feet?"

"Naw. It says *you* got black hair, weird green eyes—"

I doubted Calie had ever described them as *weird*. "There are hundreds of shades of green. Would that be tequila lime, Douglas fir, clover, peppermint leaf, or another shade?"

Paint chips do come in handy.

"Shut up, smart-ass," the lead guy snapped.

"More olive green, I guess," the reader said. He took the paperback away from his *compadre* and leafed through it. "It also says you got a lean athlete's body—"

"I hope he's a good sport and doesn't mind me borrowing it, then," I said.

"—a square jaw, a long pointy nose, and that if you stand up straight, you're close to six-two."

I immediately stooped to appear shorter.

"Yeah, it's him, Ham," the reader said. "The smart mouth gives him away."

Who'da thought?

"You want my autograph?" I asked.

"We want you should come with us," Ham countered.

"I'm on sorta a tight schedule. You could make an appointment with my associate here," I suggested, indicating the short-statured hellhound on alert at my feet. He'd stationed himself directly in front of me, insanely expecting to be a canine barrier between me and... well, these idiots.

"That won't suit the guys we work with, Raven," he said.

I'd seen the puncture marks each of them had on the jugular. They weren't vampires themselves, but they were all Renfields. Handy snacks when required.

23

"It's not even noon, fellas. The *guys* won't be awake for hours yet. Why don't we all go about our business and meet back here at, oh, let's say moonrise?" I suggested. No intention of turning up, of course. I'm not entirely stupid.

"Then we don't gotta be polite no more," Ham announced.

This was polite?

"Get him, boys."

Damned if they didn't make an attempt. Even the reader, who really should have known better, having read one of Calista's books.

Unless, of course, I was no longer the man I was within the pages of that book.

Beelzie wasn't hampered by such thoughts. The sleek black demon took one guy down with a bounding attack to the crotch. That was the last I saw of the hound for a while, though I could hear his snarls and the snap of his teeth, the howls of his victim. I was busy enough blocking, dodging, and avoiding the sharp blade of a knife when it materialized in the hand of one of the goons. A quick twist of his wrist, hitting the pressure point just right, and I was the possessor of the blade. Ha! No magic needed!

The battle moved within the close confines of the alleyway, and the scents that attacked my virgin sense of smell nearly brought me to my knees. Still, to survive the current confrontation, I plunged deeper into the disgusting essence. My sort of magic needed at least a few paces between me and whoever was going to receive the benefit of high-grade prestidigitation.

Three of Ham's horde followed me in, grins of confidence on their ugly phizes. My back against the crumbling brick building, I planted a foot in the nearest guy's gut. He flew back against the adjacent edifice and bounded off, smacking face-first into the dumpster. As two others closed on me, he crumbled into a heap in the muck.

The next dudes decided on using a pincer maneuver. I threw up a shield, or at least I tried. There wasn't even a fizzle of power in the air. No shimmer from an invisible force field. I tried to pull a thought-produced rug from beneath the nearest thug's feet. He plowed forward without even a temporary wobble.

I was royally screwed! Definitely up Battle Creek without an outboard motor.

Fortunately, good old dirty street fighting was more effective and satisfying. I'd worry about where my freaking trump card was hiding later.

A quick duck of one blow had the guy to my left swearing as his fist kissed the wall, but he wasn't down, and the other bonehead was closing in. Ham was waiting patiently for his turn, in the event a miracle happened and Beelzie and I kicked four men's asses between us.

I still held the knife. It felt right in my hand, which meant I still remembered how to use it. But did I really want to prick any of these pricks with it?

While the guy with the brick-bitten hand swore, his partner scooped up the battered remains of a tailpipe and swung it like a baseball bat at my head. I threw up an arm to deflect it. If magic had followed me across from the printed page, the dude'd slam back against solid brick at a crippling speed. If the magic hadn't come along as part of my package deal... well, then, this was going to hurt like hell.

No magic sparkled into being, but the strike never came. The guy froze in mid-swing, and his mouth opened in a snarled war cry that warbled strangely, strung out in time.

It wasn't just the one attacker suspended in motion. Beelzebub was hanging in the air, having finished savaging one hood and turned to chew up the Ham himself. The man with the newly crushed hand had his other out, ready to claw my face, and the fellow I'd attempted to slam dunk into the dumpster had been caught awkwardly scrambling to his feet. Even the few people hustling by on the opposite side of the street were caught in mid-motion.

The only things moving were the three garishly dressed Sukis and me.

I swear, in twenty volumes of The Raven Tales, I've never been able to manipulate space and time, much less do it selectively.

The fox-tailed Suki reached the alley first. She yanked the tailpipe from the goon's hand and smashed it up the side of his unmoving head, then in a smooth motion spun it around and rammed its end into the guy on my left. Deer Woman swept Beelzie out of the air, rammed an elbow hard into Ham's midriff, then stomped on his foot for good measure. The man on the ground got a kick in the ribs.

Meanwhile, the Suki with catlike features grabbed the hair of the guy next to the dumpster and rang his chimes against it again.

As time and space returned to normal, every one of the Renfields dropped to the ground insensible or moaning.

"Honey," the fox-tailed Suki drawled, "you gotta be more careful who you talk to in this neighborhood."

I lowered the knife, then remembered I'd no idea what it had been up to prior to my arrival and tossed it in the dumpster. "What just happened?"

Deer Woman chuckled as she cuddled Beelzie like a long-shanked baby. The damned hellhound was eating it up, too, attempting to lick her chin.

"Magic, sweetie," she said. "We thought you knew all about that already."

"What with being The Raven and all," Cat Girl added.

"But I'm not," I said. "I'm just a guy with the same name as a fictional super-something."

"Right," Deer Woman said, clearly not buying that at all.

"So, I repeat, what just happened?"

The ladies shared a smile. *Ah, poor deluded Raven,* it seemed to say.

"Kitsune threw a time bubble," Cat Girl explained.

Kitsune. That meant Ms. Foxtail was a Japanese succubus. Fortunately for me, they were the only ones of her species rumored to be able to bend time and space.

"Nice job," I said. "Very timely."

The vixen swished her tails—seven of them, which meant she was old and powerful—with saucy pleasure. To create the illusion of a bustle decorated with fur, she'd added froufrou bits of gathered net and verdant-shadows (yes, a paint chip color) ribbons that trailed nearly to the ground. Forest green, sequin-covered cloth draped in an apron across her stomach before being caught up with the trailing bustle. A boned and front-laced black corset cinched her torso. Her slender arms were covered by long satin gloves, their color moving from dark green near her shoulders to a solid black near her hands, mimicking the natural coloration of a fox's paw. Well, except for the green part. Her black fishnet stockings and mid-calf-laced, high-heeled black boots definitely had my approval. A thick mane of deep red hair was bound up in a further tail that swung, rather than twitched, beneath a ridiculously small black top hat. Overblown steampunk, head to toe.

I gazed into her soft brown eyes and fancied myself in love. I'd always been partial to redheads, and when one of them could tinker with time and space, what wasn't to love?

Even if she was a life-sucking demon.

I stuck out my hand. "Bram."

She slid her gloved paw into mine. "Kit."

"Thanks for saving my ass."

"It looks like a very tasty ass," she observed, then gestured to her companions. "Doe and Bakeneko."

Deer Woman inclined her head slightly, but Cat Girl shouldered Kit aside. "Neko, please, Raven."

"Bram," I insisted. "I'm not sure I'm The Raven or not yet."

"Well, one thing we know is that you aren't human," Doe said. "Kit configured her bubble to affect humans and demons. That's why the hound was affected."

"But none of you were," I pointed out.

"We wear amulets to counter it," Neko said, unconsciously grooming her cheek as she would whiskers. In her present form, they were missing, of course.

Of the three, Neko wore the most subdued outfit, though her golden catsuit seemed to replicate the glossy coat of an Abyssinian, clinging to every curve. She'd used heavy doses of dark shadow around her eyes, elongating their Oriental shape. Her mane was a king-of-the-beasts gold and brown Afro.

Despite the Indonesian look she wore, I knew a bakeneko was another Japanese demon. But she wasn't a succubus. Oh, she was a shape-shifter and a killer, all right, but she'd once genuinely been the cat she attempted to resemble now in human form.

"Can I buy you ladies lunch in appreciation?" I asked. Neko in particular would be interested in something carnivorish, since her talents weren't those of a Suki.

There was a grunt from the ground as Ham stirred back to life.

"You can't go off with them," he said. "The masters would be hurt, considering we issued the first invitation."

"*That* was an invitation?" I demanded, incredulous. Let's hope I never ticked them off. No, wait, I was bound to do that somewhere along the way. I had a knack for it. "Your principals are snoozing, dude! Hours till they're ready to bite something. I on the other hand need to bite into something now!"

Nothing like a bit of unexpected exercise to work up an appetite. Besides, I still was clueless about bacon.

"Send your men back to their hole, Hammer," Doe said, "but you join us at the table. We need to cooperate right now. The community needs to know what The Raven's appearance at this point in time foreshadows."

"It's why we rescued him," Kit explained. "You know we don't generally use magic against your kind if it can be avoided."

Once I would have said the same thing, but damn, what I wouldn't give to know if I had a lick of magic now or not. Not that I'd had all that much in the books, but some is always better than nothin'. It hurt that the power thrust had deserted me in my time of need. Or that I'd needed to be rescued at all. I rubbed my jaw, suddenly conscious that it felt a bit out of alignment thanks to someone's fist.

"So you know this chump?" I asked, indicating Ham as he pushed painfully to his feet.

"We work the same neighborhood," Doe said. "That doesn't mean I totally trust him, but on this occasion, I think we should."

Only as far as I could throw him, and considering the bulk he was carrying, that would be a very short shot put.

"Then which of these fine dining establishments would you suggest we patronize?" I asked.

Deer Woman set off, trusting that the rest of us would trail along. Ham limped painfully behind at a slower pace, favoring the foot Doe had stomped with a hoof. Neko took pity on him and slipped beneath his arm to act as a living crutch. Kit tucked her arm in mine and leaned close as we brought up the rear of the parade. Beelzie, of course, was a very complacent spawn of hell in Doe's arms yet.

"You smell good," I told Kit. "What's your perfume called?"

"Fox pheromones," she purred. "Not usually found at the cosmetics counter."

"Much nicer than the aromas in that alley. Remind me to avoid such places in the future."

"You think we have a future, Raven?"

"Bram," I reminded. "It's always good to stay friends with a time bender in my book, particularly such a fetching one."

She gave a short, barking laugh. "We'll see," she said.

Doe had reached her destination, a long narrow bar that looked battered enough to date back to the days of Fort Detroit. The joint went by the unlikely name of The Bridge, and though there was nothing bridge-like about the place, it did have the required beer signs in the barred window.

As I pulled the door closed behind Kit and myself, the bartender turned to give the group the once-over.

"Grendel's balls," he snarled. "What is this, the opening line of a joke? Three man-eaters, a hellhound, a preacher, and a piece of shit walk into a bar."

"A preacher?" I echoed.

Ham grunted. "That would be me."

Which left yours truly being the piece of shit. That was certainly going to gain this joint the Farrell five-star recommendation.

But the name of the bar made sense now. The bartender was a troll. Well, mostly troll. He was taller than I would have expected a full-blood (or whatever substituted for blood in his veins) to be. Far uglier than sin, since sin is usually quite attractive.

"Play nice, Ralph," Doe counseled. "The Raven is buying us all lunch."

"That includes you, big guy," I added. "Nice place you got here."

Lying through my teeth.

He gave me a rictus grin. "Then drinks for everyone are on you, too."

As there was only one passed-out drunk at the end of the bar, I thought my funds might stretch that far.

"I don't carry that Evan Williams you're fond of," he said, "so you'll have to make do with the house bourbon."

"Fine with me," I said, hoping it wouldn't also do duty as a varnish remover. I'd had to stomach that sort a time or two back in fictionland. Talk about manning up!

The ladies slid into a cramped booth, Neko and Kit both choosing the innermost spots next to the wall while Doe and Preacher

Ham took the outer seats. Ralph kicked a chair my way as he came over to take orders.

Unsurprisingly, Doe ordered a salad, Neko asked for fish, Kit for chicken, and Ham a triple cheese burger with the works.

"Something with bacon," I requested, "and whatever the hellhound wants." Beelzie barked an order that left me clueless, but Ralph ambled away after that. He must have understood Hellhoundese.

Deer Woman didn't waste any further time.

"What exactly are you doing here, Raven?" she demanded, those large doe eyes looking anything but soft and meek.

"You mean in this neighborhood?"

"In this dimension," she said. "You belong between the pages of a book. You aren't real. You're a figment of the witch's imagination. If she brought you across from nowhere land, there must be a reason."

"I'm sure there is, but I'm clueless as to what it is," I admitted.

"The Lilin don't do things without a reason," Kit said. "And the reason usually is only to their own benefit."

"The what?" It isn't often I'm clueless about the supernatural community, but she had me on this one.

"The Lilin, Lilith's daughters. The ones she bred with Samael."

"The archangel who went south?"

"Yes, Satan himself." Her soft fox eyes narrowed as she gazed down the table at me. "You don't know, do you?"

"Know what?"

"What your scribbler is," Doe said.

Ham frowned. "How could he not know she's a witch?"

"Calie's a witch?"

"Well, duh," Neko said. "Doe already said she was."

Yeah, well, she had, but I thought she'd merely been referring to my creator's autocratic attitude. It did explain why Calie had been able to give me a physical presence, if not a nebulous sort of life.

"Okay," I said, drawing the word out. "I suppose the facts do support that supposition. She does keep a sorry excuse for a hellhound around the house"—said hound growled threateningly beneath the table—"and it explains that overly dramatic rubbish last night to bring me across from the page."

"Wasn't the coven gathered for the ceremony that turned you into a physical manifestation?"

"Nope. She did it alone," I said. "Stepped out into the storm, somehow carved a hole in the clouds for the moon to shine through, and *wham*, there I was."

It seemed best to keep secret the fact that I'd stumbled like the worst sot when the senses all kicked in. It would sound sorta, oh, I don't know, weak? This wasn't a group that would countenance a weak guy surviving.

But if Calista was a witch, it was logical that she was part of a coven. My pseudo cousin Delia was probably a member too, though what her standing might be, there was no telling. P. T. had told me Calie's friends came often and that occasionally they did picnic dinners in a clearing in the woods. Probably at each solstice, as well as at every full moon. And they were also coming to feast on poor man's kraken that night, with the intention of looking me over.

"She did the ceremony alone?" Doe repeated. "Then she's more powerful than we thought."

"We all felt the moment you arrived," Kit said. "Every Otherworld being in the city did, I think."

"The masters had us put out calls to blood communities around the world to see if the message rippled out," Ham said. "Every one of them felt it."

"And we all knew who'd arrived, too," Ralph, our troll host, added as he plunked a cloudy tumbler down in front of me. My new sense of smell was appalled at how distant a relative of my Williams the stuff in the glass was.

"Santa?" I essayed hopefully.

"Da Raven," he said. "No other."

"But I'm not so sure that's—"

"You." The huge hand he thumped down on my shoulder was very emphatic.

"Okay, me," I said. "That doesn't mean I have any idea what I'm doing here. This world is foreign to me. Won't say I was dragged here kicking and screaming, but I didn't even know I was being drawn into it until it was a done deal."

Doe accepted the carton of milk the troll placed on the table and passed it to Neko, then moved one of the two bottles of spring water over to Kit. Ham got a bottle of some beer I'd never heard of and gave our reluctant host a hearty thanks. Apparently Beelzie hadn't ordered a drink. Ralph wasn't giving any of us a chance to place further orders, though. The door to the kitchen was already swinging shut behind him.

"If the coven wasn't convened for the ceremony, perhaps they are unaware of her motives," Doe said.

"Don't think so." I hated to disabuse her of that notion. A lone antagonist was always easier to best than one with minions. Particularly when a hero lacked a horde of his own minions. "One of them arrived this morning eager to see if Calie had been successful. She gushed enthusiasm like a thrilled puppy."

"There is a member who is nearly as old a soul as I am," Kit said. Which was saying something, considering the number of tails she sported. "Perhaps she was your visitor."

"As age frequently equals power, she could easily attract a following if she decided to break with Calista." Doe was clearly musing on the possibility.

"But would she?" Neko asked. "I was under the impression she functioned as the beta to Ms. Amberson's alpha in their clowder. Bram was probably conjured to further secure the leadership and discourage a split, if one was even in the wind."

"We've been going on the assumption that Calista Amberson is merely *calling* herself one of the Lilin to indicate she wishes to be considered a descendant of Adam's first wife and her lover," Kit pointed out. "But what if some of the other members of the coven really are far older than they appear? A witch's normal lifespan is already long, but a true Lilin could count her age in centuries, even millennia."

Which sounded like storytelling hooey even to my fictional ears.

"You aren't suggesting that Calie and some of the other members are descendants of an archangel, are you?" I demanded. That was, well, too scary to contemplate. Particularly if they appeared human. They might act human, and there is no species more dangerous than a human with a plan. The supernaturals tended to think they didn't need plans, what with awesome power stomping folks so nicely and all that.

"Some of them might honestly consider themselves Lilin whether they are in truth," Kit said.

"But they aren't really immortal," I persisted.

"That's your job to discover," she said.

Oh, so now I was part of the gang. Wondered what the induction program consisted of. Something like surviving my assignment?

"Let me get things straight," I said. "One: I'm supposed to find out why trouble was taken to metamorphose me. Two: I'm to discover whether the idea is the entire coven's or merely Calie's. And three: I'm to ferret out whether the coven members are measly humans or whether they're something more ancient in truth or merely fancy."

Deer Woman nodded. "Plus one more thing."

As if the list wasn't long enough already!

"Find out if the coven is behind the deaths of various members of the nonhuman world."

"Which ones?" I asked, a bit suspiciously. It was beginning to sound like I was going to be the only one detailed to sort out the answers.

"The deaths that match those of characters you took out in books," Doe said.

"Which ones, and in how many books?"

They all exchanged looks. All but Beelzebub. He had his nose raised and turned toward the swinging door that led to the kitchens.

Kit gave the disturbing answer.

"All of them," she said. "And the beings were all murdered in the same way you dealt with them in each of the twenty books Calista has written thus far. Does that help?"

The short answer was no. Not only as to whether it was helpful to learn that my crimes had been repeated outside of the covers, but as to whether I wanted anything to do with this investigation.

"The entire series?" I gasped instead. "Didn't the police center their attention on copycat perps when that came to light?"

"This is the real world, Farrell. The police don't investigate the deaths of nonhumans. They don't even know other beings exist, much less care if someone is bumping them off," Ham said. As the speech had made him winded, he chugged down half of the mystery beer.

"In any case, the deaths weren't copycat ones. If anything, *you* were the copycat, because they all happened before they were recounted as having occurred in one of The Raven's adventures," Kit said.

I stared at her. "You're kidding."

"Cross my heart," she said, following the words with a leisurely sketched *X* across that delectable corset.

"Hell spawn," I groaned. "The murders didn't even garner a headline in one of the tabloids or a mention on a conspiracy site?"

"We found ways to keep the conspiracy types quiet," Neko answered.

"Don't tell me you killed them," I said. Okay, pleaded is probably more like it.

"Okay, I won't," the cat declared.

"Were the rest of the circumstances around these murders identical to those in the books?" I had to know if my adventures were all redundant. Yeah, it was an ego thing. So sue me.

"No, just the way the executions were carried out," Doe said. "Names were different, backgrounds were different, circumstances prior to the murders were different. Only the method in which your executions were carried out had that eerie *déjà vu* feeling. Once we recognized the pattern, a committee was formed to read, deconstruct, evaluate, compare, and contrast each of The Raven Tales with real-life events as the books were released."

They'd gone to a lot of trouble, but they'd missed one thing.

"You're talking about over twenty years' worth of stories. Twenty murders. Why didn't you just ask Calie about it?"

Doe and Kit laughed softly. Neko and Ham smirked.

"For one very good reason," Kit said. "Whenever we confronted her, she pretended that she couldn't see or hear us. That she couldn't *feel* us."

"And you gotta admit *that* proved she was faking it, because there ain't a human alive who doesn't get the heebie-jeebies when an Otherworld being is around," Ham said. "I oughta know, as I *am* human."

Which, despite the bite marks on his neck, was true. The vamp who owned him hadn't begun the process of turning him into a bloodsucker yet. Couldn't fault them for that. Minions are hard to find.

"Heck," the unlikely preacher admitted, "even *you* creep me out. But 'cause I am human, the witch had only one reason why she wouldn't respond to me."

Because he was butt-ugly?

"She ain't never learned to be courteous to people. Hell, I was being damn polite, too!" Ham said.

He probably turned up with only half his crew to threaten her. On the other hand, it did sound like Calie to tune out anyone she didn't want to be bothered with.

She couldn't tune me out, though. I was part of her. The child of her pen. Scary, huh?

"I'll need a list of the victims' real names, their species, information about where they were found, who found them, and details about their personal lives," I said, figuring that would slow them down.

"The files will be copied and messengered to you by this evening," Doe said.

Damn, so much for that ploy.

A cell phone seemed to materialize in her hand from a hidden pocket. She had whoever she was contacting on speed dial.

"Unless, that is, you have an encrypted email address we could use," she added, already texting.

"You're looking at everything I own," I said. That would have to change, and the sooner the better.

"Hope that includes a lot of cash," Ralph grumbled, turning up with a hobgoblin girl toting a serving tray loaded with plates. He made short work of passing orders to the others, even setting a soup bowl of beef tips swimming in gravy down on the floor before Beelzie. I got a plate with six dry, overcooked strips of what I supposed was bacon, nothing else.

"What, no garnish?" I asked.

Ralph made an impossible anatomical suggestion and left us to the sustenance. He'd slipped a handwritten tally of the feast next to my plate. It's really amazing how little two hundred bucks will buy a guy in this world.

Having been soaked by Ralph on the check, and graciously paying for the Sukis' time with another bundle of bills, I whistled up the cab to get Beelzebub and myself back to the ranch—er, estate. Had to borrow Doe's cell to give the driver a call though.

Calie was at her desk when the dog and I trotted in. She glanced at us over the top of her computer glasses but didn't shut the laptop down.

"Did you boys enjoy yourselves?" she asked, totally ignoring the evidence that we'd both been battling something. My jaw was probably going to develop a bruise, and the evil doxie's coat was smeared on one side with something he'd picked up in the alley. Something I didn't care to identify.

"Well, we spent the five hundred bucks, so I'd say it was a successful trip. Met some nice ladies under a lamppost, chowed down with a thug who got his divinity degree online, and learned that you really shook up the supernatural community last night by effecting my entry into this world. Oh, and Beelz went off his special diet. It was his idea, so don't blame me. I'd no clue about what he ordered at the bar."

Her head tilted to the side, she stared at me in silence, then turned back to her computer.

"I wonder why I gave you such a punch-drunk speech pattern," she said.

"Hell alone knows."

"No doubt. Did you learn anything on your jaunt?"

"Yep. That to function in this world I need a cell phone, a no-holds-barred credit card, both bank and email accounts, additions to my wardrobe, a valid driver's license, a car, and a hell of a lot more background story on who I am. Then you can tell me why the hell you manifested me in the flesh after twenty volumes."

Calie pulled her top desk drawer open and began unloading it.

"Cell phone," she said. "It's a burner. No one will be able to trace it. You'll need to set up the message-taking feature. I thought you'd prefer choosing a password yourself."

"Gosh, Mom, thanks," I said, claiming my new toy, enjoying the way it nestled in the palm of my hand.

Calie sighed. "Sarcasm. Well, I did build it into your character template."

"Did you program in the same ringtone I've got in the series?" I asked as I dropped into one of the tall-backed wing chairs she'd placed to face the desk, throwing one leg over the padded arm.

"Of course."

Well, that would have to change. I already knew I wasn't the same man I'd been in fictionland. Fast evolver, I guess.

Calie had moved on, sliding a manila folder across the desktop toward me. "Bank account and debit card. One hundred thousand dollars is now at your command. With it, you'll be able to take care of those clothing and transportation needs and have sufficient pocket money."

A smaller envelope was placed on top of the closed folder. "Driver's license and birth certificate. The date is based in part on your age in *Raven Takes Rook*, and the day and month I began writing the first book in the series."

I'd still have to remember it myself, in case anyone asked. In the series, I aged extremely slow. I wondered if I still did or not. Whether only poisoned ink could do for me.

Calie swiveled her chair around and grabbed the most recent run of sheets from the printer. "This is your family history in further detail. Encapsulated: I am your mother's younger sister, a widow who never remarried, by choice. Delia is the daughter of our older sister. You are an only child and traveled often with your parents. Your father had a restless soul and liked to keep on the move. He inherited sufficient funds to maintain a family in modest style. You were educated by tutors. That, by the way, was a ploy that kept me from needing to hire a hacker to insert your name into any school databanks."

"Glad there were a few corners to cut," I said, scanning through the various features on the phone.

"I also gave you a job," Calista announced.

I struggled to sit up and fumbled the cell to the floor. "A what?"

"Job," she repeated. "You need some cover for any covert activities in this world."

Covert. Like not telling her of the assignments the nonhumans had already dropped into my lap?

"You're a freelance travel writer, visiting me between assignments."

"Not because Detroit could use a boost from vacationers' bucks?"

"Add what you wish to the story. These are merely basic background elements that you can build on."

She slid her glasses back into place and revived the laptop. "I know you did a lot of internet surfing last night, however, I am leaving it up to you to purchase a tablet or whatever device you'd prefer. Beyond that, P. T. tells me you have already opted out of dinner this evening. I can understand you would prefer not to be treated like a petri dish culture under microscopic study, but if you can join my friends and me later for drinks, I would appreciate it. If you need to rest, the bedroom to the right at the end of the upstairs hall is yours."

Since her eyes returned to the laptop screen and the keys began their hollow, sucking sound as her fingertips struck them, I felt well and truly dismissed.

She'd covered a lot of territory in our few minutes together but hadn't given me answers to the only question I really needed the answer to.

What the hell was I doing in *this* world?

It didn't take the further shooing motion she made with her hand to send both Beelz and me on our way. I knew a brick wall when I met one, and apparently he did, too. I'd simply bash my head against it again later. In the meantime, I had other things to do. And since the dog trotted off toward the kitchen, I suppose he had an itinerary of his own.

Considering I'd entered the real world less than twenty-four hours ago, I was getting quite a full plate of problems to chew on.

With Calie tuning me out for the afternoon, P. T. up to her pretty elbows in tentacles, and the almighty hellhound zonked out—and under—his cushy nest of blankets in a corner of the kitchen, I headed out on my own to explore the grounds. There had to be a gardener, because the lawns near the house were pristine. Weeds had been frightened off, but they could easily have taken refuge in the wooded grounds. Was clueless about the acreage Calie's estate might encompass, but with a decorative iron fence hedging in all but the front drive, it would be easy to tell when I hit the edge of the property. In any event, the gardener was not available to point a finger toward my destination.

I was gnawing on the idea of Calie's witchy connections when I set out. That she was the head of a local coven made perfect sense. The evidence of my own eyes—and person—proved that she was a power wielder. Her personality was not that of a follower, either. She was autocratic, liked to get her own way, and could probably win a stare-down competition with Satan himself.

Whom, if what the Sukis had told me turned out to be true, she considered to be her dad. Whether she believed she was better, or knew better, than anyone else via a link to his gene pool—if archangels *had* gene pools—or that of the legendary Lilith was anybody's guess.

Sheer arrogance led to the private test of her capabilities. If she failed, the women who would be arriving for dinner in a few hours would have been none the wiser. If the group had attempted to yank me from the pages and failed, she would no doubt have picked them apart, assigning blame for the failure in small, confidence-killing rebukes.

But she *had* succeeded in manifesting my debatably substantial self, and that meant even within the group she gained more power. How long would she be able to rule them, though? Even as I exited the house, I could hear the cough get her in its grip once more.

I needed to know the lay of the land, and finding the meadow fit into my schedule nicely. I set off in a waxing direction that would lead me back to the front terrace as I waned. I might well be waning by then. It looked to be quite a jog.

The grounds beyond the carpet of grass felt like primeval territory. The trees were a combination of hoary old giants and of new growth. Sunlight dappled the forest floor. Fall had settled in, giving the woods a coat of many colors and a rustling carpet to match. A slight breeze was blowing, making shadows sift.

I pushed past overgrown bushes, climbed over raised tree roots or under low-hanging branches. Despite the violence of the storm the evening before, there was little evidence that it had pushed through the multicolored canopy of leaves. I didn't stumble across any lightning damage, although I'd seen a strike the night before. Oddly, there was no birdsong, no scurrying squirrels or other small rodents, no buzzing of insects to break the silence, just the occasional whisper of the leaves.

If those whispers *were* leaves. Sometimes they seemed to form words, but words from a language that wasn't in my repertoire.

Acting brave—or stupid, depending on your view of things—I kept an eye out for a path or a break in the canopy that would signal a meadow. Then, between one blink and the next, a path appeared. It was rough, more of an animal track than a trace for humankind to tread. Still, it was a welcome change from plowing through heavy, prickly undergrowth. I took it, heading in the direction of the property fence.

The unidentified twittering increased behind me. Scanning the woods for its source, I missed the trap of an upraised root, stumbled in the bright glare of open meadowland, and slammed my face into a waiting fist.

Reeling back into the dappled shade beneath the trees, I caught my balance on an old-growth tree trunk. There were both spots and stars tumbling before my eyes.

Whoever lay in wait was enjoying letting me know they were there. I heard a grunt, a rustling of underbrush, and then silence descended once more. They'd moved to a new position, but not one that placed them between me and my goal. The meadow shimmered there just beyond the dappled shade, looking like a waiting portal into a different dimension. There was a chance that was exactly what it was.

The area was bigger than it should have been. I'd been through enough of the woods on the estate now to know the depth from terrace to fence, and this was nearly four times that length. Therefore, it was either enchanted, or this was the only meadow that used Time Lord technology. It certainly was bigger than it had any right to be.

In the center of the meadow, a huge buck raised its head at my entry, sized me up, and lowered an impressive rack of antlers threateningly in my direction.

Time to leave, I thought.

The buck thought differently. He pawed the ground. Snorted like the bull he was.

Why he bothered, when there were no does around to witness his territorial stand, was beyond me. Perhaps I was carrying a trace of Doe's scent and he didn't like sharing anything that could be added to his harem.

"Easy, boy," I murmured. Whether I was giving myself a pep talk or attempting to reassure the buck is a toss-up.

In any case, the words were translated as fightin' ones.

Bodies began raining from the branches overhead. Others erupted from the bushes on either side of me. One sprang from the ground before me, his clothing consisting of squares of turf lashed to his body with something that looked like raffia.

A short branch, not entirely shed of leaves, smacked my already injured jaw and then moved on to berate my neck.

"Hey!" I yelled. Like that was going to stop the attack. I ripped the weapon from the attacker's mitt and tossed it aside. "I just want—"

That was when the unknown troop used the head of one of their number as a battering ram, hitting me squarely in the solar plexus.

For a second or two I thought I'd go down, but the terrain came to my rescue when my back hit one of the stripling trees. I might not be down, but I certainly was not winning. Another of the attackers had found a sturdier branch and was having a go at my ribs. Yet another sank teeth into my forearm, while a third gnawed on an ankle.

When the ambulatory battering ram sprang to his feet, I met him with my unencumbered foot, inadvertently sending him sailing six feet back into the forest. No magic involved on my part; he was both short and lightweight. Still, the crash he made descending earthward was heartening.

I turned to ridding myself of clingers. A fist pounded down on the arm-nosher had his teeth briefly sinking deeper into my skin, but then he too fell away, swooning like a faint-hearted damsel. I yanked the ankle biter off and held him up by... well, I suppose it was by the scruff of his neck.

"Knock it off!" I shouted at him.

In answer, he thumbed his nose and then stuck out his fists in a boxer's stance. The fact that I still held him dangling three feet off the forest floor didn't seem to faze him at all.

Whatever the thing was, it was fearless. Or stupid. He was humanoid but appeared to be a combination of mushroom, tree bark, and moss. Short feet kicked as he swung suspended, still trying to engage me.

"Transgressor!" he shouted.

A host of voices rose from unseen throats in the woods, echoing his cry. "Transgressor!"

41

The damn word echoed through the woods.

"Transgressor, my ass!" I snarled and shook my captive. He swayed like a marionette with half its strings cut. "This is private property, dude. If anyone's transgressing, it's you and your butt-ugly buddies. This is Calista Amberson's estate."

It made no difference to the runt. Or to his friends. Those I'd tossed aside regrouped with a half dozen of their buddies and were stalking forward in formation, armed now with last season's antler castoffs.

"Release our comrade, transgressor!" snapped the one who'd led the charge.

I'm usually not very good at following orders, but this one I couldn't resist.

"As you wish," I said and granted it by tossing the ragged little imbecile dangling from my hand at them.

The entire group collapsed and rolled off the path.

They were game little... er... whatevers. Only took them forty-five seconds to sort themselves out and snag those antler weapons once more.

Their faces were broad and mud colored. Their hair looked more like bracken, straggling from beneath helmets that resembled mushroom crowns. They weren't naked but they weren't wearing anything store bought either. Chests were covered by that odd combination of raffia and cut or torn turf with their lower extremities hidden behind slabs of bark in a manner that reminded me of soldiers' skirts in ancient Rome. One of them, in the front row, had added a set of beat-up peewee football shoulder pads, no doubt nipped from someone's trash, to his ensemble.

"Cool it with the centurion maneuvers," I demanded. "I'm bigger than you are. Rather than crack your heads together, I'd prefer it if you'd just talk to me."

"If the lord so allows," they said in unison, thumped fists to their chests, and looked past me to the buck in the meadow. Unconcerned with our comedic battle, he'd gone back to grazing.

At a signal, most of the patrol melted back into the brush, leaving three to wait with me.

The buck bided his time before condescending to look up. He nodded regally, then went back to having lunch.

"You may advance ten paces, transgressor," the leader of the remaining soldiers announced.

"Thank you," I said, but when I stepped back onto the path, three points of sharpened antler poked into the center of my back.

I swung partially back to keep them in sight.

"Dudes, I'm unarmed!" I insisted.

"You lie, transgressor. You have two arms and have used them against us."

"In self-defense!"

The snort the speaker gave clearly showed we were not in accord on that.

"You are the transgressor!" the leader's hoarse, gravelly voice snarled. "How dare you enter the high lord's presence without being summoned?"

"*You're* the trespasser here, pal. This is my aunt's property, and if she found you here... well, I wouldn't envy you. She's a real bitch when riled."

"We know of no female hound on the premises, though there is a male," one of them said.

"He's more of a demon than a hound," I pointed out.

"Yes. He is the familiar of the witch." The whatsits moved up, ready to stroll companionably at my side, apparently.

"Yeah, my aunt," I said, since they were more literal than I was in identifying her.

The leader frowned and dropped back briefly to give me a reproving poke with his weapon.

"You are not of her house," he said. "There is no blood connection."

"Blood, ink, what's the difference? She is my creator. Mom, sorta."

Football Pads gave me a prick in the kidneys. "He is a golem? Activated by a sacred word written on parchment and inserted within to animate him?"

Ah, the schoolboy in the batch, still learning his monsters.

"Not a golem," I said. "Born of words, conceived of ideas, made whole by a mother's love. Sorta like Harry Potter but not."

The commander laughed. Sounded a lot like he was choking to death. "The witch has no love of anyone."

He had that right.

"I'm something new," I offered. "You've never heard of anything like me, but then I've never run into anything like you either. What the hell are you?"

The commander appeared to have training in interrogation. He ignored my question and produced one of his own. "What are you, intruder? You are not golem, but you don't smell like a human."

"I asked first," I insisted, mostly because I really didn't have a good answer for him. Was I a *fiction* or a faux human?

"It is true," Football Pads said. "He did ask first."

"And the first rule of the forest is politeness," the third guard reminded.

It was the first I'd heard of that rule, but what the heck!

The leader scowled but withdrew his antler sword from where it threatened to do damage to something I might want to use in the future.

"We are the theophylaktos."

Never heard of them? Me neither. The word is Greek and means God Guard. It sounds more like a disease to me.

I glanced toward the magnificent and silent buck. "So you guard a god. If the beast yonder is that god, he looks like he could take out a half dozen guys like me and never break a sweat. You sure you're needed?"

"It is an honor to serve," the leader insisted.

"We would not be assigned if we were not needed," Shoulder Pads said.

"Actually, I think he's right," the third guy—obviously the smart one—said. "The lord is quite capable of defending himself against such as this one."

"Yep, stomp me good," I agreed. "Besides, I've not come seeking him, to harm or even chat with. I was looking for the coven's sacred place."

"Then you have found it," the buck itself said.

A blink later, there was a buff Chippendales dancer type, in camouflage fatigues and combat boots, standing where Bambi's dad had been a moment before. He'd bypassed the beret rather than cover the spiked blond buzz cut, hadn't bothered to shave for three days, and was sans sleeves, displaying arms that could probably bench press an elephant.

Why is it that gods always manifest as chick magnets?

All three theophylaktos fell to the ground, prostrating themselves before G.I. Joe. "Lord! We bring you the transgressor, as is our..."

"Wont?" I offered.

"Reason for existing," the commander barreled on. "We exist only to protect you and serve you."

"Then scat," the former buck ordered. "Return to your mission in the bracken."

Rather than scramble to their feet, they inched backward into the forest, never raising their eyes to gaze on their master.

"Forgive my followers," the meadow lord said. "They are overenthusiastic. Few make it this far without my handmaiden drawing them forth."

"And that would be Calie?"

He nodded graciously. "So she calls herself. Might I offer you refreshment, child?"

As buff as he was, looking fit enough to win all the Olympic events from opening ceremony to closing ceremony singlehandedly, I had six inches on him. To be called *child* by him ticked me off. I decided to go on the attack—verbally, of course. Hey, if I was guessing right, the dude was an archangel. I don't have a self-destruct button, even if at times a gag might come in handy.

"A buck isn't one of your usual manifestations, is it, Samael?" I said.

He laughed. "Anything horned and hooved works. Join me for a beer."

"I'd accept if you drop that 'child' thing. You might be an ancient creature but I'm a brand shiny new one and already programmed not to take any guff from dweebs with small followings. Even adding devil worshippers and angel nuts to your tally, I've got you beat, with sales in the millions around the world. More readers care about what The Raven will get up to next than they do on the chances of you really existing."

Sam slapped a fond hand down on my shoulder. "Yeah, you're one of mine, even if you aren't anything identifiable yet. My girl does good work."

"Calie's your daughter, then?"

"Didn't say that, son. Let's get that beer. After a good grazing, I need an equally good bit of quaffing."

A moment later, we materialized in the cab of a mud-spattered, black Ford F-150. It was already parked behind a honky-tonk, though the lot was only half full. Too early in the day yet for the regulars to roll in.

"At least when looking for transportation you went local," I said. Puzzlement colored Sam's perfect face.

"Ford." Like an idiot, I pointed to the insignia. "This is Detroit. You're driving one of the Big Three."

"Oh, yeah, I guess," he grunted.

This was the almighty fallen archangel who ruled Hell? And he grunted? When this guy threw himself into a role, he totally outdid Ledger, Bale, *and* Nicholson on method.

"Just saying it's good for the local economy that you bought this truck," I said.

His expression morphed to one of diabolical amusement. "Bought? I'm the king of sin. I just took the damn thing."

My day just got better and better. Now I was sitting in a stolen vehicle with a fallen angel looking to get his jollies.

"Just don't start a bar fight on my account. Three's usually my limit each day, and I've already been in two. I'm trying to cut back."

Samael's laugh was far from quiet. "You amuse the hell out of me," he announced.

Great, now there were bits of Hell lying around Detroit as well. As if the city hadn't been shit on enough already.

"Let's get that beer," he said. "I'm sure you've got questions."

I was sure I must too, although not a one came to mind.

"It's whether I get answers that aren't seeded with further questions that I worry about," I said, and yanked the truck door open.

Music leaked from the building, but the moment Samael sauntered through the open door, I could tell it was merely background on a commercial blaring from three big screen televisions hanging in the rafters. A flicker later, two guys in navy blue jackets and pale blue Polo shirts welcomed us back and rolled into discussing the outcome of the next gridiron showdown.

Samael gestured to the bartender. "Can ya turn that shit down? Who the crap cares what the Browns are doing?"

"Not me," offered a guy firmly ensconced on the end barstool. "Lions or nobody for me."

I didn't care either way. Calie hadn't given me a sports fan bone in my entire body. It impressed me that His Nemesis knew the league teams, until I realized a well-placed derogatory word in the right crowd would incite a riot. Doing *that* was right up his Autobahn.

The bartender shrugged, reached to an unseen switch, and dropped the sound level by a lone decibel.

"What'll ya have, gents?"

"Two of whatever ya got on draft," my demon host ordered, then dragged me off to a table that allowed both of us to keep our backs to the room. In his place, I would have forced him into the Bill Hickok spot, back to the open door. Not that anyone could take him down. Not even a raving religious lunatic with a cement mixer filled with holy water. Samael's origins were in Heaven. If doused in a sacred bath, he would simply have laughed, asked for a specific brand of soap on a rope, then strangled the idiot with said rope. It'd be a waste of good rope otherwise.

Not saying I wasn't in favor of getting rid of the monster. Sam, not the lunatic. Okay, maybe both of them, but that warn't gonna happen, pilgrim.

Samael tossed himself back, tilting the chair against the wall, and swung the combat boots to the tabletop to stretch his legs.

I gave him my best satanically arched brow. "Making yourself at home?"

"Testing," he smirked back.

When the bartender arrived with the drinks—in frosty mugs, at that!—he stared at the Devil's feet, then into his face. Sam stared back.

"These are not the droids you seek," I said. Not that it worked to defuse things. What Force I had, had taken a holiday.

"Know you guys have it bad in the field," the bartender snarled at the devil, slamming the beers down, "but that's no call for you to treat us taxpayers like we're scum when you get back home."

"We won't be here long," Samael said. "Fact, once the beer's gone, you won't even know we were here."

The bartender tried another stare down, didn't win, and headed back to refill another of the bar sitters' tumblers.

"I take it he won't remember we were here at all?" I essayed.

"Already forgot us." Satan raised his mug. "To the clever Calista."

"To getting some goddamn answers and no more freakin' questions," I countered.

"Can't be done, lad. All answers create new questions." He clinked his mug with mine. "To new and more interesting questions!"

47

He downed the entire mug like a college kid chug-a-lugging his way through a fraternity induction, then slammed the empty down on the table. Neither the bartender nor the few customers in the place gave any sign that they heard the ring as the glass yelled at the unnecessary abuse.

"What did you want to ask me?" he queried.

I downed enough of my own beer to get foam on my upper lip. "Not a thing. I wasn't looking for you. I was searching for the meadow where Calie and her pals have picnics, nothing more."

"Right," he said, obviously not believing a word.

"Had no idea you even hung around that neck of the woods," I said.

Samael chuckled. "Now that I do believe. But if I was a newly formed being, I'd want to know what strengths and weaknesses came with the package."

I leaned the top rungs of my chairback against the wall as well. "But I'm not all that new. I've got twenty volumes under my belt, and they taught me what those strengths and weaknesses were long ago."

"That was the fictional you. Things might have changed."

"Might have," I agreed. "So far it's been adjusting to things I only knew through written descriptions."

"You fixate on small things. Big picture could kill you," he said.

"I was always in mortal danger until the final page anyway."

"Don't think being the central protagonist in the series meant you were ever in any real danger, dude," Samael commented. "Sorta like I knew the Big Man wouldn't toast me in that ancient battle. He couldn't kill one of his favorite pets, just banish 'em."

The draft beer really wasn't to my taste. I pushed it away.

"You aren't really comparing Calie and me to God and yourself, are you?"

"Shoe fits..." he said, not bothering to finish the cliché. "Smaller scale, maybe, but same three-act play."

"Top gun creates bullet, bullet gets sick of doing all the dirty work and turns on the top gun?"

"And the gun smites the bullet. In your case, no more little bullet if Calista doesn't get what she wants," he said.

"What does she want?"

"Thought you didn't have any questions for me," Samael murmured with a smirk. He lifted his mug for another guzzle. The damn thing filled itself to the top once more. Even frosted up. Apparently, Hell could freeze over whatever the hell it wanted to freeze over.

I stood up. "Not sure I'd believe what you told me in any case, Sam."

He laughed. "Hell, kid, Calista wants what she always wants."

"Fame, fortune?"

"To live forever," he said. The next moment he was gone.

The burner cell worked as promised. I whistled up Calie's on-retainer cabdriver and trusted him to deliver me to a haberdashery. We hit a Target to replenish my wardrobe. To be accurate, *replenish* is incorrect. Calie never described me in anything but the duds I'd arrived in. Ergo, I was open to all manner of items.

Burt—for so the cab driver's parents had dubbed him—bought the tale I spun about losing my luggage on the entirely mythical flight I'd taken to Detroit. The black Diesel Wieter jacket had survived numerous fictional battles, though I doubted the real-life one I wore retained the enchantments that kept the zipper and snaps from reflecting light. And I wasn't sure wearing anything with epaulets was a solid choice for a guy who attracted fights in the real world. Still, neither the gross alley nor the prickly talons of forest growth had done the jacket any harm. I kept it.

Otherwise, I bought my usual uniform. A week's worth of boxers, socks, black T-shirts and jeans filled the shopping cart quickly. Burt's fashion sense recoiled at the boots Calie stuck me in decades ago, so I added a pair of black running shoes. No doubt I would be running a lot—running for my life, if this existence was anything like my fictional one.

A stop at a florist allowed me to expand my scent education by purchasing a batch of mixed posies for P. T., to thank her for making dinner reservations for me far from the octopus. Since I had a few questions about this world, I asked Burt if he had someone to return home to. Finding he was a carefree bachelor, I invited him to join me at the steak joint. He would be driving me there in any case.

The ladies were still chowing down when I returned. I swung around to the back door, presented the flowers to P. T., breathing beef fumes on her, then headed up the rear stairs to the room I'd been allotted but had yet to see.

Calie liked the best that royalties could supply and had eclectic taste. Don't get the idea that I was floored by my assigned room when I entered it. Not a decorator kind of guy. It had a bed, one big enough to accommodate an orgy should I feel the urge. There were dressers, a dinky twenty-four-inch flat-screen TV, a couple nicely padded armchairs—alas, no recliner—a walk-in closet that looked even emptier when I deposited my new purchases on the wire shelves, and a private bath with a glass-enclosed shower large enough to suds up a Clydesdale in. I think the color scheme of the entire suite was some subtle gray. I'd have to check my paint chip guide to be more specific.

Not having wished for a Clydesdale, I had the entire shower to myself. I let hot water teach me that there was such a thing as too hot; then the cold faucet took me to a frigid zone. Thoroughly invigorated, I gave my face serious consideration in the mirror once the steam cleared and wondered whether I'd always had a couple days' growth of beard. I couldn't remember ever shaving, in twenty volumes. Rubbing my shaggy batch of hair dry had me wondering if it had ever been cut. Probably not. Such mundane things they were. And there was nothing mundane about The Raven.

I had a feeling there was a lot of mundane waiting to burst free from this version of me, though. I didn't look anything like the guy pictured on the cover of any of the books. Sorta disappointed at that—he was a good-lookin' guy.

Dressed once more in clean T-shirt and jeans, I Raven-footed it down the stairs with barely a whisper of sound, eased up to the archway of the main room, the one where Calie yanked me across whatever dividing line existed between fiction and fact, and took my accustomed pose against the doorjamb.

There was a ripple around the room as one after another of the ladies noticed my manifestation and stopped in mid-conversation to turn and stare at me.

"There you are, dear," Calie cooed. "Ladies, I believe you're all familiar with The Raven."

I lifted a hand. "Just Bram, please."

"I don't remember you being so modest in the stories," one of the hens said.

"I don't remember socializing much with humans in them, either," I confessed. "Maybe that has something to do with it."

Calista did pit me against all types of magic wielders, but never beings who were power-wielding humans. Perhaps that hit too close to home?

"True," another contributed. "It is amazing that you're here with us now. Isn't Calie magnificent?"

As Calie went into one of her coughing fits, *magnificent* might not have been the appropriate word.

"Here, dearest," pseudo cousin Delia offered, pouring Calie a glass of brandy. "This should help."

Calista waved it away. "Don't be ridiculous. I need my wits about me. Bram, stop hovering and sit down."

One of the younger women scooted over to make room for another person on the sofa, but I was determined to keep my distance from the lot of them. I might not be human, but what a witch could do with a single hair was enough to chill my blood. I'd already gathered up any hairs shed during my shower and done a little non-ceremonial burn on them with matches cadged from the kitchen. No way was I getting within plucking distance of any of these babes.

Instead, I manhandled an armless chair in from the dining room and straddled it.

"Shouldn't you introduce each of us to Bram?" the forward minx on the sofa asked.

"Don't be ridiculous, Neva. I manifested him for an assignment that has nothing to do with any of you. You're simply here to bear witness to the fact that he exists," Calie snapped.

Neva pouted. "You should have waited for the gathering, then," she said. "For all we know, you simply hired an out-of-work actor to pretend to be The Raven."

"I could have," Calista agreed. "It would have been far less taxing, but an actor would have been insufficient to the task at hand."

"Besides," Delia added, "your senses should tell you Bram isn't entirely human."

Thanks for the slam, coz, I thought, but decided being enigmatically silent would work better for me. Silent and watchful as a sphinx was the way to go.

If Neva thought she'd make a point by flouncing from the room, she rethought the action before moving. Arms crossed over a nicely ample bosom, she leaned back into the cushions of her perch, her expression sullen.

"Then what exactly is this task that only The Raven can deal with?" one of the slightly older women asked. "Does anyone besides Calista know? Do you know, Delia?"

I sure as hell wanted to know!

"Well, not exactly," Delia admitted. "I only know it has something to do with the future."

"That certainly covers a lot of territory," a thirtysomething brunette said dryly. "Whose future? That of the coven, of one of the members, or of one of our enemies?"

That answered one of my minor questions. They did indeed consider themselves a coven, rather than a canasta group.

"Think for a change, won't you, Zeta," Calie snapped. "If the assignment requires The Raven, then it obviously is Bram's future that is at stake."

"Mine!" I barked, startled out of sphinx mode.

Calista turned cold eyes my way. "Yes, yours. Be grateful that I'm attempting to supply you *with* a future."

"What the hell does that mean?"

"It means," Delia said, "that Calista has advanced stage cancer. She is dying."

As revelations go, this was a doozy. Shook the other coven members at a seven-point-eight Richter level, too.

"Calista, no!" one squeaked.

"Oh, dearest!" moaned another.

"Sister, is there anything we can do to..." a third attempted.

Calie cut them all off with a sweep of her hand. "Enough. It's time for me to move forward to the next stage," she said.

"The doctor mentioned treatments to extend your time," Delia reminded.

"I'm not going to radiate myself into a half-life," Calie said.

"We have potions," Neva said. "Don't we?"

"Of course we do," Zeta answered. "They can alleviate the side effects of radiation."

"But they can't kill the cancer," Calista declared, overriding their twittering concern. "Therefore, Calista Amberson will simply fade from the mortal world. And I do not wish my creation to fade with me."

The ladies exchanged puzzled looks.

I cleared my throat. "I believe she means me."

That only made them look more befuddled.

"Correct," Calie said. "I do mean Bram. We need to discover someone capable of carrying on The Raven Tales in the future. As no one knows the demands of the series as well as you do, you are the perfect person to seek the writer best suited to receive the torch."

As assignments went, this one was anticlimactic, compared to what the nonhuman community expected me to do.

"Find a writer? Hell, Calie, put a call out on the website. You'll get a gazillion applications to consider." And I wouldn't be stuck doing it.

"A waste of time, and I have a limited amount of that. The person to take up my pen needs to be found by Samhain."

Although she'd refused it once, Calie now picked up the brandy Delia had poured for her and sipped a dose of restorative.

"You have got to be kidding," I said.

"You're used to working on tight deadlines," Calie reminded me.

"Yeah, when I know what the hell I'm doing! This is virgin territory! I haven't got a clue where to begin."

She smiled, and I knew that superior grimace. She was up to something, something I wasn't going to like in the least.

"That's why I asked everyone to dinner tonight," she said. "Each of these ladies has read The Raven Tales more than once—"

She'd probably made it required reading and passed out quizzes for them to answer afterward.

"—and each can contribute elements she feels are worthy of note. The author you find to replace me will need to be able to incorporate these ideas into future plots, plus be able to replicate my prose style. You'll go forth with clues enough, Bram. In fact, I will start the list with a request that the chosen one be female and in her twenties. That should weed out quite a few of the possibilities."

Just what I needed: even narrower guidelines.

"Your All Hallows deadline is only days away," I pointed out, hoping to angle out of the assignment or at least buy a bit more time.

"There is time enough," Calie insisted. "I intend to transfer all Raven properties to the girl you find by 12:01 a.m. on November 1.

Having everything come together on the festival of the dead seems fitting, don't you think?"

The rest of the coven hadn't tumbled to what she intended, but I knew how she thought. They'd all gather in that damn meadow-that-shouldn't-be-there, and she'd commit ritual suicide before the bunch of them.

"You really think I'd let you kill yourself?" I demanded.

The coven did a collective gasp, inhaling sharply in sync, but Calie ignored them.

"I hope that you will do everything I ask of you," she countered.

I pushed up from the chair to loom over her.

"Take the problem to Samael. I'll bet even cancer couldn't take him down in arm wrestling."

That surprised her. Not the arm wrestling, but that I knew about Daddy Dearest.

"I've never written that particular archangel into a story," she said carefully.

"Didn't have to. I had a beer with him this afternoon. Interrupted him while he was trimming the grass in the moon temple," I explained. "Probably all it takes is a stroll into the woods, and when the theophylaktos munchkins pop out, make an appointment to see the almighty Sam."

Cousin Delia's face grew red. "You cannot speak of a greater being like Samael so disrespectfully, Raven."

I raised my right hand, pointing finger aimed heavenward. "Ah, but I'm not under his auspices. He deals with folks with souls for sale and outcasts who fell with him and are stuck in middle management jobs now. I'm not human, ergo I have no soul. I'm also not a supernatural, so I can't be labeled a demon either. I'm a fiction. A real nowhere man."

"But a being *willed* to life, nonetheless," Calista murmured. "By *my* will."

Looked like I was about to be tossed off the debate team, but I stayed where I was, glaring down at her. Daring her to prove her words.

"Don't push it, Calie," I snarled.

Make a note: never try a showdown with someone who less than twenty-four hours ago *poofed* you into physical existence.

One moment I was looming, the next I'd put a dent in the wallboard on the opposite side of the room with the back of my head and slid ingloriously to the floor. She hadn't even lifted a hand to throw the spell. Geez!

Calie left me alone to drag my sorry self to my feet. The coven members stared alternately at me, then at her, some with their mouths parted in stunned surprise.

Calie went beyond the dollop of brandy this time and nearly downed the remaining restorative in a rush, then turned to her guests. "Now, who would like to give Bram a suggestion to work with during his search?" she asked calmly.

Day Two, October 28

I was a full twenty volumes and twenty-four hours old before the coven flew out the door. Calie made her way up the stairs slowly, without a word. While she'd prodded her sisters into spilling asinine clues of what I should look for in an authorial replacement, I'd gotten the silent treatment from her all evening.

Which was fine by me. While duly jotting down the elements the ladies whipped free of the stratosphere—the only place such far-out suggestions could have originated—I went over every word my creator had uttered before smashing me against a vertical bed of reinforced two-by-fours and gypsum. She had slipped something of importance in there, no doubt to test my dull wits, but narrowing in on it wasn't going to be easy. I knew from experience that Calie delighted in dropping the most important element in a story into the early chapters but misdirecting readers—and me!—away from it until nearly the final page.

Once I heard Calista close her bedroom door, I headed for the kitchen. P. T. had been gone for hours, but she'd told me there was beer in the fridge. The Evan Williams called to me, but that sort of smooth bite wouldn't keep my brain functioning on all pistons. By comparison, a single bottle of quality beer would ease the knot in my neck but not befuddle my mind. Heck, it was already befuddled enough.

When I opened the refrigerator door, I found P. T.'s imprint in the liquor choices as well. She'd laid in a stock of Bell's Lager, a Michigan brand, and there was a note taped to the frontmost bottle.

A package was delivered at the kitchen door while the ladies were interrogating you. I put it in your room. Lemon scones with cranberries for breakfast at nine?

No bacon. No pancakes or waffles swimming in melted butter and maple syrup. I sighed. Allowing Burt to believe I'd spent most of my life elsewhere in the world, rather than in an elsewhere world, had resulted in him regaling me with tales of calorie-laden delights. He pointed out that a plate of nearly burnt bacon such as Ralph had served me was not bacon as the true gourmet knew it.

The only way to get decent food during my sojourn in Detroit would be to leave the house before P. T. arrived. I'd leave her a note of regret... regret that I'd miss staring into her pretty blue eyes, not regret missing the healthy fare she was determined to shove down my gullet. I hadn't come across the great fictional divide to be bombarded with things that were good for a guy!

Which brought Kit to mind. She wasn't good for me, in an entirely different universe of sensation.

I snagged a beer and poked around in the cabinets until I came up with a bag of pistachios. Comestibles gathered, I headed upstairs to look over the information that Doe had sent. I mean, who else was I expecting a package from, right?

In The Raven Tales I had an office, a secretary, file cabinets, a computer. In the real world, I had diddly-squat, unless I wanted to board horses in the bath. I also had a new problem. If Calista was determined to make a dash for the light at the end of the tunnel on Halloween, did that mean Samhain also was the end of my existence on this plane? Would I return to the pages of a book? If I did, would I be a different fellow as words flowed from someone else's pen?

I knew what Calie expected me to do in the real world; I knew what Doe and her associates expected me to do. Maybe it was time to decide what I wanted—and if that was even possible to achieve.

Twisting the cap off the beer, I settled on the floor, my back to the bed, and sorted through the sheets the Otherworld community had sent along. Twenty books; twenty deaths that had reappeared as justice from my hand.

Book 1: vampire staked and roasted.

Book 2: zombie flambéed.

Book 3: kraken. Let's just not go there.

And so it went. By the time there were twenty sheets spread in a horseshoe around me, not to mention a number of pistachio shells, I'd taken a thorough trip down memory lane and wanted to take another long, hot shower to wash the filth from my mind. Unlike in The Raven Tales, I couldn't see that any of the real-world victims had deserved what they'd gotten. Their only crime was being nonhuman in a world that named anything out of the human realm as demonic.

These beings met prejudicial killers, not a crime-fighting vigilante like The Raven. The vampire, for instance, had been turned against his will and staked to the exterior wall of a convenience store to greet the dawn. The zombie had been jumped and set aflame on his way back to the cemetery after visiting relatives on the Day of the Dead. Another victim had been a banshee who was a hospice volunteer. I wasn't eager to piece this world's events with those perpetrated by me between the covers of a book.

Like the good investigator I was in print, by dawn I'd made a list of the crime sites and names and addresses of the victims' relatives, coworkers, and friends.

Beelzie scratched at the door not long after. I cracked it enough to allow him to slip through, then closed and locked it. I still hadn't slept, but I had no idea what the need to sleep felt like. Figuring I'd know it when I dropped, if it happened at all, I stripped off the clothes I'd donned the night before and headed for the shower. The hellhound joined me.

"You ready for another day of watching me get beat to a semi-pulp?" I asked.

He yipped in answer. Apparently, he'd enjoyed entering the fray in the alley.

"Too bad you were too tuckered out to deal with the theophylaktos dudes. You'd have got along well with them. They're height-deprived, too," I said. But even the insult didn't seem to divert him from the treat of taking on the world again.

Once dressed, I folded my lists into sizes that would fit in my front pockets and tucked the burner, the debit card, and fake driver's license in my jacket pocket. The demon hot dog took off the moment I opened the door, but I lingered long enough to hide Doe's documents. When I reached the front door, Beelz had gathered his leash and slobbered over the end I was supposed to be gripping.

I called Burt as the two of us strolled toward the front gate.

"I need a really indecent breakfast," I told him. "You know a good place?"

Turns out he knew several. To narrow things down, I asked which had the best-looking waitstaff, and that's where we landed forty-five minutes later.

"You prepared to be my private chauffeur all day?" I asked, once a plate the size of a manhole cover had been placed before me. The only decision was whether to start with the sunny-side-up eggs, the leaning tower of pancakes, or the far more tantalizing strips of bacon. "I've got a long tally of things to accomplish."

"What sorts of places do you need to hit today?"

I gulped down some orange juice, probably the only thing on the table that P. T. would find acceptable. "Car dealership. Computer store. Back to the doxies to pick up Kit, then visits to places you'll like even less than our first stop yesterday. You game?"

"Ms. Amberson paying?"

"Yup, and I'm tipping. Did you notice last night that I'm a big tipper?"

"I did," he admitted, cutting into a breakfast steak. "What kind of vehicle are we looking for?"

"Black. Fast would be good, too. As close as we can get, off the lot, to the Batmobile. And, naturally, of local origin."

"You ain't plannin' on burglin' places, are you? 'Cause I gotta say—"

I raised my fork—empty at the moment—to stop him. "I'm an investigator. Legal as sin."

"Sin ain't usually legal," Burt said.

"It should be. There'd be a hell of a lot less of it. But now that you bring it up, there are two other things we need to add to the shopping list: an office and business cards." What should I call my business, though? In a way, Raven Investigations was already taken, by me, in a shitload of books.

"You want to do all of this before going back to the neighborhood where you got beat up yesterday?"

"I wasn't *beat up*, merely accosted by missionaries. The preacher and I clinked glasses and absolved each other of blame."

Burt grinned. "Accosted, huh? They accosted you pretty good, judging by the bruise on your jaw."

I'd hoped the extra day's growth of scruffy beard was hiding it. Probably should add razors to my purchase list before I started to look too much like Robinson Crusoe. The bruise on my shoulder looked far worse than the one beneath the beard, probably because what Hammer's men had started, Calie's magical slam against the wall had perfected.

Burt chewed slowly, either savoring his meal or thinking. It was difficult to tell.

"Likely be middle of the afternoon before we get back to the preacher's stomping ground," he warned.

"Kit won't mind."

"You makin' do with one of the flophouses there, or are we adding a posher hotel to the fare, then?"

"Neither. The little vixen is my way into the doors of the places I need to visit. People will accept her. If they see me without her, they'll be grabbing the nearest cleaver."

Burt shook his head slowly and dunked toast into the broken yolk of the remaining egg on his plate. "Gotta tell ya, Bram, you got some weird shit ways of enjoying this fine city."

"It's all in the perspective," I insisted. "So, car dealer first?"

"Damn right," he agreed.

When you know what you're looking for, Batmobiles aren't difficult to find. The Ravenmobile choice came down to two models of Ford. Since Beelzie couldn't get himself inside the butch SUV, we went with the Mustang Shelby GT500, which he bounded into as easily as he scrambled up to a sofa seat. I took every upgrade that was offered, but I told them to lose the spoiler. When making a run for it, you don't want anything on your vehicle that an adversary with nice long claws can grab onto.

Acquiring wheels put a major dent in the bank account. I scrawled my name on the papers. The signature looked suspiciously like Calista's handwriting. At least she didn't have what one would term a feminine hand. It looked more like demon claws had scratched something indecipherable on the dotted line.

Because of all the additions and alterations, I wouldn't be revving the thirty-two-valve supercharged V8 engine, playing with the six-speed transmission, using the Sirius navigation system, toying with the Shaker Pro audio, or filling either of the two cup holders with comestibles until later the next day. Luckily, Burt was willing to stay on the job a while longer.

It took far less time to add a computer and printer to my purchases. I wasn't nearly as picky when it came to work-related electronics. We tossed them into the cab's trunk, let Beelz have a necessary tree stop, then screeched to a halt at the first office building with a leasing sign out front.

It was a remodeled, two-story mid-century building, anchoring one end of a strip mall. Another scrawled signature, and I had an address other than Calie's to use. When you have limited expectations, it's easy to line up everything a guy needs. The realtor dude insisted on pointing out the security system, the super-duper heft of the outer door, the newly soundproofed walls, and the thickness of what was now my very own office door. These tour details went in one ear, found there was a no vacancy sign turned on, and hastily existed.

Burt and I probably spent more time deciding on the Mustang than on the visits to Target, the computer store, and the office building combined, including the time we waited for the realtor to arrange a security code pass and cut new door keys. For a hefty additional charge, the print shop a few doors down ran the business cards while we waited.

I was now officially on the clock: B. Farrell, Investigations.

Still, we stopped for another gastronomically adventurous lunch before heading for Kit's corner.

The two Sukis and the bakeneko were in place, looking just as delectably bad for any man with a healthy sense of self-preservation as they had the day before.

When Burt pulled up to the curb, Deer Woman leaned over, resting her forearm on the open window next to me.

"Bram and my darling Beelzie," she cooed. The doxie barked a welcome at the doxie. "And who's this you've brought us?"

"My keep-your-mitts-off chauffeur," I said.

"Burt," he said, reaching a hand across me to shake hers.

Doe caught my glare and released him without taking a single little sip of his life force. Of course, if he returned on his own and she enjoyed a gulp or two, it wouldn't be on my beat. He'd be weak for a few days, but happy. Unlike the succubi of legend or as depicted in The Raven Tales, the ones on the streets of *real* Detroit apparently just took a nosh. Killing a host tended to make the marks avoid a district, for some reason.

Yes, sarcasm. It leaks out.

61

"Got the documents," I told Doe. "Disturbing, rather than thrilling, reading material."

"Isn't it just," she agreed.

"I noticed that the earlier events didn't have current contact addresses for the relatives. Does that mean they left the area?"

"No, just that circumstances forced them to relocate. It was the breadwinners who were targeted if a family was involved. For the most part, the victims were single, and it was friends and lovers left to mourn."

"A significant change from the books," I said. "There were never any family members, much less mourners, in Ravenland Detroit. However, I am operating under a bit of a handicap here, Doe. If you were one of these people, would you open the door to a guy who introduced himself as Bram Farrell?"

She chuckled. "The curse of the fictional doppelgänger?"

"I'll suggest that as a title Calie can consider for the next book."

If there ever was another book. If I was still me in it.

"I've seen the titles, Bram. Far more likely to be *Raven Times Two*."

Hmm, that wasn't such a bad title, actually. I'd hate to have to live through all this twice, though.

"I doubt you dropped by just to tell me you got the files and are suffering from a case of confused identity," Doe murmured, "so what brought you to our corner today?"

I grinned. "A little red fox. I'd like to buy her full attention for the remainder of the day."

"Ask her yourself, then," she said. Blowing separate kisses to Burt and Beelzebub, she stepped back.

The swish of Kit's multiple fox tails tended to draw my attention from her face, but when I forced myself to focus on her eyes, they were crinkled in laughter.

"See something you like, honey?" she asked, a lilt in her breathy voice.

"Well, I did buy a bitchin' Mustang a bit earlier," I said.

"She couldn't have made you as happy as I can, Bram," she insisted, flirting. "After all, what's she got that I haven't?"

"Heated front seats and a good chance of environmentally lousy gas mileage. But I don't take possession until tomorrow."

She gave her delightful—well, to me it is!—bark of laughter. "A car? Sugar, don't you know I purr better'n any engine and will heat up your front seat anytime you want?"

Burt shifted uncomfortably behind the wheel.

"We'll test-drive that supposition one of these days," I said. Heck, maybe it was a promise! "Come on, climb in the back with Beelzie. I want you to be my liaison with the next of kin."

She pouted. "Aren't you going to crawl in the back with me?"

"For one thing, His Noir-ness has let me know my place is riding shotgun."

"And the other?" she asked.

"Time and place, darlin'. Time and place. Get in."

Kit climbed in. From the growls and woofs in the back seat, I think she and the Mighty Hellhound soon forgot I existed.

According to the reports I'd read last night, Pavan Banerjee and his wife Farha had left Bengal in the late Eighties. They'd come to Detroit because it was where an American missionary they'd befriended in India lived. Banerjee was an engineer, a math whiz who was fascinated with aerodynamics. He soon had two pending job offers within the automotive industry and went out with his old friend to celebrate the prosperity that was sure to follow. Farha was ill that night, so the two men feasted on a curry-heavy meal, toasting Banerjee's new start in his new country with multiple cups of tea. Neither was intoxicated by anything other than goodwill when they left the restaurant.

It was a pleasant evening, and as neither was far from home, they made the journey on foot. They parted company at the cross street that would lead them in opposite directions. And it was on his lonely walk, in the neighborhood where he lived, that the vampire fell on Pavan Banerjee. Long hours after she expected him home, Farha opened the door to find her husband unconscious on the doorstep. His shirt had been torn open, and the collar and front were covered in blood. Though it was small compared to the gore that coated her husband's clothing, the wound frightened Farha most of all: two small punctures on the side of the neck.

Unsure of how the injury would be treated by either the medical or law enforcement community, Farha called the missionary friend, who rushed to her side. Together, they decided to remain silent and simply watch over Pavan.

Banerjee recovered, but not to the health he'd enjoyed previously. Daylight began to bother both his eyes and skin. When he went for final interviews with the automobile giants, he seemed distracted and unable to concentrate. The offers dried up. Needing to support his wife, Pavan worked his way through employment agencies, through ads in the classified sections, through an agency that assisted immigrants in finding positions. In the end, he took a late-night shift working for another Indian family at their convenience store.

Where the vampire attacked again. The security camera footage showed Pavan stocking cigarettes, then a darkly clothed and hooded form grabbing him and leaving him once more unconscious. The shop owner discovered him in the morning and, also fearing what the authorities would say, called Pavan's wife. Together, they got the wounded man home.

The third time Banerjee was accosted, there were two attacks. One by the vampire and one by the unknown agency that came to be associated with me.

Well, with The Raven, after he did for the rakshasas in Book 1 what had been done to the unfortunate Pavan Banerjee.

In the event you missed it, yeah, it was an Indian version of a vampire I'd done in. Can you say *déjà vu*?

Pavan Banerjee certainly didn't sound like a fellow asking to become something other than he was. Unfortunately, someone wanted to make sure that his vampiric life was damn short.

After her husband's death, Farha Banerjee hadn't stayed in the apartment she'd shared with him. Her circumstances had changed drastically. Dreams of the future burned to dust like a vampire in the sun. Now she rented a minuscule flat over the dry cleaners where she slaved during the day.

I knew she was going to hate me on sight. Through no fault of my own, I would be a reminder of what she probably preferred to forget and couldn't. Once I started asking questions, the odds were good that she'd break down in tears.

"You mind if the Beelz stays in the cab with you while Kit and I see if Mrs. Banerjee is available?" I asked Burt as he pulled up to the curb in front of the dry cleaners.

"How long you think you'll be?"

Good question. The answer was anywhere from ten seconds to infinity. Okay, maybe not *that* long. If Farha Banerjee wasn't very cooperative or got overly emotional, it would just feel that long.

I picked what I hoped was a logical number. "Ten or fifteen minutes maybe? I'm hoping she'll be able to take a break to talk to us."

"Then I'll find a parking spot and let the mutt stretch his legs," Burt said. "Stretch mine a bit, too."

The long black demon in the back seat barked his approval of the plan.

The redheaded demon swung her long legs out of the car. If she'd been on the traffic side, there would probably have been fender benders due to driver distraction. I wasn't driving and I was damned distracted as it was.

Kit flowed to her feet and linked arms with me as Burt pulled away.

"Does your driver believe in beings like me?" she purred.

"Doubt it," I said. "Humans either wear blinders or believe wholeheartedly where demons are concerned. No middle ground. He seems more of an unbeliever, or if he does believe, it's just in demons who torture the damned in Hell, not demons who come to Earth for human groceries."

She pouted. "Is that what you think I am? Just a being in search of a meal?"

"Depends on whether I'm in a book or walking around on the outside," I admitted. "I find things look quite different out here."

"Like me?"

I grinned down at her. "Fishing for compliments, little fox? I'll give you enough to tide you over for weeks, but right now I'm on a tight schedule. Let's get Doe's assignment behind us first."

And Calie's, I added silently. If I survived past All Hallows, there would be more than just a relationship with a Suki to sort out.

No one was at the counter in the dry cleaners, but the door jangled upon our arrival. A few seconds later, a woman rounded the partition that screened the work area from sight. There were gray streaks in her short-cropped dark hair, but her ancestors had hailed from the Dark Continent, not the Indian subcontinent. As she walked, I could hear the slap of flip-flops against the cement floor. She gave us a quick glance, brows rising a bit over the outlandish drama of Kit's working clothes, then seemed to notice we weren't carrying any garments to be dropped off.

"Here for pickup? Do you have your ticket?" she asked, her voice pure Bronx.

"Actually, we're looking for Farha Banerjee," I said. "Is she working today?"

"We all work every day," the woman countered, bristling a bit. "What do you want with Banerjee?"

Lovely coworker, wasn't she?

"Is she available? I'm investigating several cold cases and was hoping to ask her some questions about her husband's demise." I slipped one of my spanking-new business cards out of my jacket pocket and slipped it across the counter.

She picked it up. "You Farrell?"

I nodded. It kept me from quipping, "Me Farrell." This wasn't a book, after all. Had to tone things down when dealing with *real* people.

"She won't want to talk to you."

"Could you at least *ask* her if she will?"

She shrugged. "She doesn't like talking about that. It was a bad time for her."

If she worked here seven days a week, this wasn't all that great a time for her either.

"I understand," I said. "Still, the perpetrator was never brought to justice. My associate and I would like to remedy that if we can."

The woman stared at Kit.

"Your associate?" she repeated, doubt and sarcasm mixing equally in her voice.

Kit smiled, radiating friendliness. "I hope you'll forgive the way I'm dressed. Mr. Farrell just pulled me off an undercover job, and I didn't have time to change. We're really sincere in wanting to see justice done. We wouldn't willingly cause Mrs. Banerjee pain, but she may be able to tell us something that isn't in the files."

"You're part of one of those groups like the shows on TV that look into old crimes and solve them?"

"We try, at least," I said. The idea wasn't that far from the truth. In fact, the idea of a fictional hero and members of the nonhuman community becoming crime fighters certainly sounded like a network pilot, if not a full season's worth of shows, to me. Maybe Netflix or Amazon would pick it up.

"I'll ask her, but I make no promises," the woman said. Shoving my business card into the pocket of her slacks, she slap-slap-slapped her way around the partition once more. As another woman rounded it barely fifteen seconds later, I figured Banerjee's widow had been listening to our conversation all along.

Her dark hair had more than a scattering of gray in it. Pure white streaks peeled back from her brow and were bound in a tight knot at the nape of her neck. Her sun-warmed skin looked dry, parched. Deep furrows trailed over her high cheekbones and down from thinly drawn lips. She looked two decades older than her true age. A spare woman, short of stature, she maintained a ramrod posture, spine stiff and shoulders thrust back. Despite the heat of the pressing machines, she wore a long-sleeved blouse with a high, tightly buttoned collar and rows of neat buttons marching down the front. A simple cross hung from a chain around her neck. From the stance she took behind the counter, she hadn't let circumstances rob her of pride, though they might have made her wary.

"I am Banerjee's widow," she said by way of introduction. Over two decades of living in Detroit had tempered the rise and fall of her native accent to a mere echo. "I understand you wish to speak to me?"

I whisked another business card into sight, introduced myself, then my accompanying vixen as Ms. Fox-Jones, and explained once again that we were investigating cold cases and that the file on her husband's death had intrigued us.

"Such a file does not exist," Farha snapped. "I was advised at the time that the police would not be interested in investigating. They were not called."

"Nonetheless, someone in the community did look into it at the time, Mrs. Banerjee."

"What community?" she demanded, then leveled a finger at Kit. "Hers? Do you think I don't know what you are?"

67

As she was glaring at Kit, I wasn't sure whether I was also included in the accusation.

"After Pavan's death, I made it my business to learn all I could about such *communities*." She said the word like it was an anathema.

Kit drew herself up, eyes narrowed. "I am not like the thing that killed your husband. It was not one of my kind that pinned him."

Farha had no intention of backing down. "Was it not? It is what the *community* does to humans. Destroys their lives."

"We believe a human did the deed," Kit countered, tossing her head, making her red hair swing like a twitching tail.

"Like this one?" Farha demanded, turning on me. "He looks capable of such a thing. In fact, he *is* capable. I know the name Farrell, and it is not one I would care to wear come Judgment Day."

Now that presented me with a conundrum. Did I tell her I wasn't human or that I was? In either case, I was the despised Bram Farrell. The Raven. The man who had killed a vampire in the same manner that her husband had been murdered. The fact that it had happened in the pages of a book didn't make a difference to Pavan Banerjee's wife. His death had been hellish, and her existence since then probably had been, too. Particularly if she had not moved forward with her life.

"If you could just tell us about that night," I tried, "perhaps we can—"

She tossed my business card back in my face. "Leave. And don't come back. No matter how much *investigating* you do, you cannot bring my husband back. Whatever killed him is gone. Look to your *files* if you don't believe me. There have been no other deaths like my Pavan's, have there?"

Not in the Raven books. That would have killed sales. Calie had moved on to recounting the death of a different species of Otherworlder. And while I'd been the perpetrator in print, in rereading the real case files the night before, I was fairly certain that if I ever did feel the need to sleep, my rest wouldn't be undisturbed. My victims would haunt me now.

"No, there haven't been," Kit answered her. "There have been different, equally vicious murders."

"Then investigate them," Farha snarled. "Let my husband find what rest he can."

I certainly had no counterargument to that. "I'm sorry we bothered you, Mrs. Banerjee. If you change your mind, please call me."

To ensure she had the number—or something to set on fire to soothe her anger—I put another business card on the counter, grabbed Kit's arm, and hightailed it.

"Well, that went particularly well," I said as the door closed behind us.

"If you were looking to be pilloried," Kit agreed. "I don't know whether to pity her or despise her. Either way, she isn't doing herself any good. Such hate will destroy her soul faster than any demon swallowing it could."

"Bad karma."

"Really bad karma," Kit agreed. "Where to next?"

Had to grin at that. "Where else? The zombie's family if you're up to it."

She laughed. "Takes more than a halka spitting at her to put this little hunter off the trail."

"A halka? Isn't that one of the Indian names for a witch? You think Farha Banerjee is one?"

Kit shrugged. "She has the personality for it, but no, she's just acting like one. Besides, *you* would know if she was one. You live in a witch's hive."

Hive wasn't really the right term, but the way the other members of the coven buzzed around Calista, it did ring true in a different context.

"You're right. Farha isn't a witch, just a very bitter woman."

Kit curled her fingers with mine and tilted her head coquettishly. "Which isn't going to stop you from looking for the human who killed her husband."

I sighed deeply. "Nope. Not a bit."

She looped our linked hands over her head so that my arm rode comfortably on her shoulders and she could cuddle closer.

"My hero," she purred, smirking.

"I wonder," I mused, my mind on what she'd said. "Do you really think a human—a *lone* human—could have overcome a newly turned vampire and held it in position against a wall while driving a stake through its heart with enough strength to impale it *on* that wall?"

Kit withdrew her hand from mine and pushed away. "It was not one of the Otherworld community that committed the atrocity. We investigated thoroughly, and our investigations aren't regulated by any governmental laws, Raven."

She sounded proud about that lack of policing.

"You mean beings were tortured, killed, in an effort to unearth the killer?"

"Perhaps," she said.

"No one, human or demon, tells the truth under torture, Kit. They simply tell their local Torquemada what he wants to hear."

"Yet even then, we didn't find the murderer."

"That means that, like Farha, you believe the perpetrator left Detroit rather than hang around waiting to be caught?"

"It's one theory," she admitted. "But not the one you believe."

She knew me that well already? Or had all the knowledge she'd gathered about me come from reading Calie's damn books?

"Not saying yes, not saying no," I said. "Let's go round up Burt and the hound and see if Xavier Botello's family is more accommodating."

Either foxes have short memories, or I'd been forgiven, for she snuggled back beneath my arm again. "Do I get to be Ms. Fox-Jones, undercover operator, again?"

I laughed. "Hell of a lot better than them thinking you're a forward *puta, zorra,*" I told her.

Fate likes to fuck with a guy's itinerary. The Botello family was missing when we reached their home. Not as in abducted, but as in vacationing.

"They're in sunny Acapulco," a neighbor said. "Youngest daughter caught herself a doctor. The entire family headed to Acapulco for the wedding. They'll all be back day after tomorrow, though."

It was nice to hear that at least one victim's family had moved on with their lives, but it left me wondering what to investigate next. When we crawled back in Burt's cab, I fished one of my lists from my jeans pocket and handed it back to Kit. Beelzie already had his snout resting on her thigh and was gazing up at her with hopeful red eyes. She must have read that look right, because she took the list from me with one hand while beginning to scratch his belly with the other.

Next time around, this fictional hero is interviewing for a job as a crime-fighting dog in a mystery series. Dogs get all the attention from females.

"You're more familiar with the neighborhoods and the lifestyles of the people involved," I told Kit. "Since the Botellos are out of the picture for a couple days, who should we hit next?"

She chewed on the corner of her lip in a very humanlike way as she studied the tally. "Rolph Lund," she suggested.

I took the list back and scanned it. "Book 11, *Raven Breaks Even*." The victim had been a numbers-running troll. I won't go into the details. It was messy. "Why does that address sound familiar?"

"Because it's the street that I work," she said. "You really need a map, Raven. Learn your way around town."

Burt glanced over at me, his expression clearly asking for a location.

"Back to more familiar stomping grounds, then," I said.

He took a gander at the road behind, via the rearview mirror, and did an illegal U-turn.

"Is this address right?" I demanded. "666? That's not very encouraging."

"Mark of the beast," Burt grunted.

Kit made a noise that sounded a bit like a sneeze, though I think it was a snort of disgust.

"That's ridiculous superstition," she told him. "Besides, if there was a 666 address, it would be in the middle of the block, where they knocked down the old hotel."

"They knocked down a building in your neighborhood?" I was stunned. Most of the buildings looked like they should have been included in such thoughtful urban rehabilitation.

"Admittedly, it burned down first," Kit said. "The Lunds' address is 966. The first number is loose and swings down to look like a six, so everyone just writes it down that way. Even delivery services know which door it is."

"How far is it from your corner?"

"Just a couple doors. You've been there, Bram."

Considering that other than her corner, I'd only visited a noxious alley and The Bridge Bar and Burned Comestibles Lounge, I groaned.

"Not Ralph's place?"

"Of course, Ralph's place," she said. "Rolph Lund was his brother."

"Ralph and Rolph Lund?"

"And their sister Ruth. They anglicized their first names to something close to what they sounded like in their native language."

When grouped as a trio, the names sounded like noises Beelzie made when he found me wanting in some manner. Of course, troll names are incredibly difficult to pronounce correctly by unaccustomed palates. Mine had never been so accustomed.

I twisted to look back at her as I shoved the list away again. "Is that why Ralph burned my bacon yesterday? Because he associated me with The Raven?"

"No one *associates* you with The Raven, Bram," she declared, humoring me. "You *are* The Raven."

"Fictional character, Kit," I countered.

"You're investigating for the community and for Calista," she said. "Ergo, Raven."

Burt gave me a look that clearly said "Women!" Had to agree— with both of them, unfortunately.

"You thirsty?" I asked him.

"Always."

I fished out a twenty and handed it over. "Then after you drop us at The Bridge, head for a safer bar. I'll call when you're needed."

"Pooch staying with me?"

I spared the hellhound a glance. "You in, Beelz?"

The bark was definitely an affirmative. He probably remembered the beef chips backstroking through thick, rich gravy. Personally, I was hoping leg of troll might appear just as tasty to him, if the occasion required it.

Kit's neck of the woods wasn't far from the Botellos' neighborhood. Burt dropped us off on the opposite side of the street from The Bridge and took off. I dawdled, releasing Beelzie from his leash. We might be breaking a major law of pet management, but he needed to be free of encumbrances if things went south—and I do mean to Hell, sans any pansy-ass handbasket.

72

Free of his leash, Beelzie surprised me by looking both ways along the street before crossing it. Could be he'd been looking for something other than vehicles, but the road was practically deserted. Down the way, Neko was chatting up a mark. Deer Woman was nowhere in sight. Kit tripped across after the hound and I trailed just far enough back to grab the door when she opened it, holding it for my troops to take the forlorn hope position.

"Hi, Ralph," Kit called. "Have you got time to talk about Rolph?"

The bartending troll had been wiping down a spot on his counter, but at the sound of her voice, he looked up, caught sight of me beyond her shoulder, and made a grab for something beneath the bar.

Double-barrel sawed-off shotgun time, I thought.

He came up with an axe, an axe with an edge so sharp it glinted hungrily even in the dim light of the bar.

I gave Kit a push, sending her tail over tail—Hey! She's got a lot of those red fox tails!—into the nearest batch of tables and chairs. Grabbed Beelzie up as well, tucking his long body under my arm as I dived for cover.

The axe bit deep into the edge of the bar top, barely three inches from my head.

"Take cover, Beelz," I urged. "Get Kit out."

Waste of breath and words, of course. Kit launched herself at Ralph, her teeth turned sharp and wickedly ready to rip into him. Her claws were extended beyond the tips of her gloves. My feral goddess.

Ralph backhanded the succubus hard enough to send her sliding down the highly polished bar. She gave a cry that was half pain and half surprise and zipped off the far end onto the floor.

As red tails and green satin tumbled out of sight, Beelzebub went into demon mode. His eyes glowed like hot coals. His canines had extended even further than Kit's, but then he still had a muzzle and she hadn't gone entirely ninja fox. I swear the dog had powers of which I was unaware for the leap he made for Ralph's throat was beyond awesome.

Next to my associates, I felt like unnecessary furniture in the room. So I did what neither of them had considered—or, in Beelzie's case, could do. I picked up a chair and slammed it into Ralph's back

73

while he was busy multitasking, fending off the hellhound and trying to get his axe free of the bar.

It took more than one strike. Fortunately, the chair was sturdy enough to last through the punishment. It was still in fairly good shape when Ralph no longer was.

When he crumpled to the floor, I calmly set the chair down (it only wobbled a little bit), grabbed a mug, and drew a tall, foaming draft beer. It was ready when he pushed upright, one massive hand against the floor to support his weight.

"Here," I said, handing him the drink. "I'd say it's on the house, but as it's on my tab, that doesn't really apply, does it?"

He glared at me but took the beer. While he downed it, I yanked the axe free.

"I'm not here to cause trouble, Ralph," I said. "I'm here to help. Doe set me to finding who murdered the twenty supernaturals Calie based part of her stories on."

"Supernaturals," he growled and then spat on the floor. "My family ain't former humans. We ain't demons either, not like these two."

He gestured to where Beelzie sat on his haunches at Kit's feet, his eyes still burning as he stayed on alert. Behind him, Kit leaned back against one of the booth supports setting her toy-sized top hat back at a jaunty angle. Her teeth looked human again, and there wasn't a claw in sight. Her fishnet stockings had suffered, but the rips only made a man's eyes drop to them faster: warp speed rather than Mach Two.

Neither of the demons took offense at the troll's words, which was a relief. What we didn't need was another fight to break out. The loss of a pair of stockings, and the gain of a chair with more personality, would be minor to what could happen.

"Damn right you aren't," I said. "Trolls are legendary folk. Ancients born of this land long before the place was overrun with humans."

He grunted as he straightened his back, arching it. I swear I heard it groaning like weathered boards on a span of historic bridging. "You know your history, then."

"It pays to know the folks one lives among and I've never lived *among* humans, just existed in their minds thanks to a string of words."

"Words are powerful things," Ralph said.

"Clearly!" I spread my arms to indicate that I was the proof of that. Then I asked what I'd come to ask. "I understand that you think I had something to do with your brother's death?"

He snarled, showing really nasty teeth. Trolls and dentists didn't mix, apparently. "There were ten deaths before his. By then everyone knew it was The Raven what done 'em."

"I wasn't of this world yet," I reminded. "Only been on this side of the fiction line less than two full days."

"You did for him, Raven. Everything pointed to it."

"What? Evidence? There are no law enforcement personnel investigating crimes in the nonhuman world. This isn't some story where you can hire a PI with powers to look into things. It's Detroit's hidden world; well, unhidden really, every being front and center for humans to see if they didn't have their netherworld blinders on. Talk to me, Ralph."

He rubbed that giant hand over his far, far, far from Adonis-like features and sighed deeply. "I need another drink," he said.

"I'd like one as well," Kit requested. "So would Beelzie."

The dog dipped his long demon snout in confirmation but kept the security light blazing in his eyes.

I shoved a hand into my pocket. "Hell, so do I," I said, slapping down another twenty.

At the rate I was spending money, I'd make Calie's hundred grand disappear quicker than David Copperfield could manage it. The stage illusionist, not the one in Dickens's books, though I had met that one in fictional character land. There's a bar, The Hero's Rest, that characters in frequently read books... er... frequent. Considering someone in the world was always reading *David Copperfield* for a class assignment or one of the Raven books for chills, thrills, and fun, we two fictional characters never get a night off. Not even after becoming physical beings. Too many people expect great things of us—well, okay, of me.

We all settled in a booth, Kit and I on one side with mugs of over-foamed beer in our hands, Ralph and Beelzie on the opposite side. Beelzie's beer was in a soup bowl, his paws were on the table and his tongue was lapping faster than I could talk. I was definitely a bad influence on the demon canine; he'd downed people food the day before and would return to Calie's estate a bit tipsy today.

"Rolph weren't a bad guy. Not for a troll," Ralph said into his beer. "Sure, he had this numbers thing, but he ran an honest game."

I glanced at Kit for verification. She rolled her eyes.

"Sounds like someone else didn't think so." Yep, me living dangerously.

"Me and Ruth never thought it was the game that got him dead. It was prejudice."

"Someone who didn't like trolls?" Go figure!

"Yeah. Those fairy tales don't 'zactly paint us in rosy terms, ya know?"

You ever read the original versions of those stories? Hell, enough to give children nightmares for life! In other words, yeah, I sympathized with the plight of trolls. Sue me.

"That mean I should be looking for someone who is racist about trolls?"

"Racist when it comes to anything that isn't human," Kit corrected. "Even my kind hasn't been exempt."

Book 8, *Raven's Run*. An incubus, the male of Kit's species, had been dispatched in it. In fact, now that I thought about it, the Sukis were being very quiet about the death of Tado Gallo.

Now was not the time to bring up Gallo. I had to concentrate on Rolph Lund first.

"Tell me about your brother's last day," I urged Ralph.

He laughed. It sounded like chains straining to support a heavily laden vehicle as it crossed above the surface of a river. "Sure you want to hear about a troll's daily grind, Raven?"

"No detail is too small in an investigation," I said.

"Remember that you asked for it," Ralph grunted, then reeled out some horribly trite stuff that I could have done without. When he finished, I knew what brand of toothbrush Rolph preferred and that he went commando beneath his rough-textured trousers. I knew he fancied freckle-faced women, the worst rotgut liquor, and cage fights. Only two of those sounded promising, but while the numbers-running brother had liked to mentally strip down those freckled dollies to see if the dots were connectable, he hadn't been brave enough to ever approach any woman except his sister Ruth, who, according to Ralph, had warts rather than freckles. And a mean left hook, Ralph added, apparently having felt it himself. With those sorts of brotherly compliments, I thought, he deserved it.

The cage fights, however, were another thing entirely. Rolph had run book on those, too, and had paid off a couple of guys to take falls to increase the take.

I pulled the list of victims out of my pocket again and turned it over to the blank side. "You know these guys' names?"

"Yeah," he said. "Spli—"

"You got a pen or pencil on you?" I asked Kit.

She raised her arms. "Where would I keep it?"

Ralph groaned, pushed to his feet, leaned over the bar—don't even try to picture that—and returned to the table with a deeply chewed pencil. "Split-Nose Erskine and Paps Pacheco."

"Obviously old family names," I said, scratching the monikers down. "You know where I might find them?"

"It's been ten years or more, Farrell. And I ain't inta doing illegal things like my brother was. Look what it got him," the troll rumbled.

"A hint, then? Maybe the name of a gym, or a zoo, or wherever worn out cage fighters go?"

It sure wasn't going to be Heaven.

Ralph glared hatred at me. No surprise but, geez, I was looking for a killer that had done for his brother. And I was still next to clueless about this world I'd stumbled into. Kit was right, I *did* need a map. I needed more than that though. Like my head examined.

"Binky's Boxing Arena," an even more gruff voice said at my elbow. Odd, because I was sitting down, which would put the speaker at about three feet tall.

I'd been wrong in identifying the girl from the kitchen as a hobgoblin the day before. Now that she was up close and personal, it was clear she had troll blood, but mixed with dwarf.

"Shut it, Ruth," Ralph snarled. "You don't know nothin' about such things."

Her laugh was nails on a washboard. I was beginning to long for the days when a description like that was nothing but words.

"You wish," she coughed, laying a hand on my arm. "Split-Nose and Paps don't do the cage no more, Raven, but they train idiots to climb into it. Go to Binky's and ask for Split-Nose. Tell him Ruth sent you. He's sweet on me."

"Sweet on you!" her brother snarled. First time he'd heard of it, I guess.

She ignored him. "Don't talk to Paps unless Split-Nose is there. That Spaniard has a nasty temper, and what few brains he did have were ripped out in the cage."

I wondered if she meant that figuratively or literally. In any case, I scrawled the name of the boxing joint down as well.

"Did you hear what Ralph told me?" I asked her. "Anything you want to add to it?"

She sighed sadly. "Rolphy was sorta my twin, only we obviously had different fathers, since he got Ma's build, like Ralph here."

Ralph ground his teeth. Not a pleasant sound. Hard for a big guy to live down a mother's weakness for a sweet-talking guy with a height management problem.

"You were close?" I essayed.

"Like that," Ruth said. Since she crossed her fingers rather than just stick them close together, I wondered whether there was a lot I didn't know about the mating habits of trolls. It *was* generally a small community of close relatives. "I even gave him some ideas on how to set things up to make a killing on the fights. Rolphy had game, but no creativity."

I stopped myself before a sarcastic "uh-huh" left my mouth. Made a nod suffice.

"If you have any more questions about Rolph, you come to me, Raven," she said, then glanced across the table. "Your dog all right?"

Thinking she meant his eyes, I fell back on Calie's explanation. "Gene pool blooper, that's Beelz."

"He's a demon," she said, sounding as though she was surprised that I hadn't noticed that myself.

"He's also drunk," Kit said.

Ralph grunted. "Probably gave him too much for his size. I'm used to feeding decent-sized hellhounds."

Beelzie's nose was in the empty soup bowl, and the glaze in his peepers looked about right for all the pink that generally painted what should have been the whites of his eyes.

"It's pretty potent stuff," Ruth agreed. "I brew it myself."

Kit's mug was nearly empty, but her metabolism seemed to be holding its own. My glass had barely been touched. But that was because I was a bourbon sort of guy, as a rule. And troll beer and embalming fluid have a lot in common.

I got to my feet and reached across to grab the mighty little demon by the scruff of his neck and lift him out of the booth. Kit took him from me immediately, cuddling him like an infant.

"Thank you for your help, Ruth, Ralph. I'll look in at Binky's, and if I learn anything that might be helpful, I'll pass it along to you," I promised.

Ruth swatted her brother's massive arm. "See, I told you he wasn't like you thought."

Ralph turned an evil stare my way. "Remains to be seen, sister. I could be the one in the right yet."

We left them engaged in a glaring contest. Could have been what trolls did for fun.

Outside on the street again, I gave Burt a call. "You still sober enough to pick me up? If you are, we'll take Beelzie home, I'll let you soak me for another dinner, then you can drop me at a bookstore and be done for the night. You game?"

He'd already decided on the restaurant.

Kit grabbed the front of my jacket and dragged me down to receive a smooch that if I was a real boy would have sent smoke jetting from my ears, then sashayed those foxy tails of hers back to the corner to twitch them at paying customers.

Beelzie's legs wouldn't work when I set him on them, so he played dead dog on the sidewalk while I propped up the building, waiting for Burt to arrive.

Naturally, that's when Hammer and his morons decided to amble out of the alley across the way.

"Yo, Raven," one of them called out. "You got time for that interview with the bosses now?"

"Let me check my appointment book," I said and mimed removing a nonexistent book from my jacket and flipped through it. I really should have upgraded to an imaginary electronic tablet of some sort.

"Sorry, *now* seems to be taken already," I said and tucked the invisible day planner back into an equally nonexistent inner jacket pocket.

"We ain't takin' no for an answer," another of them said.

I looked at the preacher. "Did I say no, Hammer? I didn't hear myself say no."

"Sounded a lot like it ta me," he countered.

"Really? I must practice my diction. Let me ask you this. Are the dead ones interested in talking to me about Pavan Banerjee?"

"Who?"

Well, that *did* answer my question. "If not Banerjee, then what is this about? Don't tell me the Vamp Scouts are taking orders for cookies already? Put me down for four boxes of anything with peanut butter in it."

Hammer glared at me. "You ever get tired of rattling off rubbish?"

I gave it a moment of fake thought. "Nope. It's your own fault for turning up with such asinine requests. I'm a busy man. Take a damn freaking number!"

His fists clenched, as did his jaw. He took a step toward me, but stopped as Beelzie's growl amped up.

"Back off, Hammer," I warned. "He's had far too much to drink and might be one ornery drunk to tangle with. I'll make a deal with you. Go back and find out if the neck-biters will give me information on the vamp that turned Banerjee a little over two decades ago, and I'll meet them at moonrise tomorrow in a location of their choosing."

He considered the offer, then turned his ugly mug to the side to crack his neck. Sounded like a two by four splitting to me, but then I'm still new to the world of sound, right?

"Give me a minute," he said and walked away, a cell phone already to his ear. The rest of the boys stayed, blocking traffic in the street. Odd how quickly drivers in the area found new routes to take.

"So," I said to them, "how about those Lions? Think they got a chance of making it to the Super Bowl this year?"

Apparently, they weren't football fans. Which on one hand was good, because that was all I had.

Hammer's bosses had obviously given a quick answer, because he was back among our happy crowd before anyone's scowl broke their face.

"Moonrise tomorrow," he said, then rattled off an address but gave no directions. I'd have to Google it.

"Shall I bring a hostess gift, or will the ladies be absent?" I asked.

No one thought that merited a response, including me. They skulked their way back to the alley—maybe it had a clubhouse—and I was free to go.

Burt pulled up two minutes later.

After dropping a worse-for-wear hellhound back at Calie's estate, we took the scenic route to the restaurant, swinging by my new office to drop off the laptop and printer, then feasted on things that would no doubt have given P. T. nightmares. Once more replete, I had Burt drop me at the largest brick-and-mortar bookstore in town and then hightail it for a good night's rest. I'd call him in the morning for the next round of fun and games. In the meantime, I needed to devote some time to my creator's quest.

It was the reason she'd brought me over the divide. Idiotic as it seemed.

The helpful staff at the store told me I was in luck: There was a writer's group meeting that very evening, and they welcomed new members. Having an hour to kill before they were scheduled to gather, I did some more shopping.

Kit was absolutely right in that I needed a map. I needed two of them: one to deposit in the glove compartment of the shiny new Ravenmobile when I picked it up (because GPS could get me where I was going, but it wouldn't give me a sense of where I was in the city), and one to pin to my office wall.

There was a small but sufficient office supply area in the store. I picked up a collection of multicolored markers and pushpins with and without numbered flags. I added a spool of string, a box cutter, two more ruled legal pads, a box of pens, a ream of printer paper, and a nifty thing that looked like a pen but held a microphone and recorded voices to a flash drive doohickey.

The enthusiastic salesperson helped me find the largest, most detailed map of Detroit in existence, and once we'd added two of them to my pile of goodies, he stood guard over the pile while I headed for the fiction department. I needed some personal research materials, and the only place I could come up with that sort of information was in The Raven Tales. Probably because Calie was a local author, they had complete sets. A quick swipe of the debit card and the whole kit and caboodle was mine. Oh, and so was a giant latte.

I settled in one of the chairs in the area where the writing group was due to meet and pulled out the first volume. By the time the first scribbler turned up, I'd scandalized employees and customers alike by turning over the corners of pages where information that I thought might be pertinent fell.

"Hey," an overly enthusiastic voice said as a young woman swept into the rough circle of love seats and chairs. "Welcome to your first meeting of the Clueless Scribblers."

I closed my book but didn't put it away. "Hey, yourself. That can't be the official name of the group."

"Well, no, but it describes most of us fairly well. I'm Naomie, with an *ie*, by the way." She plopped down in an adjacent seat and held out her hand.

I moved forward in my chair to give it a pump. "Bram," I said.

She pointed to the tome resting on my thigh. "Like in the Raven books."

"It's what attracted me to them," I said, making the statement sound like a confession.

"Just to warn you, there are *those* within the group who despise fantasy. Well, really, they despise everything except what they fancy writing themselves."

As Naomie with an *ie* had accessorized with silver, skull-festooned jewelry, I figured she had paranormal literary inclinations.

"You wouldn't by any chance be published, would you?" she asked.

"Me? No, sorry. Why, is it a requirement?"

She laughed. "No, but we've got this poet lady and this dude working on his PhD who think writing for money is selling out."

"Idiots, in other words," I said. Calie had run into those types herself. I was just quoting her.

"On the nose. Oh, geez, here they come!"

Which of the six people headed our way were the idiots, I wasn't sure, but they were all carrying neat stacks of paper in their arms.

I dropped my book back into the bag on the floor between my feet.

"Readings?" I asked Naomie.

She was bent down, dragging neat file folders from the bag at her side.

"Yeah," she said. "If you decide to join, you might want to bring a flask of something strong to tip into that latte in the future."

Naomie did the introductions, but the names washed over me. Until I heard each read their masterpieces, it didn't matter who they were. I was looking for the right voice, the promise of plot twists, for someone who had the potential to write the kind of drivel that I spouted all the time. Each of these, along with a few other elements, were things the coven members had come up with the evening before. Calie had forced me to write them down. It looked like at least three of the new arrivals met Calie's gender and age requirements, Naomie among them. But not a thing any of them read came close to Calie's style of prose.

When the last of them finished reading, collected comments from the others, and started to clear out, I noticed Naomie was blinking back tears and attempting a smile. Wished I could have saved her from their harsh criticisms, but even I could tell she was a novice wordsmith.

I found my helpful salesperson before leaving.

"I really appreciated your help tonight," I told him. "But I need two other things, though the store isn't going to carry them. The phone number of a cab company and a phone book. Any ideas?"

He supplied both in a flash. "We never use the phone book, so you might as well take the one behind the counter."

I got one last latte to go and slipped him a grateful twenty by shaking his hand.

Day Three, October 29

Luna was swelling toward a full harvest moon, although in October the more official designation would be a Hunter's Moon. This hunter was definitely off his game in this world. That needed to change.

When I reached it, the rest of the office building where I'd leased space was semi-dark. The security lights created more shadows than they diminished but made it possible to avoid walking into walls. I paid off the cab and took my purchases, which now included a burger and fries courtesy of a drive-through window, inside using my virgin building key. Since my visit earlier in the day, someone had taped a sheet of paper to the door of my niche. I wondered whether a brass plate would follow quickly enough for me to see it before Calie shuffled me off-planet again.

One of the reasons I'd gone with this office was the free Wi-Fi. Plus, I had better things to do than shop for quarters.

The office was already equipped with desk, wheeled desk chair, two four-drawer filing cabinets, and a desk lamp. There was also a telephone. Doubted it would ever ring.

I flicked on the lamp, rather than the overhead lights, and set to work. The computer connected to the Net in a blink. The map fought me until I gave up on having it straight and allowed it to look tipsy when I pressed push pins into the wallboard at its corners.

Google and Yahoo both gave me free email addresses. A variety of real estate companies were happy to let me sign up with those, along with my cell phone number. With access established, I began searching for the average income level of various neighborhoods in the Detroit area. By dawn, my colored markers had created a vibrant landscape of primary, secondary, and in a few cases where borders overlapped, tertiary colors.

Neighborhoods like Calie's were now highlighted in green, since living there required lots of moola. I'd checked crime reports from the newspapers, too; yes, I had to buy subscriptions to do searches of the archives, but it was money well spent. The areas where drive-by shootings, domestic abuse, and civil disturbance were the norm were allotted red, for all the blood spilled. I might not know streets, but I knew the parts of the city now, or at least where to find them.

I was adding flagged pins to the map to indicate each of the death sites when the receptionist arrived and cranked up the coffeepot in the outer room. It was time to give Burt a call, but I called the estate first to see how Beelz was faring. From the barks I heard in the background, I think he wanted P. T. to give him the phone. I promised to pick him up before we claimed the car. He seemed cool with that.

Burt had been doing a bit of his own thinking and realized that I needed to insure the Mustang before I could drive it off the lot. Dealerships were such sticklers. This meant that while he and I returned to what I already thought of as our favorite breakfast place, I gave P. T. another call.

"You have any idea who writes Calie's insurance policies?" I asked. "I've got a car to pick up later on today, and I need to be covered."

"Why don't you call your aunt's friend Neva?" she suggested. "Ms. Amberson doesn't use her, but I believe that's because she's already been with the same agent for years."

Neva of the ample bosom and cougar-ish designs?

"You wouldn't happen to know her last name, would you? Auntie felt names were superfluous when she introduced me."

P. T. sighed. Yes, poor put-upon chef that she was, though she did have that fault of depriving a man of true carnivore fare.

"Fitzsimmond. Two *m*'s and a *d*."

"Gee, I thought there would be more letters than that in it," I said.

The sigh was deeper this time. "Is there anything else, Bram? I've got a chickpea stew I'm putting together for lunch. Will you be back to join Ms. Amberson?"

As I had a forkful of waffle dripping syrup onto my plate at the time, I sincerely doubted it. I mean, *chickpea stew?*

"Better not count on me making it," I said, "but yeah, there's one more thing. Do you know the names of the women who were at the octopus extravaganza the other night?"

"You are going to owe me so big, Bram Farrell," she snarled, but she rattled off their names in nothing flat. Fortunately, I'd fumbled the magic voice recording pen from my pocket and flicked it on to catch all the information.

"It's difficult to pay off this sort of debt when the lady in question probably cooks circles around any restaurant's staff," I wheedled.

"Not if the lady in question is fine with drinks and a movie," P. T. said.

"Done, but it will have to wait until after Halloween. Calie's got me doing some research for her."

"That's not long to wait," she said. "Besides, she is planning a special meal for her friends and associates on the thirty-first. I'll be busy getting ready for it."

I said goodbye, hoping she wouldn't feel stood up if I zipped back to fictionland before she could be wined and movied.

"Halfway to insurance connection," I reported to Burt. "Have a name, now need an address."

He whipped out his cell phone. It was a lot fancier than mine, but then mine was of the toss-away variety, not the long-term contract genus. "What's the name?"

I supplied it. A moment later he waved his index finger across the screen in a series of quick flicks, apparently found what he was looking for, and handed the phone across the table to me. It was ringing.

"Fitzsimmond Insurance Writers," a perky voice said a moment later.

"Is Neva available?" I asked.

"Who may I say is calling?"

"Bram." It seemed enough, although I fancied the perky one would read romance into it.

She put me on hold. Barely five seconds later, Neva was purring into my ear, cougar-ness definitely flicked on.

"Brrraaammmm, I'm pleased that you called."

"You'll be even more pleased when you hear why." Truthfully, she'd probably be disappointed. "Picking up a Mustang later this afternoon and am in need of a policy rider or something like that."

Neva switched off cougar mode and into business gear. "I'll need more than just the model."

I gave her the name of my salesman at the dealership. He'd be able to answer her questions better than I could, anyway.

"You need me to sign anything? Give you the bank account to suck the premiums from?"

"I can get the bank information from Zeta," she said. "Although Calie doesn't use Zeta's bank, she did use Zeta to set up your account."

Hmm. "Interesting. What fields are other members in?"

She supplied names that still meant nothing to me, but with businesses that did. One was in real estate, another in politics, a third in law enforcement, a fourth a member of the Board of Education, a fifth a stockbroker.

"And, of course, Delia is in public relations and promotions," Neva added.

"Sounds like nearly every element of community life is covered by at least one of you," I said, pitching my voice to appear amazed instead of suspicious, which I was. Very suspicious.

"We like to think so." Neva sounded like she was preening, proud of the coven and her part in it.

"When should I swing by to scratch my name on the official paperwork?"

"Two to three hours?"

I promised to be there.

Burt had cleaned his plate and was nursing a fresh cup of java. I handed his phone back and mentioned that part of the day's itinerary.

"Where else we headed? More shopping?"

"More investigating," I corrected. "First we swing by and pick up Beelz. I promised him."

Burt took that in stride. "And then?"

"I need to visit the scene of a very old crime," I said and gave him the address of the convenience store where Pavan Banerjee had greeted the morning sun one final time.

All Hallows was closing in on me, and I needed to pick which of the cold cases to concentrate on. Certainly there was no time to delve into all twenty. By concentrating on Banerjee, Botello, Lund, and Gallo, the incubus Doe and Kit could probably fill in the gaps on, I'd be sectioning things into the earliest two and a couple in the middle of the sequence. I would only need to decide which of the later deaths to look at for a decent, if skimpy, correlation sample. I had a vampire, a zombie, a troll, and an incubus thus far, so perhaps I should consider looking at other sections of the nonhuman community. Time for more lists, but not until I took care of a few more priorities.

For a hellhound with a hangover, Beelzebub didn't look much the worse for wear, but perhaps as a breed demons have harder heads than we sorta mortals. He bounded into the back of the cab and offered no comments.

"Will you be joining your aunt for dinner?" P. T. asked.

I'd be preparing for the meeting with the vampires, but she didn't need to know that.

"What's on the menu?"

"Seafood couscous paella. It has scallops, shrimp..."

"Gosh, look at the time," I said. "Don't go out of your way to make enough for me. I'll pick something up while I'm out."

I'm sure that she heaved a massive sigh as Burt peeled down the driveway.

The Grab It Quik convenience store, where Pavan Banerjee had spent his last months working the late-night shift, was in one of my secondary color sections, but so close to the primary red one that there wasn't much of a distinction. It didn't feature a filling station area, though the requisite ice locker, stack of soft drink cases, and trash receptacles bracketed the front door. Specials for primary-colored shaved ice monstrosities and sixty-four-ounce soft drinks were featured on the windows, the sheets taped just far enough apart for a cruising cop to glance inside and have a clear view of the aisles and counters.

Just inside the door was a rack with a stack of the daily newspaper's latest edition on the top tier and free issues of rental brochures, vehicle-for-sale papers, and a publication promising job openings on the lower ones. The place was neat and clean but had seen better days.

The man behind the counter was pure WASP.

"Hi," I said, giving him my most sincere smile. "You the owner?"

"Yes, I am," he said, though not proudly. More like warily.

"Recent acquisition?"

"No. I bought out the previous owners couple decades ago."

Not surprising, really. They'd probably unloaded it at a bargain price after coming in one morning to find their store unmanned and an employee-sized burn mark on the side of the building.

I magicked a business card into existence—okay, so it was sleight of hand.

"You wouldn't happen to know where they could be reached? I'm investigating a cold case, the murder of one of their employees."

"Far as I know, they headed back to Delhi. Never heard from them again, if that's your next question."

It wasn't even on my list.

"Do you mind if I look around your property? Just the outside."

"There ain't gonna be any clues around here, buddy."

"Just getting the lay of the land in my mind," I promised. "Won't take but a couple minutes. Five, tops."

"Fine with me," he said, "except first you gotta buy something to make it worth the time I just wasted with you."

Apparently, there was a very good reason why the neighborhood looked run-down. The convenience store conveniently relieved people of twenty bucks for three small coffees and a bottle of water.

Once out of sight of the dipshit who owned the sorry place, I poured one of the coffees onto the patched but still cracked blacktop, washed out the cup, and refilled it with water to give Beelzie a few refreshing laps. Then he and I circled around to the easternmost exterior wall. Burt sat in the cab, both guarding it from local marauders and downing his coffee.

From my brief period reading the first of The Raven Tales the evening before, I'd been reminded that my fictional self could sense things about a crime scene. It was partly an empathic thing, since Calie had concentrated on describing emotions, but with a hint of something else. I was hoping some of that remained in my present form. I hadn't used it on the page in a book in years, which is probably why it had slipped my mind. Probably Calie's as well.

It had been over twenty years since Banerjee's death. The building had received a slap or more of paint in that time, but not recently. What paint remained was flaking off or gone, showing the layers from the current dirty yellow to a hard aqua to a dark gray. The paint was described as white in the file I'd read; obviously, the dark gray had been added to cover the burn marks of Pavan's passing. While the paint had worked rather effectively, the patching of the holes driven into the concrete block clearly showed.

Yes, *holes*. While I'd done for the vampire in the first book with a single, really sturdy and sharp metal-tipped wooden stake, that hadn't been the way Pavan Banerjee was nailed up.

There were a couple empty wooden pallets piled up next to the large dumpster on this side of the building. I got as close to the wall as I could and stretched my arms out to where two inexpertly patched marks showed through the layers of paint. Banerjee had been pinned up like a butterfly on a collector's board, his arms wide, railroad spikes driven through the palms of his hands. The stake through his heart had been nearly an afterthought.

Or a guarantee that he wouldn't be able to escape the rising sun, whether he was still half alive or not.

Doe's file made no mention of wounds to Banerjee's hands, only to the stake in his heart.

I didn't realize I'd gotten really close to the wall until it dawned on me that I'd actually *seen* those railroad spikes in my mind. There was no way I could have known what had been used from the patched surface, and there was no mention of them in the file, just the single stake.

Beelzie yipped, pulling my attention away from the wall. Could have been he merely wanted more water in his Styrofoam cup.

"What did this guy do to tick someone off *this* bad?" I muttered, hunkering down to refill the cup. From what the file said and the impression I'd gotten from Banerjee's bitter wife, I'd been seeing the guy as rather meek and mild. An engineer, a geek who wanted to make vehicle and wind work in sync.

"I need to find the missionary and get his view of Pavan," I told Beelz, who dipped his long black snoot in agreement and put the slobbered-on end of the leash back in my hand. He was ready to move on.

Burt had finished his coffee but hadn't left the cab to get rid of the cup. "Find what you were looking for?"

"Cold case, remember? Nothing to see after this many years." Rather than drink my coffee, I finished off Beelz's bottle of water, grabbed Burt's empty, and deposited it all in the trash container outside the store's door. Give me a gold star for citizenship, hey? I gave the glaring guy on the other side of the glass wall a two-fingered salute.

And made a decision.

"You know of any Indian restaurants in this neck of the woods, Burt?"

"You thinking lunch already?"

"Nope, thinking I need to find a church within a few blocks of an Indian restaurant."

There were three churches in the right vicinity.

The one thing the demons hadn't bothered to include in their files was the name of the missionary, hence all I had to go on was that I was looking for a man whose ministry placed him in eastern India, in the area the Banerjees hailed from. It was a big territory, but there couldn't be that many missionaries with that particular locale in their résumé of stations. I was hoping that when the man returned home, he'd settled near whatever ministry had sent him forth to do good works. Twenty-some years might be too far back for some people's memories to spit out details, but churches kept written records.

Farha Banerjee could have given me the name, but I doubted she wanted to see me again, much less be quite that helpful.

The first church I hit was closed up tighter than a chastity belt, but there was a contact number posted on a board. The operator who answered said she'd take a message. I left my phone number. The second one had a parson so new to the job he looked shiny. He happily called in the guy using a weed whacker to trim around an ancient and crumbling stone fence at the rear of the building, because the man was a longtime member of the congregation. Struck out there, too, since the maintenance volunteer claimed he'd never heard of any members going off on a mission anywhere, in thirty-plus years.

I was tempted to cross my fingers when I pressed the intercom outside the office door of the third house of worship.

"Welcome to the Lord's House," a pleasant male voice greeted, sounding only a bit tinny as it pushed through the electronic box. "Just grab the door on your left when you hear the click of the lock opening."

"Thanks," I said a bit stunned that he hadn't wanted to know my business before allowing access to the building.

91

It was dim inside, but my eyes adjusted quickly. All those midnight Raven adventures had trained them to refocus in record time, I suppose. Fifteen feet further down the corridor, a man bustled through an open doorway. The hair on top of his head had packed its bags, leaving him with a natural tonsure of graying fair hair. A pair of reading glasses were pushed up to rest on the no-longer-seeded area. His girth and the lines around his eyes announced his age as either late fifties or early sixties. His wardrobe was basic shades of brown and rested safely in a non-fashion zone, being baggy and comfortable. He wasn't wearing a clerical collar, but then perhaps that wasn't a requirement for day-to-day church business.

"I'm Reverend Timothy Halston," he announced, hand already out in greeting. "How can I help you, friend?"

"Bram Farrell," I said, pumping away.

He smiled wider. Mischievously, even. "Like in the books?"

Ah, the curse of the local bestselling author striking again.

"I'm Calista Amberson's nephew," I said. "Seems she had absolutely no imagination in coming up with a name and nipped mine when she started writing." At least that was the story she'd given me to trot out.

"Oh, now I'm disappointed," Halston said. "I thought she'd been very clever, since in old Gaelic, 'Bram Farrell' translates to 'raven hero' or 'raven man of courage'."

That probably had been why she chose it, still it was news to me.

"But you came to the door today on an entirely different sort of quest, didn't you?" he asked.

I whipped out one of those handy-dandy business cards.

"I might not be a raven hero, but I am investigating a cold case and am in search of a man who might have been a member of this congregation in the past. All I know of him is that he served as a missionary in the Bengal area of India over twenty years ago."

Reverend Halston's face fell into tragic lines as quickly has it had lifted into pleased ones moments earlier.

"A cold case? You wouldn't by any chance be referring to the death of Pavan Banerjee, would you?"

Talk about ripping the rug out from beneath a guy! If there'd been a handy mirror behind Halston, chances are it would have reflected one stunned raven hero gaping at him.

"Ah," Halston said, "I see that it is. Perhaps we should both sit down."

We did more than that. Once settled in his office, me on one side of the desk, him on the other, the man pulled open a lower drawer and extracted two plastic tumblers and a bottle of Jim Beam. Without asking, he poured us each a generous dollop.

"It's not The Raven's regular Evan Williams, but it should suffice," he murmured, sounding apologetic.

Neat and room temperature though it was, it kicked my brain back into action.

"You were the missionary who made friends with the Banerjees," I said.

He kept his drink in hand while resting his wrist on the edge of the desk. "Yes."

"So you know what really happened to him."

Before answering, he tossed back the rest of the whiskey in his glass.

"If one travels the Third World frequently, one sees and hears things that the Western world calls ridiculous superstition today. Demons do exist, Mr. Farrell. I've seen them and what they can do, and I've felt helpless before their power."

This explained why Halston had sided with the Banerjees' decision not to report the original attack to the police and why he had not stepped forward when Pavan was murdered.

I put my own empty glass back on the desk. "You saw and heard, but you didn't believe, did you, Reverend Halston?"

"Didn't want to believe," he admitted. "Demons were merely a concept, a way mankind found to give substance to something that was so terrible they couldn't bear believing that these creatures existed in their world."

"Beings, Reverend, not creatures. Beasts, perhaps, but beings, with spirits, free will, and a desire to survive," I said.

He laughed softly, self-consciously. "You sound like your fictional counterpart, Mr. Farrell."

I smiled wryly. "My entire adult life has been a reflection of The Raven's, in a way."

"Does that mean you're a vampire hunter, a stalker of zombies, too?"

"As much as Queen Victoria or Abraham Lincoln ever were," I said, widening my smile. After all, between the covers of books, both historical giants had smote a few paranormals. "More of a researcher. I investigate the odd, the curious. The fact that the villainous vampire in my aunt's first Raven book mirrors what I've since learned actually happened to Banerjee makes this case of particular interest to me."

"Considering Farha and I kept quiet about it, as did the family he worked for, I'm amazed that you found anything about the event," Halston admitted. "But I suppose someone must have let something slip, since your aunt depicted it in chilling detail. Was it someone who lived in the neighborhood and happened to see or hear something?"

He wasn't going to like my answer.

"Local law enforcement might not have been involved, but the local nonhuman community was very concerned, and they kept records. Unfortunately, they are just as biased as many humans are and didn't consider your name worth including in their files."

"A local nonhuman community!" exclaimed Halston.

I wasn't surprised when he reached for the whiskey again, though when he offered me a refill as well, I waved it aside with a shake of my head.

"The vampires?"

"Brace yourself, Reverend Halston. That's like singling out one ethnic group from the conglomeration of people who call the U.S. home. There are various types of shape changers and legendary creatures as well as those who were once human, like the vamps, the weres, and the walking dead."

When he attempted to pour another dollop of the Beam, the bottle rattled against the plastic lip of his glass.

"Then the apocalypse is upon us," he muttered, nearly under his breath.

"Nothing close," I assured him. "They've been here as long as mankind has been, some longer. They are predators, I'll grant you that, but the same can be said about some humans in prison—and some out of it, in big business, in politics, in any position of power. You can pass them on the street and, if the glamour is right, you wouldn't know Otherworlders were any different from any person in your congregation on Sunday. There might even be some among them. Even demons occasionally long for spiritual connections.

"But I didn't come here to rock your view of the world."

"No, of course not," he agreed. "You came in search of information about Pavan Banerjee's death."

"Frankly, I was hoping to find out what sort of man he was."

The minister took a moment to refocus on his lost friend.

"A brilliant one, Mr. Farrell. The job he had when I met him in India bored him, didn't make use of his talents. He was manic about the way the power of the wind could be harnessed simply by the shape of an item. One night I jokingly said that the automobile industry needed a man like him on their design teams. From that point on, he began working on plans of aerodynamic perfection—his term, not mine—with which to tempt the Big Three. As a native of Detroit, I did know a few people who were in positions at Ford, GM, and Chrysler; I got him some initial interviews. I think his wife went along simply because she couldn't bear to resist when he was so excited about prospects here.

"I was due to return home around the same time, so we made the journey together, and they found a small home near me. We were in daily contact. I have never met a warmer, more open person than Pavan was."

I noticed he didn't include Farha in that assessment.

"The tragedy is that I not only lost a best friend, I lost two friends the day Pavan died," Halston said. "During your investigation, have you met Farha Banerjee?"

"I did," I admitted. "To say she was pleased to meet me remains to be seen."

Halston shook his head. "She's not the same woman I knew in India, nor even the one who immigrated with her excited husband. The light of warmth went out in her in those weeks before Pavan's death. As his dreams evaporated, she hardened."

Halston hadn't done more than run the edge of his forefinger along the curve of his cup throughout the story. Now he gripped it and downed the entire shot in one quick gulp.

"Thus ends my confession, Mr. Farrell. At least, it feels a lot like one. My best friend's wife thinks I was instrumental in his death, but the true sin is that in encouraging Pavan I inadvertently ruined the lives of two good people."

I'd clicked the spy pen on at the beginning of his story. Now I clicked it off.

"I'm no confessor, Reverend Halston, but I'm sure the man whose teachings you follow would place no blame at your door."

The minister smiled faintly.

"Unfortunately, it isn't His forgiveness I need. It's my own," he said quietly, then rallied. "Did anything I said fulfill your needs, Mr. Farrell? Do you have any further questions I could answer?"

Only one.

"The morning that you accompanied Farha to the store and found Pavan, did you notice whether there were any other people about who might have seen something?"

He gave the request a moment's reflection, then shook his head. "No one, which now that you mention it, appears odd."

"How so?"

"Because it is a working-class neighborhood, the majority holding blue-collar or low wage positions. There should have been people up, people leaving for work, for school, at that hour of the morning. But there was no one about that day. Not on the street, nor looking past the drapes. If I understand these things correctly, Pavan would have burst into flame when the rays of the sun struck him. You'd think someone would have called emergency services or come out to gawk, wouldn't you?"

After my visit with Reverend Halston, Burt and I swung by Neva Fitzsimmond's office to sign away another small fortune. I hadn't exactly purchased a vehicle with modest rates, *and* the driver's license I carried was of nebulous manufacture anyway. I probably didn't show up in computer databases. I'd never passed a driver's test and was rather vague on whether I even knew *how* to drive. Calie just plunked me down in a situation and never explained the transportation element in the books.

The stay in Neva's office took five minutes. She would have preferred longer; I would have preferred shorter. The deed done and paperwork for the glove compartment in hand, Burt, Beelzie, and I headed back to Kit's corner. I needed backup for the visits to the boxing joint where Rolph Lund's old buddies hung out, and having a Japanese fox demon with ninja reflexes along might help me later leave the vampire's lair in one piece as well.

At first I didn't see her. Weird, huh? I mean, each of the Sukis and the bakeneko dressed to catch the eye, usually. At least, these versions did so. But while Deer Woman and Neko were strutting their stuff, Kit appeared to be absent.

Then she strolled out of the shadows.

Gone were the fishnet stockings, corset, long gloves, and cocked top hat. Gone too was the trail of bushy, red fox tails. In place of my sex demon cohort stood a slim, shapely woman in a dark pantsuit and a white, open-necked blouse, with red hair bundled into a tame bun at the crown of her head. She looked more like a female homicide detective on TV. And part of that was that she still wore shoes with incredibly high, knifelike heels.

"This the Ms. Fox-Jones look?" I asked, getting out of the cab.

She pirouetted, arms spread. The jacket flared with the spin, and I noticed she probably had more buttons left open than considered kosher in business. Didn't mind it at all, myself.

I brushed my mouth against her ear and murmured, "Where're the tails?"

"Still there, just glamoured," she whispered, feathering a fleeting kiss on my cheek.

I held the rear door open so she could slip in next to Beelzie, who welcomed her with disgusting slobber. Kit didn't seem to mind. She ruffled his sleek black coat in response. Probably knew the spots where a rub felt exceedingly good, from when she was in fox form.

"Where we off to today?" she asked.

"The delightful-sounding Binky's Boxing Arena." I shut the door and dropped back into my shotgun position in the front. "Burt's really looking forward to that."

"You have me take you to so many of the better neighborhoods," he commented, putting the cab back in gear. "Still, I've eaten well along the way."

"See? Compensation above and beyond the fare. Tomorrow you'll be back to driving Beelzie to his beauty treatments. The good times will have passed by."

"Unless, of course, your Batmobile gets stripped in one of these neighborhoods and you need a ride," he added.

"True," I agreed. More likely I'd wreck the damn thing through incompetence or because I ticked off the wrong beasty and they ran or flew faster than the Ravenmobile could move within five seconds.

97

As had happened often during this quest, it turned out Binky's wasn't far from Kit's stomping grounds. It wasn't the most prepossessing sort of place. The sign was small and bolted into the door rather than mounted on the side of the building.

This had once been a thriving concern of some sort, dating back to the early decades of the twentieth century. Now many windows in the upper stories were broken and not even boarded over. The ones that remained hadn't been cleaned in more years than I cared to guess. The once-red brick was nearly black in places and crumbling a bit in others. Maintenance wasn't a priority either inside or out.

Burt opted to stay on duty in the cab while the rest of my troops gamely trailed behind me to the door. Kit lagged a step or two on my left, and the long, dark, and dangerous length of the dachshund from Hell took a spot to my right. He was leashless and ready to rumble. Probably hoping to. I know that was why Kit was along. Nothing either of them savored more than a fight. Chances were neither had been in many situations that held out the promise of one, until I'd poofed into their lives.

With the danger junkie twins bookending me, I took the nearly minuscule welcome legend on the door as an invite and pulled the damned thing open.

Beelz took point, dashing a few steps within, giving the joint a quick once-over. Then, I swear, he jerked his head to tell Kit and I the coast was clear.

If you can call a coast clear when it's filled with sweaty men punching giant bolsters or grunting as they lift weights, or with gathered advice givers shouting at a couple of opponents in a raised ring. Judging from the number of men (and belatedly noticed musclebound women) crammed within, Binky's was a popular spot.

Other than a few support columns, the arena was open and probably covered most of the building's ground floor. If the ceiling hadn't been high before, the removal of the flooring for what would have been the second story made it a soaring height.

They could have done with a better ventilating system, open windows, or a gazillion air fresheners. The stink of overworked bodies was enough to knock a visitor out faster than a right hook.

As I had no description to go on to identify either Split-Nose Erskine or Paps Pacheco, I pretended an interest in the various equipment around us. The Beelz settled down on his haunches, content to wait. Kit looked like she was doing some yoga meditation, but then I realized the men nearest to us had gone a bit slack-faced, so she was probably grabbing a quick snack. In the long run, that should help, as there would be at least a few guys incapable of ganging up on us if it came to a rumble. There was no telling how either of Rolph Lund's buddies would react to questions.

"Yo! Dude!" someone called. "You interested in a fight?"

Odd, how I'd just been thinking along those lines.

"Honestly, I'm interested in talking to a couple guys who used to fight in the cages."

The man moved a few steps nearer. If he'd been green, I might have mistaken him for the Hulk.

"We don't do cage fights, man. They're illegal."

"I said *used to*," I clarified.

He looked Kit and me over. "You the cops?"

"Do cops travel with wiener dogs?" I asked, indicating the Big B, who was now reclining at my feet. Tired of waiting for the fun and games to begin, I suppose.

The guy squinted at the hellhound, which was doing an excellent job of blending into the shadows. The place wasn't all that well lit.

"What's with his eyes?" the guy demanded, taking a step back.

"Gene defect. Not catching," I assured him. "All I want to do is talk to Split-Nose Erskine and Paps Pacheco. Are they here today?"

"Eugene and Fabio are here every day," he said. "They're trainers."

They had first names! Not exactly ones that sounded like fighters' names, of course.

"Are they training anyone currently?" I asked.

He squinted at me. "What do you want ta talk ta them about?"

How sweet that he wanted to protect them, but the clock was ticking for me. If it took knocking this idiot's block off to get past him, so be it. Reading the tension in the air right, Beelzie raised his head and revved his growl.

Seemed today was Kit's day to read minds. She stepped in front of both of us.

"Tell Split-Nose that Ruth Lund sent us," she said.

"Well, why didn't you mention that before?" he grouched and stumped off toward a closed office door on the far wall.

Kit swung to face me. I fancied I felt the brush of her currently invisible tails across my jean-covered shins. Strangely enough, it felt comforting.

"Why didn't you mention that earlier?" she demanded.

No idea. I shrugged.

She did that exasperated eye roll that clearly said "Men!" and fell back to take a position in our miniaturized attack wedge. Beelz still had the point. He got to his feet as the muscle-bound cretin returned with two men in tow.

As the one was short and had muscle gone to pot, trading it in for fat, I figured he might be the very un-fab Fabio Pacheco. The way his once impressive pecs hung like breasts beneath a T-shirt with the sleeves torn off was sort of a giveaway. There was a distinct sheen of gray on his otherwise shaven head, and his skin tone was swarthy, with a hint of illness tainting it. The frown riding his battle-scarred features was far from prepossessing.

Split-Nose Eugene Erskine didn't exactly have a comely mug either, but his was less intimidating, more open. He had straggly blond locks past his shoulders, probably grown since his days in the cage. I mean, there weren't exactly *rules* in that arena. A fighter wouldn't want to give the competition something to grab hold of, right? His blue eyes had burst veins radiating from the center, indicating he self-medicated whatever ailed him, and he did indeed have a nose that in the past had been split. There was a nasty-looking scar running from his right nostril up over the rise to a spot near the left side of the bridge. He was taller than his compadre by maybe an inch or two and scrawny rather than... er... ample? His knuckles showed recent contact with someone else's face. My recently battered jaw whined in sympathy for the other fellow.

"Ruth sent you? What in the hell for?" Split-Nose spat out. I do mean that literally. Spit flew in concert with the words.

"To tell us about her brother Rolph's business with you," I said. Smoothly, I hope. "We're investigating a slew of cold cases, and Rolph's death is among them. Ruth thought you could give us a more rounded personality profile of her twin."

The scar on Split-Nose's phiz twisted as he scowled. "A what?"

"Tell us what he was like when away from home," Kit translated. "*Capisce?*"

100

"He was what he was," Paps said.

"Right. A dickhead," Split-Nose agreed, expanding on the theme.

"I was under the impression you were friends of his."

"More like business acquaintances, until he gypped us out of our share of the dough," Erskine said.

Ah, a new side to Rolph Lund that might cough up something useful. "He reneged on your deal? He do that with others, too?"

"Oh, no," Paps declared. "We was special."

Apparently, I don't own the franchise on sarcasm.

"He was in deep ta some guys, but don't ask me who," Split-Nose said.

"Because you don't know, or because they'll come after you like they did Rolph?"

"Who says they came after Rolph? A dead guy can't pay debts. Ain't you got no logic?" Paps demanded.

"I say he got done in by a dame," Erskine offered, then looked at Kit in her official Ms. Fox-Jones getup. "No offense meant, ma'am."

"None taken," she said.

"You really think the way he died was an act of passion?" I asked.

Of course, if you haven't read the eleventh volume of The Raven Tales, you don't know how to kill a troll, do you? They're big, ugly, strong, and incredibly thick-skinned, and have lousy people skills; reference Ralph Lund if you want a good example of one. But we're talking *kill* here.

Let me give you a spoiler for *Raven Breaks Even*: You find the troll's bridge and destroy it. Helps if he's under it at the time, of course, but all trolls have a bridge somewhere. They don't build them, they simply adopt them, protect them, form some sort of psychic link with them. Get real attached to them. You see a bridge that's in disrepair, it's a clear sign the troll hasn't been in residence for a long while or was killed by another of its kind; trolls don't need to use the bridge connection for a whack.

But if you aren't a troll and want to kill one, you've got to break its heart by destroying its pet bridge. As in Rolph's case, the troll doesn't have to be anywhere near the span, or even see it fall, to have his lights go out.

Beyond weird, right? But effective. The act had been more dramatic in the book, of course, but Rolph Lund had collapsed while attending a rave—yeah, go figure—at the same moment when an unknown person drove a truck loaded with explosives into one of the supports of a historic bridge located on a farm fifty miles away. The resulting fireworks sent half the old structure tumbling into the rill it crossed and set fire to the neighboring woods. According to the report I'd scanned my first night on this side of the binding, the fairies living in the mini-forest had escaped unharmed as their home burned, but they were majorly ticked off. The farmer was pretty livid about the vandalization of his property, too.

Anyway, Rolph's death didn't sound like it'd had even a kissing cousin connection to a crime of passion, which is usually a spur-of-the-moment sort of thing. This attack had been well planned, the truck striking the bridge at one of the two spots that would bring the beyond-vintage structure down. The real trick, to my mind, was the attacker having discovered which was Rolph's bridge. Trolls don't exactly advertise that sort of thing.

"The dude's been dead a long time. His heart exploded," Paps said.

It had, too. Quite literally. Those who'd been dancing anywhere near him were no doubt still in therapy after being soaked in his blood.

"Rolph's family are the only ones who insisted he'd been murdered. Personally, I think his arteries was clogged."

"Yeah," Erskine agreed. "Don't know why you want to dig up anything about him."

"So that justice can be served?" I suggested. Yeah, what *was* I thinking!

Pacheco snorted, then waddled away.

Erskine enjoyed a silent chuckle over my naivete. His narrow shoulders and sunken chest jerked with unheard mirth.

"Tell ya what," he bargained. "You go a couple of rounds with one of my boys, and I'll give you a bit more about Rolph's business dealings."

"You want me to box someone?"

"Naw, I want you to bare-knuckle *fight* someone," Split-Nose corrected. "By the looks of that jaw, you've some experience in that."

In being on the receiving end, definitely.

"'Sides, I heard that a fella matching your description held his own against Parson Hammer and his boys the other day."

Ah, my reputation preceded me. Lucky me.

"I go a couple—that's two?—rounds with your boy, and you'll talk. That the deal?"

"No, you gotta *win* the fight," Split-Nose said. "Then I'll reminisce about old Rolph."

Yeah, I thought the original suggestion sounded a bit too easy.

"Okay. We have an accord?"

Yeah, I've been living in fictionland far too long. Plus, a hell of a lot of the old magic wielders haven't bothered to update their language in a couple hundred years. I was used to speaking Thesaurus.

"We got ourselves a deal," he said, clarifying it, and wrung my hand. It smarted enough when he let go to make me think he'd been trying to break bones in it prior to the fight.

As he strolled off toward the roped pen, shouting that he had a sucker lined up for annihilation, I took Kit's arm.

"If I go down," I said quietly, "you have my permission to suck that idiot down to the point where he'll spill what he knows without much encouragement. We need that information."

She leaned in close. "And what about the man in the ring with you?"

"Hell, suck him down to a manageable size, too. Maybe he won't beat his girl tonight."

"You think he does that?"

"I think any of these Neandertals are likely to do that," I said, then hunkered down to Beelzie's level. "Don't interfere. Let Kit handle things." He didn't look happy, and he didn't do his nod thing, which meant I really better win these two rounds.

I stripped off my jacket, handing it to Kit.

"Think they'll keep a round to three minutes each?"

"I think you'll be lucky if they don't let the first round go until there is a knockout involved," she warned. "Which is why you need to concentrate on the events in *Ring Around The Raven*."

Light dawned. In the spoiler category, here's how the scene in that book played out. Me, surrounded by goons hired by a siren. Then, the only thing I'd had to comfort myself with was the fact that she hadn't bothered to enhance any of their abilities. They were brute strength and, if necessary, they were disposable. I'd been a very dependable disposal unit on those pages. And I hadn't used a lick of magic to do so, which was good, considering I was currently lickless.

"Got it."

Before I climbed into the ring, she planted a long wet one on me. Whether the hoots and the whistles meant someone just might bet on me winning this one was debatable, though.

You want the short version of what happened? *Ouch* pretty much sums it up. The long version might be more interesting, though.

With Kit's kiss still ringing chimes in my system, I ducked through the ropes and into the ring. Eugene had lied about my opponent being a "boy." Mutant gorilla was closer to the truth. He had at least three inches on me, and those simian arms were going to be difficult to get within to do damage and then nip out of again.

Eugene climbed in the ring with his "boy."

"Gents," he announced, "we got us a new contender for Joey to toy with."

That would be me.

"We want this fight to be a good one, so here's the rules. Elbows to the ribs..."

For illustration purposes, Split-Nose drove one of his elbows into my ribs.

". . . perfectly okay to do," he said.

"And this..."

His fist rammed into my kidneys

". . . also okay."

"Glad you made that clear," I gasped. "What about this?"

I slammed my fist into his solar plexus.

"Or this?"

Cleaned his clock with a blow on the chin.

As Erskine keeled over, I cocked a questioning eyebrow at Joey. "Those okay, too?"

"Fine by me," he said.

"Great. Any other rules we should discuss, or should we just move to name calling and posturing?"

He was already posturing, legs braced, arms bent, hands flexing into fists then relaxing briefly before knotting up again.

"Pansy," he said.

Insults it was.

"Flower picker," I countered, and cracked my neck. Some thoughtful soul hastily dragged the unconscious Eugene out of stepping on distance.

"Motherfucker." Joe was upping the ante.

"Probably," I agreed, "but not likely yours."

It took him a minute to ponder that one before he recognized it as an insult.

"Why, you..."

I ducked his blow.

"Obviously, she wasn't my type," I said.

"You tell him, Raven," Kit yelled. Her idea of encouragement.

The next blow brushed my unshaven chin as I leaned back to avoid it. The follow up wasn't as easy to escape. I manfully took it on my already bruised shoulder. Satan's spawn! The real world hurt like hell!

While I lollygagged over that revelation, Joey jabbed at my stomach. I flew backward, hitting the ropes.

"Don't think, act," Kit instructed.

Beelzie barked some instructions of his own. She'd picked him up so he could observe my being taken down a few pegs.

"Hey, I'm still on my feet!" For how long was debatable.

Gorilla Joe closed in, ready to re-pummel my solar plexus. Leaning back on the ropes, I kicked him in the nuts. Big mistake. The crowd turned rabid.

Joey'd had worse than my love tap, though. He shook it off. Well, I hadn't really put my heart into that kick anyway. I'd just been buying time.

Before he had a chance to land any fury-fueled hits, I damaged my knuckles on his jaw. He staggered back a step, his brow working; gears turning, I supposed. I ducked under his next blow. On my feet behind him, I slammed a foot to the back of his knee. Joe crumpled forward, catching himself on his hands.

I danced off to the corner where Kit was.

"How many hours have I been in here?"

"Maybe ninety seconds," she said.

"Shit. Any new suggestions?"

Beelzie rolled his lip back, showing nice, sharp dental work.

"I'm not going to bite him. He hasn't been cooked properly," I told the dog, then turned to where Joey was pushing to his feet.

"Hey, Joe! The dog thinks you might taste like pork. I told him chicken. Which of us is right?"

He did a pretty good imitation of a gorilla's roar and, head down rather like a charging bull's, he rushed me. I let him come within a hair of ramming me and slipped aside. His head connected quite well with the turnbuckle's post.

"Foul!" someone yelled. It was the tamest word I heard.

"No rule was mentioned that said I had to stand still for this," I shouted back.

Joey was pulling himself back up. Geez, was he ever the glutton for punishment.

He waved a hand back at the crowd as if assuring them that he had this. "'Salright," he muttered. But he only had eyes for me. Burning with hatred they were, too.

Couldn't blame him. I'd be royally ticked with me too.

"Yer slippery," he said. "But yer going down."

Totally expected that.

He lunged for my feet. I jumped as hastily as if his arms had been life-sucking tentacles. Been there, survived that.

He rolled over, bowling me down to the canvas. Then he was straddling me, ramming blows at my face. At this rate, there would be no second round.

Then the bell rang.

The crowd wasn't happy to hear it. Joey abided by its message, though, and got off me. I waited until he'd returned to his own corner and was mopping down his face while listening to a now conscious Split-Nose murmur instructions to him. Then I crawled over to where Kit and Beelzie stood.

"Am I winning yet?" I asked, leaning back against the ropes, legs spread out before me on the canvas.

"You're ahead on points for stupid remarks," Kit said.

"Ah, well, as long as I've got that covered," I murmured. "How did I get out of this in the book, again?"

"By a miracle," she said.

"Could use one now." It hadn't been a miracle, though. Calie choreographed fight scenes like they were freakin' *Swan Lake*. In the book, I'd used a lot of insults and misdirection to get some of the guys inadvertently taking one another out rather than me.

106

"Here," Kit said, handing me a linen handkerchief embroidered with lotus blossoms. "Your lip is bleeding."

"It is?" I raised the dainty bit of cloth. It felt cool and smelled far better than Binky's place. Or me, for that matter.

"Other side," she said and took the handkerchief back to minister to the cut herself. "Have you got enough in you to outlast Joey?"

"Debatable," I said. "I've a feeling I was far nimbler in the book. Certainly avoided a hell of a lot more punches from a shitload of opponents."

"Then I'll give you something to help," she said.

Drawing my face around, she kissed me again. It was long, slow, and warm. Rehabilitating. Suddenly, not a bruised or battered bit of me ached.

Before she withdrew, I slid a hand to the nape of her neck to hold her in place.

"What did you just do?" I asked quietly against her lips.

I felt them curve in a smile.

"Gave you a bit of these assholes' life force. I've been siphoning bits ever since we walked in the door, in anticipation."

"And if I hadn't needed it?"

The grin widened more.

"I wouldn't need dinner," she said. "Go get 'em, killer."

Energy seemed to pulse through my veins as I pulled myself upright on the ropes, faking weakness now.

"That's some woman you got there," Joey said as he thundered to the center of the ring again. "When this is over, I'm taking her for mine."

"You'd regret that," I warned, slightly distracted by something more than just the life force boost Kit had given me. I could hear his heart thumping, was more acutely aware of his breathing. We won't mention the smell of his sweat, but even that didn't bother me now. The pupils in his eyes did a slight jig, he took a breath, and his system pushed a new dose of adrenaline. Talk about telegraphing a punch!

While his left sailed toward my face, his right was zeroing in on my gut. Before either fist connected, I smashed my foot down on his, ducked beneath his left, and landed a blow alongside his nose.

Joe rocked back but kept his balance. He wasn't their local champ for nothing. He was bleeding and ignoring it.

I jabbed again and again, connecting with the corner of his right eye, the tip of his chin, the solid brick wall of his abs.

107

He landed punches that would have had my head ringing without Kit's magic wake-the-hell-up kiss. My ears were ringing, but I wasn't sure whether it was with the yells of the crowd or the roaring of waves. Only the hellhound's aggressive bark stood out from the pulse.

"How long?" I yelled to Kit.

"Ninety seconds!"

What was this, a special number or something?

I danced back from Joey.

"Let's make it a hell of a lot less," I suggested to him.

He was beyond coherent conversation and merely grunted.

The ropes were three feet behind me. I threw myself toward them and rebounded at Mach speed. Okay, it just felt that way to me. I rammed my shoulder into his chest, felling him.

"Sorry about this," I said as I stuck his jaw, then lifted his head by the hair and rammed it down on the canvas a couple times.

You could almost see the stars and tweeting birdies circling his head before he passed out.

I leaned back on my haunches, still straddling Joey's prone body, and faced Split-Nose Erskine.

"Now, about those questions I have," I said.

"To hell with you!" Paps yelled and scrambled through the ropes. You ever see a fat man do that? Believe me, you don't want to.

He never made it to me. A streak of black fur was on him before he had both feet back on the floor.

"Maim, don't kill, Beelz!" I shouted.

Whether the hellhound paid me any heed, I had no idea, for that was when another five men leapt into the ring. They didn't look like they were interested in resuscitating Joey.

I rolled off him and back to my feet. Kit materialized at my side in ninja mode. Her claws were extended and there was a feral grin curving her mouth back from those sharp little teeth.

"You want two or three of them?" she asked.

"Three, by all means," I said. With that adrenaline shot she'd given me, three barely felt sufficient.

We cleaned clocks, mopped the canvas with them. I truly felt sorry for her two victims; those spike heels were vicious little suckers for a guy to run himself into. Beelzebub sounded like he was enjoying himself as well.

Once the ring was littered with six sleeping men—the rest of the fight fans decided they were late for appointments and vacated the premises—and Paps was attempting to wrap his bleeding arm with gauze, I'd pretty much expended that extra life force shot. Split-Nose was babying an arm that looked like it had been wrenched from the socket.

"Now can we talk?" I demanded, letting disgust with Pacheco's and Erskine's actions saturate my voice.

He looked up to where I sat with my legs dangling over the side of the ring, my arms weighing down the ropes as I leaned on them.

"What are you people?" Split-Nose asked.

"Law-abiding citizens," I said. "Doubt you can say the same. So spill."

He spilled.

"Why in the hell couldn't you just tell me that without the rigmarole?" I demanded once Split-Nose had spun his tale. Considering what I'd gone through to get it, the story was sadly flat. Here's the gist of it. No need to bore you with the ping-pong match the interview dissolved into.

Rolph had started small and built his numbers racket into a comfortable income. He'd operated out of Binky's, but he'd also made a couple bars and a laundromat regular stops on his route. Players bought into the private lottery at different price levels, one dollar, two, or five, allowing more than a single game to run every day. Buy-ins simply chose a number from zero to 999, which gave a selection from a thousand possible numbers. If Rolph charged a buck a number, he could take in a thousand greenbacks a day if all the numbers were taken, though that was highly improbable. For handling the daily lottery, he'd let his players know that 10 percent of the proceeds were his. The winner would receive the other 90 percent.

However, it was very unlikely the winner would get that percentage of the proceeds, since Rolph lied a lot. Probably the only decent thing he did was to let the money ride if no one chose the winning number. Rolph profited either way because he didn't take 10 percent, he took 50 percent, and he never revealed the true number of players in any of the games.

Making book on the cage fights brought in larger amounts, but only if the match was fixed. That was where Split-Nose and Paps and others like them came into it. Trouble started when the guys throwing the fights found out Rolph was taking a much larger share of the payoff.

"He got beat up a couple times by guys in the neighborhood as well as dudes takin' dives in the cages, but Rolphy was one big, mean sucker. He gave as good as he got. Still, when word got out about his sticky fingers, he promised to stick to agreements. Far as I know, he never fixed another fight, and payoffs on the lotteries got bigger. Seemed he was on the straight," Split-Nose told us. "Either someone didn't get the word, or the guys whose territory he was poaching decided to get even. Don't know how the hit was done but, hell, there're all kinds of drugs that can be slipped inta drinks. Rolph wouldn't even of noticed. He'd eat or drink anything on a bet."

"Lot of really disgusting stuff, too," Paps contributed.

Then he asked if Beelzie had been checked for rabies lately. Personally, I didn't think rabies was brave enough to pay the wiener pup a visit. Fleas sure as hell didn't.

Since I couldn't see a mobster admitting to believing there were things like trolls, he certainly wouldn't have found out about Rolph's obscurely located bridge. I didn't think the lottery losers would either. That left me with the spurned woman theory, yet neither Erskine nor Pacheco remembered Rolph talking about any particular woman. I'd have to visit Ruth Lund and see if she knew of a sweetheart who might have lost the warm and fuzzy feeling for her twin.

When we all climbed back into the cab, Burt took one look at me and turned to Kit. "He ran his mouth again, didn't he?"

"Right into a heck of a lot of fists," I said.

"You might want to head back to your aunt's place for a shower and a change of clothes before we hit the dealership," he suggested.

"Faster to pick up something new along the way and get a motel room to use the shower."

Burt found a Walmart this time. Kit volunteered to do the shopping. She shopped nearly as fast as I had my first day this side of the line.

At the motel, the guy behind the desk looked at what I'd scrawled on his registration form, then at me.

"What, Smith isn't good enough for you?" he asked. "You've got to use some fictional character's name? What are you, some rabid Raven fan?"

Amazing how many folks read Calie's stuff in Detroit.

"That's me," I said. "Name legally changed and everything."

The way he shook his head, I guessed I'd been written off as a nutcase.

"Just need the room for an hour," I said.

He looked past me at Kit. "I'd make it two or three if I were you," he suggested.

She gave him a wide, flirtatious grin and snatched the room card key from his hand.

Half an hour later, once more clean and shiny though looking a bit abused, I was back in the cab. Burt had walked the dog in the interim. They'd grabbed a couple hot dogs but hadn't bought any for the rest of us. My stomach growled as Burt finished his hot dog. Beelzie had tucked his away while still at the store.

"Final leg of the journey now?" Burt asked.

"Yep, unless we pass any sort of bookstore," I said. "If you spot one, pull over so I can dash in."

"Are you looking for a particular book?" Kit queried.

"Counting the number of Raven books on the shelves," I lied. "One of Calie's jobs for me."

She shook her head in what might have been wonder, or it might have been over the vagaries of humans.

"Sounds like busy work to keep you out of her hair," she said.

It sounded a lot like that to me, too. Not the counting books, which was a big fib, but the idea that *I* needed to find a replacement to continue The Raven Tales. Her editor and agent were in much better positions to do so.

"Can I borrow your phone to look something up?" I asked Burt. "Mine doesn't do net searches."

"You're going to be driving a chick magnet that cost over fifty grand, and you need *my* phone," he said.

"The universe is full of whimsy. One has priorities."

"And the Batmobile was yours?"

"The *Raven*mobile," I corrected, "but yes, it was."

Burt handed the phone over. Kit had to operate it, as I was clueless. She demanded my phone as well.

111

"I don't know how you've survived in the modern world," she muttered in disgust.

Considering I hadn't been *in* the modern world seventy-two hours yet, I thought I was holding my own fairly well.

"I need a phone number for a public relations firm where Delia Maddox works," I delegated.

She flicked the pad of her finger across the screen of Burt's phone, performing what might have been magic as far as I was concerned, then thumbed a number into my cell and handed both phones back.

"You have got to upgrade this thing, Raven."

"After the thirty-first," I promised. If I was still around, it would be at the top of my list.

Delia answered the phone herself a second later.

"Hi, coz," I said. "You got time for your bookish cousin?"

"Bram!" She sounded surprised to hear from me. "What can I help you with?"

"Finding Auntie a pen."

"You mean a ghostwriter?"

"Preferably a live one, but yes. There is no way this side of Hades that one can be turned up in one town on the deadline she gave. The net has to be thrown worldwide."

"That's what I told her," Delia said. "I even had a complete campaign planned, but she vetoed it."

I slumped down in the seat as far as the law-enforced restraint would allow and fished the spy pen from my pocket.

"Give me the highlights," I said and pressed the record button.

She reeled out a campaign featuring a designated website, social media blanketing, and mailings to agents who represented both mystery and paranormal tale tellers. "I also suggested a team to read writing samples, but Calista didn't want to be bothered. She shut me down even before I reached that stage."

"Can you put a team together now?"

"It will take a day or so, but it can be done," she said. "I'll also touch base with the Raven fanfic people. Could be there are a couple already up to par on the stories they spin."

"One more question. Does Calie surf the web news or do social media?"

"Bram," Delia murmured, "don't be ridiculous. She has people like me for that."

"Then if we simply go ahead and run the campaign, is she likely to hear about it?"

There was silence on the phone. I'm a patient fellow, though, and I could hear her breathing.

"Are you telling me to go ahead with the campaign and not tell her?" she asked at last.

"How fast can you get it up and running?"

"If I drop everything else, by tomorrow morning."

"Then make it so," I said and turned the recording pen off. "Later, coz!"

Burt glanced aside at me. "You look like you're up to something."

"Just getting the book count off my to-do list. Anybody interested in stopping for food before we hit the dealership? I'm starving."

Kit suggested Japanese and knew a place within a couple blocks of where the Mustang awaited me. She ordered for us, which meant Burt and I were stuck with something called oyakodon. Turned out it was chicken thighs, egg, and jasmine rice in some sort of stock, with liberal dashes of soy sauce and a Japanese rice wine called mirin added. I could have done with it not looking like a casserole. Fried would have been nice, with a spicy barbecue sauce to dip it in. Burt and I manfully downed it, but I read dreams of KFC in his eyes, too.

It was a relief when we reached the dealership and I could slaver over the car. Burt did a bit of that as well, particularly when we parted from him. "Call when you need me," he said, wringing my hand. I was going to miss him, too.

Still, it was a relief not to have to guard my words around him. He was innocent of the sort of things my world seemed to revolve around, and I wanted to keep him that way.

Kit slid into the shotgun spot and made noises that sounded like she might have to pay the leather seat for a pleasuring. Beelzie scrambled into place in the back, his long, glossy midnight form nearly disappearing against the upholstery. I ran my hands over the curve of the steering wheel. Yeah, we were all in happy land. Then I put the car in gear and stopped holding my breath. I *did* know how to drive!

"We've still got a few hours before the meeting with the vampires," I told my troops. "Mind if we cruise around a bit?"

"No argument from me," Kit said. "This is heavenly."

The car engine purred at the compliment. Okay, maybe it was *me* making that sound. Still...

113

"Were you in Detroit when Tado Gallo died?" I asked Kit.

She gasped, surprised at the turn in the conversation. "That's quite a leap. I take it we aren't totally relaxing before the meeting. You're interviewing me about a victim."

Well, he had been an incubus, the male of her species. Made sense that she might know him, right?

"Just trying to make best use of the time," I insisted. "Were you?"

She didn't exactly answer the question. "What do you already know about Tado?"

"What I read in Doe's file on the case and what happened to his doppelgänger in the eighth Raven tome. Both were Brazilian. In the book, he was a masseuse and sometime lifeguard at a resort. In this world, the report says, he was a swimming instructor."

Kit tilted a hand back and forth. "More of a gigolo who liked to screw his marks in the water."

"A boto, then? Shape-shifts into a river dolphin?"

According to Amazon basin legends, the boto visits young women in their dreams, luring them to the river, where relations progress and the victim is impregnated, later giving birth to a succubus. Matching an incubus with a human is apparently the only way to continue the species—the succubi, not the humans.

"Did Tado play in both pools?" I asked, since the boto were supposedly bisexual as well.

"Of course," Kit said. "There isn't as much traffic in sex with women looking for our brand of companionship as there is with men. Tado took patrons where he found them, be they male or female."

Which left the field for Tado Gallo's killer open to homophobes as well.

"He was found bound to girders at the top of a building still under construction, wasn't he?"

"Stretched in a spread-eagle position, his face turned toward the sun," Kit added. "Unlike Doe, Neko, and I, he didn't function well in daylight. He was a creature of the night, of the depths. Whoever killed him gutted him like the fish he sometimes was."

It was certainly what I'd done to the incubus in the book. Damn, but I had a nasty streak when it came to dispatching Otherworlders. It didn't sit well with me in this world.

"You think that's what people read the Raven books for? The

detailed violence meted out to the supernatural perp of the moment?" I asked.

"It's escapism, Bram."

But it wasn't to me. It was the only life I had any memory of, and the details of it were bothering me. I didn't feel like that man any longer.

"Still," I said.

"More than just the executions draws people to the stories. And, speaking as a nonhuman who has read them, I'll confess that the crimes committed by the characters brought to justice at the conclusion merited every nasty death that Calista wrote. The disturbing part is that she used the details of deaths where the victims hadn't committed the outrages of their counterparts in the books."

I had been driving by instinct, with no particular destination in mind, but now I realized my thoughts were taking us to my tiny nook of an office. I glanced over at her while we waited for a light to change. "And that's why the entire nonhuman community believes a human committed each murder, isn't it?"

"Legendary beasts are hungry, vicious predators," Kit said. "I ought to know. I'm one of them. But we kill to feed, to protect our territory, our packs, not for pleasure. That is a crime only humans commit. Only a human would hunt us for sport or for a reason we simply can't fathom."

"Any way someone might have gone after Gallo because he'd gotten a daughter or sister pregnant with a sex demon?" I asked.

"Doubtful. Tado came to Detroit because of the lake and river, but he'd been working the area for nearly three centuries, and no new succubi were conceived, much less born, in Detroit in all that time."

"Shooting blanks, was he?"

She laughed softly. "Or he was incredibly careful. We can smell when humans are in heat, you know."

I drummed my fingertips against the wheel. "And can you tell if something *is* human even if it looks human?"

Kit slid her hand to rest on my thigh, the action more comforting than sexual. "You're really asking about yourself, aren't you?"

I was so transparent, my middle name should have been Cling Wrap.

"You don't smell human, Bram, but you don't smell like one of us either. You're something different, something new."

Just my luck. Not that I wanted to be an Otherworlder. Too many people, even among their own kind, hated the various

115

nonhuman species. I wasn't sure I wanted to be totally human at times, either. I was a conundrum to everyone, including myself.

"I was curious," I confessed. "Thanks for keeping me totally screwed up."

She laughed and patted my thigh before removing her hand. "You're The Raven, Bram, whether you're painted in words on a page or walking around in this world."

I glanced over at her lovely face, with its faint fox cast.

"You need proof," she said matter-of-factly. "Okay, look at this vehicle you bought! Only someone who's sure of himself and of his abilities drives a ridiculously powerful, insanely expensive car while wearing clothes from Walmart."

"Jacket's a designer label, though," I reminded.

Kit's grin widened. Women can be so disgustingly self-satisfied about the stupidest things.

"Where are we headed?" she asked as I pulled into the parking lot next to the office building.

"We're going to start sticking pins in things," I said.

"Voodoo dolls?"

"Locations on a map. I need to see where all these murders occurred and where the victims lived. There has to be a connection. It's past time to find it."

The wall was going to give the management company a real tooth-grinding session if I landed back in fictionland in November. It was well-perforated once we'd added pushpin flags to indicate residences and murder sites. We even added in the victims' workplaces.

And when it was all done, a pattern was visible. With only a few exceptions, everything was happening within one wedge of the city.

While *location, location, location* was all very well, that didn't mean our perpetrator hadn't come from outside the area. They had, however, needed to know these connected neighborhoods well. They weren't the most prepossessing neighborhoods in Detroit, either.

There was still a shitload of questions to be answered. I just hoped I had time enough left to connect the various dots.

Moonrise was upon us now, and that meant the vampires were waiting for their conference meeting. Doubted it would follow *Robert's Rules of Order*.

The vamps were doing well for themselves, I will say that. I'd been combing the areas of the city that the downturn in the economy had kicked in the teeth for days now, but our meeting place was in a tall, elegant office building. The valet service was off duty, but the Renfields were there, looking extremely out of place as the building accentuated their low rung on the human ladder. The Ravenmobile looked right at home, though.

I pulled into a reserved parking slot. Doubted anyone was keeping track at night. Kit waited for me to come around and open her door and then took her time getting out, going for drama. Once she was upright on those incredibly needle-nosed heels, I pulled the back door open and the hellhound, with his short legs, long body, and floppy ears, made a much less spectacular exit. I armed the car's theft protection system, and we were ready to rumble.

The Beelz took point again, strutting past Hammer and his boys. Kit strolled along, her hand in mine, as though we were entering a five-star restaurant for an evening of delightful conversation. Me? Well, I was pulsing with a recent adrenaline shot kiss and hoping my Suki companion had saved enough life force energy for herself. Despite the posh location, I expected more than information would be exchanged.

"'Fraid to come without your protectors, Raven?" one of the men taunted.

"We all have dinner reservations later," I said. "They didn't want to wait in the car."

Kit ran a well-manicured finger down the cheek of one of them as she passed. "What's the matter? You afraid of a girl?"

Considering his eyes went blank at her touch, he should have been.

Hammer pulled his man back, slamming him against the side of the building.

"Don't let her touch you, idiot. Don't you recognize her? She's that fox-tail succubus. She'll eat you alive."

Kit's lips curved in a self-satisfied smirk as she turned back to me.

"He's right," she said. "They are all idiots."

117

Which included Hammer. She didn't have to touch any of them to chow down.

It wasn't the humans I was worried about, though. Since I hadn't seen the vamps yet, there was no telling how old or how powerful they were or how many would be at the meeting. I might not be human, but I wasn't going in armed with anti-vampire charms, either.

Hammer obviously expected me to be loaded with them. Before allowing me to follow Beelzie's trail, they patted me down. None too gently, either.

"No wooden stakes," Hammer reported at his cell phone. I guessed the speakerphone option had been engaged. My phone didn't have that function. "Nothing silver. No crosses, holy water, or garlic. He hasn't even eaten anything garlicky."

"Saving myself for a gastronomic feast later. Reservations made and everything," I said, every word a lie. "And I didn't bring any mistletoe, or holly, or a bouquet of roses to tart up the room, so everyone's safe."

Except me, probably.

"He did bring a dog and a succubus, though."

"We're doing that late dinner date," I reminded.

"Please escort our guests in," a man's world-weary voice instructed from the phone. I probably only fancied that the speaker hissed that plural, going for melodramatic villainous emphasis. Nailed it, though! Would that I be equally successful if given the chance to drive one through my auspicious hosts.

"Yes, sir," Hammer murmured. He'd morphed from troop commander to frequently sucked lackey in the space of two seconds, but recovered enough to snap orders at the morons who traveled with him.

They formed a very unlikely honor guard, two ahead of us, two behind us, with Hammer in the lead. No, I take that back. Beelzebub zipped between his legs and was back on point within two strides. The hound went as far as the elevators and sat down on his haunches, content to wait for the rest of us to arrive.

The elevator filled up fast. Beelz sat his haunches down, nearly on my foot. Probably trying to avoid being trampled. You get five bruisers like Hammer and his guys in a closed-in space with a shape-changing fox and a dude who's winging the hero act, and there isn't much room for a downsized hellhound.

118

When the doors opened, he was up and the first one out, though he waited patiently for Hammer to get us all in his own preferred marching order before taking a position directly in front of me this time. If the Beelz had been a waist-high wolfhound, I would have felt protected. The dachshund from Hell was more inclined to elicit warm, fuzzy feelings. Well, maybe his eyes would put the vamps off their blood cocktails.

We hiked to the end of the corridor. Hammer knocked respectfully on the door and, upon receiving a murmured invite, opened it and stood aside. The entire honor guard stood back for the three of us to enter, then nipped in to take positions along the inner wall. The door closed with a very final and ominous click.

There were only three of them. The oldest was seated behind a desk. Give him an opera cape and he was Count Dracula to a tee. A woman, frozen in time around her twenty-ninth year of life, perched on the edge of the desk, a Jessica Rabbit styled mass of platinum waves tumbling around her shoulders. Her cheekbones and jawline said Valkyrie to me; I suppose she was Swedish, Norwegian, or Danish. She had all the makings of a dame hiring Sam Spade.

The third occupant was the youngest of the three, turned maybe three decades back. Propped against the wall, arms folded, ankles crossed, he looked bored and brattish. He sported a painted-on tan, medium brown hair with artistically bleached streaks of gold, and a two-day growth of beard. He probably had the beard when he died, because I've never heard of a vamp needing to crawl out of his coffin and find a razor.

The fake surfer dude was as impeccably dressed as the other two vampires, though he sported an open-collared Ralph Lauren shirt beneath his designer suit jacket. The femme had chosen a scarlet dress that hugged every one of her curves with slavish devotion. Boss man's suit could have come from George Clooney's closet, or Cary Grant's, for that matter. He'd been walking about in the daylight when the Renaissance was more than a faire.

So, were they stereotyped vamps? Yeah, pretty much. But that was on purpose, for reasons they probably didn't intend to spill to me.

It sorta crossed my mind that I was freakin' nuts to be anywhere near them, much less to have made a deal that placed me in their territory.

While I stood wondering who was supposed to move the first piece in our chess game, Kit played pawn. She slipped her hand free from mine and headed toward the bank of windows. It put her on the side of the desk where surfer dude lounged.

"Oh, look at the view!" she cooed. "It's like a field of fairy lights."

"I'm glad it meets with your approval," the vamp master said. "It was certainly a selling feature when we leased the suite."

She turned, rotating on the ball of one foot, and glanced at me. "Your office isn't as impressive by comparison."

My office wasn't impressive even without the comparison.

"I'm not the head of a vamp syndicate," I said. "That might have something to do with it."

"True," she allowed, then turned a wide, bright smile on the man behind the desk. "I'm Kitsune Fox-Jones. And you are?"

"Your host for the moment," he said, and indicated two uncomfortable-looking, low-backed, skimpily padded, jade leather chairs, set like parallel sentries before the desk. "Please, sit. Would you like a drink? I can offer you an Evan Williams. I believe it is your preferred poison, Mr. Farrell. Yves, fix our guests something."

Yves pushed off the wall but didn't look overjoyed to be the designated bartender, though I'd chance a G-note that he'd been one when alive.

"Thanks," I said, taking the chair nearest Miss Sweden 1934. Kit cruised the room, admiring what few trinkets an interior decorator had chosen for the suite. As Beelz was still sticking by my ankles, I helped him up to my lap. He turned his watchful red gaze on the Renaissance dude.

The vampire leaned back in his much cushier seat, his elbows on the plush arms, his fingers interlinked.

"I understand you are interested in the unfortunate death of Pavan Banerjee. Rather ancient history, isn't it?"

"I'd like to hear the vampire community's side of the story," I admitted. "In my experience, different sides have different views."

He smiled, amused but too well-mannered to laugh in my face.

"In your experience," he said. "As I understand it, Mr. Farrell, that consists of adventures in the pages of several books."

"You haven't read them?" I asked, treating my borrowed hound to a soothing stroke of my fingers from between his ears, down the sleek black coat, to his shoulders. Whether it calmed either him or me is hard to say. He had his volume turned down, but I could feel the growl rumbling, could feel that he'd tensed every muscle in his elongated form. "You must be the only person in Detroit who hasn't. At least, you're the first one who can read that I've run into who hasn't."

"I prefer stock reports when in search of adventure," he said.

I pretended to look around the room but let my eyes linger on Ingrid, or whatever her name was. "Looks like you've done very well for yourself. Snagged all the accoutrements of success."

He allowed a chuckle to ripple forth, then leaned forward. "Let's cut to the chase, Mr. Farrell. Ask your questions."

"Okay," I said, but that's when bad boy Yves decided to thunk an expensive cut glass tumbler down on the edge of the desk before me. The bourbon nearly sloshed free.

"Is Surfer Dude going to hover over me or go back to his time-out session?" I asked.

Yves seethed. (I've always wanted to be able to do that, but seething and flippancy don't mix well.) He exchanged heated looks with the nameless boss, looked at Helga for backup, and received an elegant shrug in response. While he slouched off to his self-appointed sentry spot, I fought the urge to down the bourbon in a single gulp. Instead, it stayed untouched, though within easy reach.

"Who preyed on Banerjee, and why was he turned against his will?" I asked.

"Against his will, Mr. Farrell? I've heard no such rumor. As far as I know, he was a willing participant in the ritual. As to who turned him, that honor belongs to Drow Stowe."

"Drow?"

"I believe his proper name is Woodrow, though he thought it rather antiquated."

"And was he antiquated?"

"You mean an old vampire, one born in a past era? No, he was of rather recent birth. One of yours, wasn't he, Yves?" the master asked, not bothering to turn to look at his younger associate.

"Yeah, he was," the sulky brat grunted. "He ran, though, scared at what happened to Banerjee."

I turned to study him. "Ran where?"

Yves shrugged. "No idea. He didn't leave a forwarding address. He wasn't from around here. Maybe he went home. Maybe he stowed away on a tramp steamer and jumped ship in Tahiti."

"That would certainly be my preferred port of call if I had to avoid the sun," I said, going for urbane. "Where was he from?"

"Somewhere in the Northwest Territories, wherever in hell that is."

Geography wasn't his strong point, if he had any, that is.

"That's in Pretty Cold Canada," I said. Okay, so geography wasn't my best subject either, but I knew the Northwest Territories lay east of the Yukon, which was next door to Alaska. "That's mostly First Nations country. Was he a member of one of the tribes?"

Yves's shoulders lifted and fell in a "search me" action.

Well, I had a name now, and I knew that while the territory was large, it was home to barely forty thousand residents. Woodrow Stowe should be fairly easy to find. If that was his name; if he had gone home; if he was still alive.

"Did someone within the syndicate kill Banerjee?" I asked.

"Why would any of us do that?" Frida snapped. "It was monstrous what was done to the poor man. We felt his birth, and bare hours later, we felt the loss of him within our community. No, something this horrific can only be laid at the feet of one creature."

Although I knew what she was referring to, I had to give voice to the word for clarification, if nothing else.

"A human."

"Yes," she said, allowing the word to hiss with barely suppressed hatred.

"You used to be human," I said. "Every vampire was. There is no reason this side of the Styx that all your human traits died when you did."

She might have hissed at me again, but the man behind the desk silenced her with a partially raised hand.

"There are some that the turn affects in undesirable ways, bringing the worst human traits to the fore," he agreed, "though we attempt to screen applicants in the modern world."

"Yes, I can see you asking one to pass a psych evaluation first." Hell, they were all psychos to begin with. Had to be, to trade in the lives of thousands of victims to gain personal immortality. "What's the protocol for dealing with a psychopath who passes the lie detector test?"

Truda and Yves exchanged glances, but their boss had centuries of mastering control of himself. His jaw didn't even tighten.

"We take care of them quickly. Self-policing is a priority in a community such as ours."

"Paperwork to file and that sort of thing?"

"In a way." He wasn't going to give anything away without a herd of eight-legged Sleipnir offspring dragging it out of him. Odin's horse. You knew that, right?

"For the sake of argument"—not to mention my sanity—"let's say someone who had developed a god complex after his conversion didn't feel it was necessary to create a paper trail. We'll call this vampire Woodrow. Imagine him deciding to create his own little group of worshippers and not feeling it was necessary to ask anyone's permission. Not the syndicate nor the hosts he chose to be followers. If one of his newly turned converts turned on him the moment their vampiric strength kicked in, wouldn't he decide to make an example of them?"

All three of them glared at me.

Hedda was the first to break. "You are determined to crucify us for the death of a little man none of us even knew existed until he ceased to exist?"

"Just asking if there was an outside chance it could be Banerjee's maker who executed him," I said.

"You asked what we knew," the big man said. "Now you know. I believe it is time to move to the reason why we invited you to meet with us days ago."

I didn't think I was going to like this. Beelzebub had the same inkling. He hopped down off my lap and fixed his burning eyes on our host.

"And what is that?" I asked, attempting to sound relaxed. Doing my best to look it as well, I reached for the tumbler on the desk. No doubt the big man knew my heart was engaged in a classic Buddy Rich drum solo. His hearing was supernatural, after all. Mine wasn't bad either, but as he hadn't had a heart that beat in an epoch, I couldn't tell if he was gearing up for a try at my jugular. If he did, we'd all discover if I had blood or red ink in my veins.

He was smiling, which I chose to take as a very bad sign. "To destroy the one being that all the evidence points to as the executioner, of course. The Raven."

Ah, now *that* I hadn't anticipated. Cripple, yes; destroy, no.

123

I was the only one who hadn't considered it, though.

The Borgias' buddy gestured negligently with his index finger, and his army went into action while he relaxed back in his chair.

Maida lunged across the desk at me. I wasted the Evan Williams by tossing it in her face, then hurled the tumbler at Junior as he came off the wall. The blonde—yes, I've run out of X-treme Nordic names to call her—flinched back when the bourbon hit her eyes, but she recovered before I could see if my shot had beaned Yves's noggin. Snarling, she threw herself forward... to be met by the snapping jaws of a huge Great Dane with a familiar black coat, rust markings, and burning red eyes. Beelz's growl wasn't muted now as he met her in mid-flight.

I stepped back out of his way and, in doing so, noted that my shape-shifting girlfriend was wearing a different look as well. It seemed a cross between modern body armor and antique tournament gear, with a touch of shogun warrior. The total effect reminded me a bit of a cyborg. She closed with Yves, but as he couldn't find an unprotected spot to lay into her with his teeth, he fell back on back alley fisticuffs. My brief glance showed he'd never been any good at them.

With Mr. Big content just to watch the proceedings, I was left with a handful of humans to deal with. If you recall, I hadn't been very spectacular when they'd yanked me into that alley my first day in town. If they took me down now, the vampire coalition would win the day even if the hellhound and the succubus won their battles.

I did the stupidest thing that came to mind. I grabbed the guest chair Kit hadn't used and swung it at old Renaissance himself. It hit him squarely, taking him by surprise since, apparently figuring I was a done deal already, he hadn't even been watching me. Beelz's morphing into more impressive hellhound form was much more interesting. I wished I had the time to watch him, too. My chair delivery technique was enough to knock the old don to the floor, his chair tumbling over on top of him. I expected that to break his calm, but he merely lay there laughing.

"Hammer!" he called between chuckles. "He's yours for the moment."

It's dangerous to turn your back on three vampires, but there were five humans closing on me with scores to settle. Beelzebub and Kit were keeping two of the immortals busy, at least.

I still had the damn chair in my hands, so I hurled it at the approaching mini-battalion. The idiots had come forward in a wedge formation. When the chair took the point man down, a couple others wobbled, leaving me with still far too many incoming.

Have a confession to make. I held out on revealing that I'd made some calls and received a delivery while we were at the office. While I wasn't *armed*, I wasn't without a few tricks.

Supplied with distractions, I threw one of the impact smoke bombs I'd culled off a local stage illusionist against the wall. The thickness of the carpet certainly wasn't going to set it off. The sound of the strike and the blast of colored smoke startled the herd into a stunned and sudden stop. I was already running at them. A dangerous step up on the side of the discarded and wounded chair allowed me to plant my foot forcefully in the chest of one of them, laying him out temporarily. I sparked a bit of flash paper in another's face, the unexpected flare of flame in my hand sending him stumbling backward to trip over one of the already downed guys. Two of them bounded back to their feet and came at me from opposite sides, but a parkourish run at the wall took me halfway up it before I managed a backflip over their heads. Certainly got my hopes up about the outcome.

I tossed more smoke bombs, manifested more flashing flames interspersed with kicks at legs, stomped on feet. The extra speed Kit had supplied with her life force dose kept me a slippery, ever-moving target. With the electronic sparker in one hand to ignite the scraps of flash paper in the other, fisticuffs were on the back burner until I ran out of magic tricks.

Pathetic, huh? But I'd singed a couple of them with quick bursts of fire and reduced everyone's sight with the smoke so that we moved in a colorful illusionist's fog, all of us coughing on ill-advised intakes of breath. Still, while tiring, the boys were still game. The air was beginning to clear when Hammer pushed his men aside and strode forward.

Nice that they'd worn me down a bit for him, isn't it? By then I was out of the conjuring aids Kit had palmed before I'd been searched and then returned to me when we held hands again. I still had one talent I hadn't used, though.

As I'd begun with the idiot troops, I barreled at Hammer, doing some damage to an already smarting shoulder. Mine rather than his. He danced away from the worst of the blow, but I'd never intended for it to entirely connect. I'd needed him to twist aside, leaving me free to appropriate the bit of steel pipe he had tucked in the back waistband of his jeans. He didn't know I had it until I smacked it into his rib cage.

It just made him mad.

He made a grab for me, catching the open front of my jacket to drag me toward his descending fist. Praying there was still a spark left in the flash paper starter, I planted it against his neck. He flinched, but that didn't stop the power behind the blow that hit my solar plexus. The whoosh of breath that left me would have put out the fired-up birthday cake of a senior citizen. He followed it with a second hammering that stripped the starch from my knees. When he let go of my jacket, I crumpled at his feet. Since I was at a handy level, he kicked me.

Damn, but I missed having magic.

It was beginning to appear very unlikely that I'd make it to being alive for seventy-five hours this side of the fiction line when a tattooed biker materialized behind Hammer and pounded a fist down on the crown of his head. Reverend Wanna-be-a-Vamp's eyes rolled up and he fell. Someone should have yelled "Timber!"

As the men I'd downed straggled back up, Samael put them back in place with a backhanded slap. He didn't even look at what he was doing. Was I jealous? Damn right, I was.

"Shouldn't you be manning a desk in Hell or something?" I asked, wiping whatever red stuff was flowing from my split lip away with the back of my hand as I pushed to my feet.

Oddly enough, the room was dead quiet. I glanced back over my shoulder. Renaissance Dude was checking his fallen comrades. Ingrid lay in an attractive pile on the floor, looking like a well-chewed dog toy. Surfer boy was slumped against the wall, all his piss and vinegar drained away by Kit, who stood over him, fussing with her hair. She'd lost her spike heels, I noticed. One of them was driven into Junior's heart.

"The hound said you could use some help," Samael answered. "Why, did you want to finish them off personally?"

I ignored that jibe. "Beelz put through a call, huh?"

As though hearing his name, the hellhound ambled over. He was still in big box store size, and his muzzle was sporting splashes of blood. The idiot dog put his huge paws on my shoulders and slathered dog spit over my face. I swear he was grinning ear to ear, pleased that he'd been shown a good time.

"He likes you," Samael said. "Says you feed him better and introduce him to beings who are asking to be attacked."

"I do my humble best," I murmured.

The evil archangel was smirking as he vanished.

"Thanks, Beelz," I told the hellhound, rubbing his massive Great Dane side. He drooled on me a bit more, then returned to doxie mode.

Kit stepped over the nearest fallen soldier—it was Hammer—and touched my split lip. It tingled a moment and then hurt no more, all healed up with a dab of life force. Some of Yves's, probably.

"All better now?" she asked.

"What'd you do to Junior?"

She shrugged. "I'm far older than he and I know more tricks, that's all. He'll be puffed up on ego again soon enough. My heel wasn't made of wood. Was handy, though."

The vampire master checked on Yves and pulled the sacrificed heel free. Then, brushing off the knees of his trousers as he rose, turned to face us.

"You have unexpected friends, Mr. Farrell."

"You really should read the Raven books," I said. "You'll find I make friends easily."

I wasn't going to mention that I had just as much luck when it came to making enemies.

"Perhaps I will," he said.

"In the meantime, you might work on your logic," I suggested, "because the idea that a fictional character, who hadn't even been created on paper before Pavan Banerjee's death, could be responsible for that death is really asinine."

He bent his head in a microscopic nod of agreement.

"Perhaps, but the fact that you are standing here today proves that the coven has powers none of us suspected were possible. They could easily have brought you off the page to murder Banerjee and then sent you back. Publication has nothing to do with it, Mr. Farrell. You are, in many ways, merely an upgraded golem, a creature activated by words on a page."

To say that idea sat well with me would be a bigger fib than the white lies I usually specialize in.

127

"Humans killed Banerjee and most likely all the other nonhumans who bear distinct resemblances to the victims in those books. You are merely the weapon unleashed," he said. "You claim to be investigating these deaths. I suggest you also investigate the witches who gave you life."

Except he didn't term them with a word that began with a *w*.

"I believe you can see yourself out, Mr. Farrell."

If I'd had a smoke bomb or a single bit of flash paper left in my arsenal, we would have been gone before the air cleared.

Day Four, October 30

Despite the recent shot of life force Kit had given me to heal my lip, the rest of me felt like it had taken a whirl through a blender. I let her drive. Rather than take Beelzie and me back to Calie's fortress or to my modest office, she took us home with her.

Home wasn't a hovel in a scrap of forest land; it wasn't a scraggy little room anywhere near the territory she worked from that convenient corner, either. It was a luxury loft condo. Spacious, airy, tastefully decorated in woodsy tones, and equipped with every electronic device I cared to lust after. The master bedroom was furnished with the sort of sleeping facilities harem-owning sheiks would covet. I collapsed on the bed with a heartfelt sigh. Beelzie scrambled up next to me and nosed his way under the sheets.

"Food," I said.

Kit picked up the bedside phone and pressed a single button. Bless her, she had pizza delivery on speed dial.

After telling me how much cash I needed to fork over, she asked, "Beer, sake, or tea?"

From beneath the blankets, Beelz barked. I don't think he was asking for tea. I opted for a beer, and Kit disappeared.

"You want to soak those bruised muscles in a hot tub? You've got thirty minutes until the food arrives," she called back from the kitchen. "If so, towels are on the shelves in the bath."

Sounded like a heaven-sent idea to me. It got even better when I was submerged in the giant tub and Kit sauntered in, dropping items of her clothing as though she might need to use them as trail markers to find her way back to the bedroom.

I discovered a couple things that night. First, that besides driving a car, I knew how to do something else I'd never done in the Raven books, and based on Kit's reactions, I did it very well. Second, that

129

sleep was still disgustingly elusive. I looked human, acted fairly human, but I was still just a character on a page. I never got to sleep there, either.

Kit and Beelz didn't have that problem. While the hellhound dug his way under the pile of fresh towels Kit had tossed on the floor for his nest and she burrowed under the covers on the bed, I slipped away into the other room the moment they were both asleep. There were things to ponder, plan, and ferret out yet.

I now had more information to follow up on in relation to Pavan Banerjee's murder. When I dropped Kit off in the morning, I'd have assignments to distribute in the neighborhood. As a Native American demon, Doe would have connections with First Nations, but perhaps Kit could talk to Ruth Lund about the spurned girlfriend angle. Since the Botello family should be back from Acapulco and they were human, I wouldn't need a go-between. To keep up the ruse that I really cared two hoots about finding a writer for Calie, I'd need to touch bases with Delia, too.

Which got me to wondering about the vampires' belief that the coven was behind the deaths of each of the Otherworld victims. I knew damn well I hadn't been dragged from my comfy pages to wreak havoc on this world in the past, but that didn't mean the witches in Calie's group were equally innocent of vicious antisocial acts.

Kit had the latest in touch screen tech, so I made myself at home behind her glass-topped desk. Fortunately, the internet connection didn't require a password. I had my list of victims and was hoping I could learn more about them. Admittedly, the further back in time their deaths had occurred, the less I'd be able to find online.

I also needed to decide which of the more recent victims should be added to my investigation list. Currently, the list looked like this:

- Pavan Banerjee matched up to the vampire in Book 1
- Xavier Botello mirrored the zombie in Book 2
- Tado Gallo, the incubus, belonged with the story in Book 8
- Rolph Lund had come to the same end as the troll in Book 11

Two more would hopefully give the sampling the sort of detail that would show a pattern. At least, I hoped it would. October 31 was closing on me quickly.

I fished out Doe's list of the deaths in the real world. There was a yeti in Book 19. Its murdered real-world doppelgänger had been Jamyang Yontentsang, a name the file said meant "gentle voice of the family of good qualities." The rampaging Gampapa I'd executed had certainly lacked gentle or good qualities. As Jamyang's was one of the more recent deaths, I circled his name as one to be investigated.

One more.

There was a banshee from auld Éire. She'd been a hospice volunteer in Detroit. Sorta kept her in the same business without the need to maintain the carriage and horses with which to escort the dead. I passed her by.

Kuchisake Onna, the Slit-Mouthed Woman of both China and Japan, was a deadly little minx, but I already had enough Japanese seductrixs in my life, between Kit and her bakeneko associate, Neko.

The biskimi bi masa: Now, that one had possibilities. Why? Well, because they wouldn't be repeating any of the elements of the vampire, zombie, incubus, or the rest, *and* I really needed a female in my list. True, the biskimi bi masa were a group of Congo River nymphs, but they were skin disease dispatchers rather than succubi. Only adventurous idiots ever went looking for them. Amélie Lumumba had been an exchange student at the University of Michigan, nearing the end of her training to be a doctor of pharmacology. Her specialty—surprise, surprise—diseases of the skin. I circled Amélie's name as well.

The internet search turned up a mention of Banerjee's work as an engineer, but nothing new to add to Doe's data sheet. Botello was a surprise, because he still had fan sites. Apparently, he'd been an honored and famous bullfighter in his day. He'd been long retired before his relatives moved from Mexico to Detroit, where he died of natural causes while on a visit to them. One of his last requests was to be buried in a cemetery nearby rather than being shipped back to his homeland.

There was a very good chance that, like Marilyn and Elvis, he'd become a zombie because he'd been a legend in life, and being honored by fans kept that final exit door closed to him until the mysterious perpetrator I was hunting thrust him through it. I still had to visit his relatives, but his bullfighting background would help as a conversation starter.

There was nothing about Rolph Lund or Tado Gallo, but the yeti, Jamyang Yontentsang, had a Facebook page, with fresh messages from folks unaware of his demise. Google spilled even more, for he showed up in photographs taken at sci-fi fan conventions, billed as the Albino Wookiee. He looked really psyched, surrounded by the bunch of pseudo Hans, Leias, Lukes, and Landos caught grinning widely and waving at the photographer. Doe had supplied a booking agency. I added it to my interviewee tally.

Amélie had been typical of her supposed age: Her Facebook account was still up, too, and YouTube had clips featuring her with other med students. I jotted down what names were given, then headed to the university's website to identify professors she was likely to have taken classes from.

Efficient little devil that I am, by 5:30 a.m. I was at a block wall on the investigation until the rest of the city stirred awake.

Unless I took the vampires' idea seriously and considered the coven members as suspects.

What the hell, right? I had time to kill. *En route* to the kitchen for a beer refresher, I checked on my dozing companions. The huge bed was empty, but there were two muzzles peeking from the nest of towels, one sleek black, the other featuring a black-tipped nose on a rust-colored, furred face.

Huh. My girlfriend was sleeping with my best friend. Of course, the fact that one was a succubus and the other a hellhound certainly made us a threesome for an afternoon talk show, didn't it?

They were cozy; they were zoned out. My mind was still tripping along in the hamster wheel, going nowhere fast.

Beer in hand, with a side of pretzels unearthed in a search of the cupboards, I settled back at the computer. What, I wondered, did I really know about my creator?

While the search for my dead Otherworlders had supplied rather skimpy bits of info, Calista Amberson was mentioned everywhere. I hit Wikipedia first.

Young Calista Westbury's parents were academics from wealthy families. They arrived in Athens in 1948 with their five-year-old daughter. Soon, they befriended and opened their home to another American, Lovidia Smarts, who had settled on the Mediterranean in the early thirties. She was a woman with a similar fondness for the Grecian wonder years.

When Calie was eleven, her parents died in a yachting accident, and it turned out they'd given Lovidia guardianship over their daughter. Rather than remain in the vicinity, Smarts packed up her ward and headed to Philadelphia, where Calie still had family. By the time my creator was sixteen, the remaining Westburys had also died of various ailments, leaving her sole heir to a very comfortable estate.

That was when an investigator uncovered Lovidia's past as an active member of the Nazi party. With the witch hunt closing in on her, Lovidia committed suicide.

Calie was eighteen now, and the full power of the family estate, plus the private funds Lovidia willed her, made the young heiress catch of the year. She was snapped up by Cornelius "Skip" Amberson and wed him in all pomp and circumstance, if the photos that accompanied the entry were anything to go by.

The happy couple moved to Miami, where the bride threw herself into events with the garden club, learned to play golf, and hosted lavish parties. All might have been well, but Skip wasn't happy merely being rich. He wanted to be a big shot in business. He chose investments as his new hobby. At which he sucked. In twenty years they had run through their inheritances. With creditors closing in, Skip conveniently took his yacht out for one final shot at bagging a marlin, and the marlin bagged him. At thirty-eight and nearly penniless for the first time in her life, Calista was forced to look for a job.

She found it in Detroit, where an executive had an eye out for an assistant who could arrange banquets, deal with the upper class, and be an appropriately dazzling bauble on his arm when his wife wasn't around. By the time the executive retired, Calie had accumulated a substantial amount in her own bank account, but she decided that at fifty, she needed a new career. She'd chosen to be a novelist and been a success from the release of her first book, one featuring a smart-ass guy referred to as The Raven. Since then, she'd turned in a new book every year.

Except for this year.

The fan sites were rabid over the reasons why there hadn't been a new Raven book announced. Not one of their sources mentioned anything about Calie being diagnosed with cancer.

I did find one printed interview, from nearly fifteen years ago, where Calie claimed she'd borrowed her nephew's name to use. Seems no one ever realized that she didn't have a nephew from whom to borrow. Just in case, I did a web search on the Westbury and Amberson families. The only fellow who could claim the nephew spot I filled was illegitimate, the son of Skip's much younger half sister and someone she'd met and forgotten in the sixties. His name wasn't Bram Farrell. Wasn't anywhere even close to it.

There was no mention online of Calie's connection to the coven.

I considered asking her about them for about a zilch of a second. She'd never tell me anything. I might not have known as many details of her past prior to reading them on the Net, but I knew the woman who had invented me fairly well. Living in a person's head for a couple decades will do that for you.

However, I didn't think other coven members would be as reluctant to spill the beans.

By the time Kit and Beelzie stirred, my itinerary for the day was planned. I'd even hit a donut shop. If I was headed back to fictionland on the thirty-first, I was tasting every delicacy the *real* world offered first. Considering how delightful Kit looked, all tousled and heavy-lidded—well, once she was back in human form, though she'd been a really cute little fox, too—I considered tasting some of the delicacies more than once.

"Do you need me along for anything today?" she asked before burying her nose in the tall cup of latte I'd brought back.

"Nope. Don't *need,* but would always welcome the company."

"You have Beelzebub for company already."

"Giving him the option to come or not to come along today, too. Here's what's on tap: visit with the Botello family, who should be settled in once more after the extravaganza in Acapulco, lunch with Delia to find out how the project for Calie is going, tracking down the Albino Wookiee's agent, hunting up a professor or so on the Dearborn campus. Sound thrilling?"

Kit studied me over the rim of her cup.

"No," she said. "I think I'll head back to luring snacks in on the corner with Neko and Doe."

"Can you see if Ruth knows whether Rolph had a sweetheart with a reason to snuff him? I mean, since you'll be in the neighborhood," I wheedled.

Kit shrugged, a motion that sent the silky kimono she'd donned slipping down one bare shoulder.

"Should I call you if she has a name or wait to give it to you when I see you next?"

"Best call. No idea how long my day will be."

Rather than comment, she chose a donut and sank her teeth into it. The teeth looked a bit sharp and foxlike. Better the pastry than me.

Beelzie laid flat on the floor and put a paw over his eyes when I queried him on a ride along. Obviously, the two of them only wanted to be with me if there was a good chance I'd get into a fight. Today's schedule was too tame to be of interest. I sorta felt that way about it myself. But it needed to be done and done quickly. I could almost hear the clock in my head ticking the minutes away.

I called Delia while Kit donned her black corset and other finery. My pseudo cousin begged for a late lunch so she would have more information on the author search. To jump-start the wider spread of my killer search, I asked if she had a list of the coven members and what each did for a living.

"As it looks like I've got to make my way in this world, having a connection to people in various businesses could come in handy. You know, like your PR talents and Neva's in the insurance world have been helpful."

"I keep an updated file of everyone's data on my computer," Delia announced. "If you've got an email address set up—"

Which, of course, I now did, and gave her one of them.

"I'll send it as an attachment. You should have it within five minutes," she promised, then suggested a time and a restaurant.

Kit was ready to leave as I disconnected.

The trouble with dropping Beelz back at the estate was that P. T. would be there to welcome us. Not that I was avoiding her, but after being bashed about in the boxing ring and then battered at the vampires' uptown office, I wasn't exactly looking my best. Part of me wondered whether I was feeling what should have been my chronological years. I'd been twenty-nine in the first Raven Tale, and twenty books and twenty-plus years later, on paper I was still that. When I'd stepped out of the shower at Kit's, the mirror hadn't reflected any signs of aging. No gray hairs or deep creases in my face, just a mass of bruises on a lean, moderately muscled torso. Still, while Kit and Beelz might be looking forward to the next physical battle, my body sure wasn't, whatever its age.

My mind? Well, it sorta knew the respite wouldn't last. It sure hadn't in the books, and so far, life on this side hadn't been much different.

Of course, P. T. hadn't seen the Mustang. Perhaps she wouldn't have eyes for me *per se*.

The Beelz opted to ride shotgun after Kit vacated the seat. He had his head held as high as possible, to take in the scenery. His tail started a metronome beat against the upholstery when he caught sight of the house.

"You do know she'll feed you that special dog diet stuff," I told him.

Beelz made a groaning sort of sound but then appeared to remember those tummy rubs and looked excited to be home again.

If I'd had tummy rubs—and what they might lead to—to look forward to, I would have been excited, too.

I pulled the car around to the kitchen and tapped the horn lightly. P. T. was out the door before I'd stood back to let the hellhound scamper across the driver's seat and down to the driveway.

She stood with her hands on her hips, her blond hair tousled by the breeze cruising the estate. Her jeans were a shade I was sure my paint chip chart would term pumpkin, and she'd tucked a white shirt into the waistband. Her collar was open at her throat, sleeves rolled up to her elbows. Flat-heeled, brown suede boots rose nearly to her knees. Behind her, the scent of baking bread spilled from the house.

"Now what could have kept the two of you out all night?" she asked.

"You don't really want to know," I said.

P. T. stepped closer, put a finger to my chin, and nudged it over so that she could see the extent of damage my face had incurred.

"He started it," I insisted, indicating the hound. "I was just trying to get him out in one piece."

"Likely story," she said.

Beelzie tried to back me up—okay, he yipped—then tried to hump P. T.'s booted leg. Couldn't help but wonder if he was going to lay claim to every female I was attracted to.

136

"Your aunt would like to see you," P. T. relayed while disengaging from Beelzie's amorous attempt.

Well, I knew I couldn't avoid Calie much longer. I really hadn't seen much of her since she'd thrown money at me.

"About anything in particular?" I asked, going for casual interest.

P. T. grinned. "I believe her exact words were 'If my nephew waltzes in, tell him I expect him to make an appearance in my office.'" She did a pretty decent Calie imitation, considering she'd only been an employee for a few months.

A dramatic wince was called for. I gave it.

"And will you be here for lunch or dinner?" P. T. asked.

"Will you be serving anything resembling a porterhouse or a rib roast?"

"Falafel with tahini sauce for lunch."

I waited for a translation.

"Beans and chickpeas, with a sesame seed paste sauce."

I hoped I didn't look like I blanched.

"Gosh, sorry. Appointment with Delia for lunch."

P. T. sighed. "I even hate to mention dinner."

"Ah, take a chance," I urged.

"Tas kebab. It's Middle Eastern lamb stew."

"Damn. I've got so many people to see today, you'd better not wait for me on that one."

She cocked her head. "Will you ever be around for a meal I fix?"

"Consider working the words 'filet mignon' into the menu and I'd be slavering."

"You're hopeless," she decided. "Go see your aunt. I've got pita bread to make."

I lingered long enough to enjoy watching her walk back into the kitchen, then moved the Ravenmobile around to the front drive. All the better to make a quick getaway. I hoped.

Although it was hours until her usual rising time, Calie was waiting. She wasn't at her desk when I paused in the open doorway, propping the doorjamb up with a shoulder—the stance I'd been taking for a long time in her mind, thus the one she'd expect me to take. She was at the window, the sheer panels behind the heavier drapes held aside in one hand.

The drop in temperature outside was apparently affecting her more than it was me, or P. T., who hadn't bothered with a jacket when she'd come outside. Calie was bundled up in a heavily cabled, high-necked black sweater and charcoal-colored wool slacks and had a jewel tone paisley shawl wrapped around her shoulders as well.

"What is *that*?" she demanded, apparently sensing my arrival.

"The dealer swore it was a car," I said.

"Is it why you smell of cheap perfume?"

"I've no idea what any scent costs, but based on the surroundings I picked it up in, my guess is that it's expensive."

"Far too much musk," Calie insisted, wrinkling her nose as she dropped the curtain panel and turned to face me.

I really doubted she was picking up any scent. No, she knew where I'd been and with whom. The real question was, how did she know? Who was the spy?

"Is that all you wanted to see me about?" I asked, pushing free of the doorjamb. "If so, there are other places I need to be."

"I'm sure the doxie can find other customers for the remainder of the day."

Damn, she sounded jealous!

"Are you referring to Beelz or to Kit? I'm sure your informant told you her name."

"As well as her genus," Calista said, then shook her head. "I suppose it's my own fault. I didn't incorporate enough humans into the manuscripts for you to develop a rapport with your own kind."

"Far as I know, I'm the only fictional character walking around this side of the stitched binding," I said, "so who are these beings of my own kind with whom I'm supposed to develop a freaking rapport?"

Calie smiled, though I didn't see any amusement in her expression otherwise.

"Anyone who isn't an Otherworlder would qualify. There is Philomena, for example. Don't you find her attractive?"

It took me a moment to realize she meant P. T.

"Very cute," I agreed, "but clueless on what to feed the male of the species."

"I'm sure that over time she could learn," Calie suggested.

She clearly didn't know P. T. Kosmas in the least.

"You can stop with the matchmaking. I'm still adjusting to life in the real world, and already you don't like my car or my companions. Anything else you want to complain about, Mom?"

Calista's expression twisted, as though she'd bit into something sour. "Please don't use that nomenclature when referring to me. The idea of offspring has always been repellent to me."

"Yet here I am! If you don't want to be my mother, then stop the hell acting like you are one."

"Oh, I'm not upset with you over the succubus or the automobile, Bram. I'm furious with you over this!" She strode over to her desk and swiveled the open laptop around to face me. In blaring headlines, a website announced that she had cancer and that there was a search on to find a new writer to take over the series.

Okay, Delia had been wrong. Calie *did* keep track of news in the publishing world.

"You gave an impossible deadline. This was the only way to come even close to lining someone up."

Backpedaling, yeah, I know. Like that was going to get me out of detention.

"If you had bothered to search—" she began.

I could tell it was going to be a harangue without listening to the whole thing.

"No," I interrupted. "You brought me across for another reason. A reason you haven't mentioned yet. Looking for someone else to write The Raven Tales is a lame excuse. A lame idea. Let the damn series die. If that means me as well, so be it. I've been in your world for less than four days, Calie. I'll be sad to leave it, but I don't really belong, do I? Therefore, what's the real reason you made me a Pinocchio knockoff?"

Her shoulders were thrown back, her teeth gritted in fury. She could have been a statue but for the quick pace of the pulse that beat visibly in the column of her throat.

"To find a replacement for me," she growled.

I knew it for a lie now. There were other sources who might know what she wasn't telling me, though.

"The search is underway," I said, "but right now I have other things that need doing."

"Investigating for the succubi? Are you attempting to prove I was the one perpetrating the crimes I recounted in my manuscripts?"

139

She was going for an award-winning performance as the *grande dame* infuriated at what she perceived as an insult. I wasn't awarding an Oscar, though.

"Actually," I said, pausing for effect myself. This ink drop hadn't fallen far from the maternal pen. "It isn't the Sukis who think you did in twenty nonhumans. It's the vampires who do."

As an exit line, I thought it worked really well.

If there was one being who knew what was in Calista's mind, I thought I knew where to find him. I headed for the woods.

There was more of a nip in the air than on my last trip there, and more trees had shed leaves. Those retaining a tight grip on the branch were various tones of yellow and gold, but any shades of red or orange were now gone. Rust dominated. Not rust like Kit's fox coat, but junkyard, crumbling rust. Even the underbrush was beginning to look decidedly naked compared to just a couple days ago, the leaves shriveling into small twisted corpses. While there were a few evergreens, it was basically a landscape of birch, maple, elm, and ash trees.

Once the cover was gone, I wondered where the theophylaktos dudes would hide. But then again, once winter hit, Samael probably headed for Rio rather than stick around frozen Detroit. He'd simply delegate all tempting to underlings who might enjoy the cold for a change.

This time I knew where I was going.

The crunch of leaves beneath my running shoes gave warning of my approach. It was a purposeful step, I thought, but it seems my purpose wasn't clear. Three theophylaktos dropped on me figuratively from the heavens. I kissed dirt.

They laid into me with what felt like pillows while bellowing what they appeared to think were ferocious war cries.

"Transgressor!"

Had heard that one.

"Protect the Great One!"

I fancied Samael fed that one to them for amusement's sake.

"Smite him!"

Archaic, but colorful.

"Yield, lowly one!"

That one got me. I rolled over, grabbed the nearest leg and yanked. The theophylakto spilled over on his back, his surprised yelp quite satisfying to my ears. I swept two others off their hairy little tootsies with a sweep of my leg through the trampled leaves and twigs of the forest floor. Then I bounded—yeah, bounded—to my feet. As they scrambled up, I was already crouching, knees bent, arms spread, teeth bared in a grin.

"Come on, bramble boys," I snarled.

Shoulder Pads scrambled at me on all fours, hands and feet down, rear in the air. I sent him spinning away up and over my shoulder. He squealed. The commander held back, but his remaining grunt hurtled forward. I stepped aside, and he smashed flat against the tree behind me. Nice solid thud it was, too.

With his troops down, the leader tightened both his hands around the grip of the long weapon in his hand.

It was hard not to laugh in his face. He was so centered on annihilating me, but it wasn't going to be easy considering he had a blue foam sword that sported a bright yellow foam guard and a green plastic handle. Two other toy swords lay in the forest detritus, waiting to be reclaimed by my currently unarmed assailants.

"Is that fair?" I demanded. "I'm weaponless. The least you could do is let me use one of your men's swords. Even things out. I'll even use only one hand."

He took a better two-handed grip on the handle. "You were warned before, transgressor. Now suffer my wrath."

"You're kidding, right? Your lord and I had beers together. Plus, he's got better muscles than I have! In the annihilation game, I'd be toast if I tried to go up against him." Not to mention he had all the hocus-pocus to mete out as well.

The little whatever-theophylaktos-were kept his foam blade at the ready, looking rather like a baseball player waiting for the windup and the throw.

"I will allow you to make the first move," he said.

I did. I took one step forward and ripped the damn toy from his hands as it descended to wallop me on the shoulder.

This seemed to be the signal for the other two to leap at me. I smote the nearest one with the foam blade. It bounced off him,

141

naturally, but when he saw there was no cut, he was so startled that he stumbled backward and tripped over a fallen tree branch. I put my hand on Shoulder Pads's brow and held him off, though he did some awesome bull snorting while swinging knotted fists. They stirred the air six inches from me. Then the commander barreled forward and, wrapping himself around my leg, attempted to bite me. I pounded the plastic pommel down on his head to discourage that idea.

"Knock it off, guys!" I yelled. "I'm just here to ask your boss a question."

"Just one?" Samael asked.

He stood at the edge of the wood, the meadow at his back. Today he'd decided to be a middle management weekend gardener rather than a vet in camouflage or a biker. He wore light brown corduroy trousers, a sweater that stopped just shy of being an argyle pattern, Hush Puppies, and a tan baseball cap. He was leaning on the handle of a rake. Behind him, the meadow was free of leaves except for the large pile off to the side.

The three theophylaktos fell prostrate on the forest floor.

"You give them these?" I asked, brandishing the ridiculous sword.

"They take their job too seriously at times," he said, a smirk on his lips. "This seemed a logical compromise that would keep everyone safe."

"And entertain you?"

"That, too," he agreed. "Begone, my guard. The Raven is known and is powerless in my company."

"Powerless," I repeated, disgruntled. "I could have brought holy water with me."

Samael was as amused with me as he was with the theophylaktos. As the three short guards melted into the woods, he let the rake vanish as well.

"How thoughtful," he said, "but I prefer sacramental wine. The more expensive of the vintages, naturally."

"Naturally," I said.

"What is this one burning question, Raven?"

He didn't look at me as he asked, but flicked a finger at the two toy swords lying just off the path. They popped out of existence, as did the one I still held in my hand.

142

"Okay, maybe it's more than one. One with extensions, let's call it," I suggested. "What the hell is Calista up to? She's given me a cock-and-bull tale about needing a replacement so that the Raven series can continue on without her, but come on, if she's kin to you, all she has to do is ask and you'll make the cancer wish it hadn't made an attempt on her, right?"

He shrugged and, hitching the knees of his trousers, made to sit down. A patio lounge chair appeared in the nick of time. It featured a curved ironwork frame and autumn-toned plush cushions, the pattern looking a bit like dancing flames. When a matching chair followed a moment later, I sat down cautiously, just in case it vanished. A side table wavered into existence between the chairs, already supporting a bowl of caramel-covered popcorn and two tall, sweating bottles of Evan Williams apple cider. Samael chose a bottle and grabbed a handful of sticky delight. I took the second bottle and helped myself to the snack as well.

"Yeah, I could," he admitted, "if she wanted me to, but she doesn't want to repair this form. She wants a new one."

"Like an android thing? I know in sci-fi such things are possible, but this is only the beginning of the twenty-first century. No one's up to speed on that yet."

He looked surprised at the idea. "Where did you learn about that?"

"Fictionland," I said. "Characters who have been around long enough for readers to consider them nearly real people have a sort of cachet to exist even when our creators aren't working on a story. We've got hangouts just like people this side, because it was people on this side who envisioned our worlds. FYI: Don't play poker with cyborgs. They count cards. Androids with human brains are just as slick or clueless as they were when in biodegradable bodies."

"Interesting," he murmured. "I may have to visit someday."

"Oh, you're already there, and in more than one form. Some beasts, some businessmen, even biker types like you decked yourself out as last night. Nothing much is new in fictionland these days."

"Life goes on there?"

"Until we're forgotten. Then we just fade away. You can stop trying to get me off the topic, though," I said. "Calie wrote me to be hyper-persistent when it comes to getting answers to questions. So what the hell are you talking about in relation to her wanting a *new form*?"

Samael delayed by munching caramel corn, then washing it down with long swallows of cider. As had occurred at the bar, as much as he drank, the level of fluid in the bottle stayed the same. Heck, now that I looked at mine, it remained full, too.

"How old do you think Calista is?" Samael said finally.

"She was a child during World War II," I said, remembering the homework I'd done. "Therefore, she's in her seventies."

The devil chuckled. "Wrong. She's more than seventy centuries old."

Okay, it was my turn to look stunned.

Samael leaned forward. "It's like this," he said. "Those first humans—"

"The ones in the Bible, or the ones the archaeologists dig up pieces of in Africa?" I asked.

"For simplicity's sake, we'll say the biblical ones."

"Adam, Eve, and Lilith."

"The original *ménage à trois*," Samael said. "I knew them, of course."

"Of course," I echoed.

I do have the strangest conversations with beings, don't I?

"Adam was a bore, a whiner. Don't know why the Big Man put up with him. Lilith got ticked off early on. She'd already snapped on the lures I'd dropped in Eden's ponds, and she was glad when Eve arrived to take her place. Poor, spiritless Eve, though even she was tempted when I whispered in her ear."

"Heard it all, move on, dude," I urged. "My time is limited. Things to do, people to see."

"Don't sweat it, Raven. While we're here, time isn't going anywhere."

"Convenient," I said, "but even a bottomless bottle of E. W.'s cider won't make up for a story that's a yawn."

You'd think I didn't know how dangerous he was, wouldn't you? Ah, blame Calie. She wrote me to be stupid at times.

Samael laughed, not faking the amusement this time around.

"True," he agreed. "Bottom line is, our daughters took after their mother. They wanted more and considered being gypped out of immortality as quite unfair. Well, Lilith wasn't much taken with the idea of getting old, either. They were clever girls, though, and made a deal with one of the other spirits."

"Don't tell me. The moon, right?"

"It is how she brought you across," Satan said. "Just a modification on the ceremony."

"They remake themselves?"

"Not totally. Just a spirit shift."

I know it sounds idiotic, but I said, "A spirit shift?"

"You're unclear on what that means?"

"Could be see-through underwear with a name like that!"

The fallen archangel sighed. "She's taught you nothing in those stories, has she?"

"She's kept me pretty damn well in the dark and merely put me through the upper levels of Hell," I said. "Enlighten me, gramps."

He frowned at that, but heck, if Calie was his daughter and my creator, then he was my grandfather, or what could pass for one.

"It means the postulant—"

"In this case, Calista?"

"—seeks out a new form to inhabit and, under the right conditions and plea, changes places with the former occupant. *Spirit shift* should have clearly indicated that."

He was arguing ceremonial mumbo-jumbo while I was fixated on what had actually taken place.

"She's going to push some clueless person out of their body, dumping them in her aging and cancerous one?"

"She does it a couple times a century," he said, treating it like this was not a big deal.

Well, hell, not for the devil! It left things wide open for him to offer the poor unfortunate stuck in Calie's old body some pretty tempting deals!

It also meant that the last time she'd shifted forms had probably been when the real Calista Westbury was eighteen and Lovidia Smarts stole her body. Had waking up and finding an older woman's face looking back at her in the mirror pushed the real Calista over the edge to suicide, or had my Calista helped her out of the way? Calista Westbury *had* inherited Lovidia's funds, after all. I couldn't see *my* Calie turning down an opportunity like that. She'd probably arranged things to keep increasing her personal financial worth, the only setback having been her marriage to Skip Amberson.

And now she planned to steal a body again. I wasn't supposed to be finding her a writer; I had been brought across to find her a new form.

As delightful as the special brand cider had been a moment ago, it now soured in my mouth. Even the caramel-covered popcorn lost its appeal.

Samael was at ease in his chair, his never-empty bottle dangling negligently from the hand he rested on the ironwork arm.

"You look a bit green about the gills, kid," he said. "Something disagree with you?"

I nearly asked him to send me back to fictionland, but I'd already inadvertently put things in process for Calie. A worldwide search was on for writers interested and capable of taking over The Raven Tales. Once one was chosen, she'd do the spirit shift and they'd be left to die in her cancerous carcass.

But she didn't want to wait for a prolonged search. She wanted to *ascend* to her next stolen life on the night of Samhain, and she planned to ensure that the replacement died immediately this time.

"Now where, I wonder, did you develop such a sense of right and wrong?" Samael mused. "Not from Calista. If she's the beneficiary, a thing is considered right, in her mind. She's been that way for centuries worth of centuries. But you're not. You're honestly appalled at what she intends to do although she's done it over and over and over and over ad nauseam. This is quite interesting and very unexpected."

I slammed the bottle down hard on the table between us. "Tell me how to stop her."

He laughed out loud. "Do what? Why would I do a thing like that?"

"Then tell me how to get in touch with someone who can stop her."

"You mean like the Big Man himself? Bram, Bram, Bram. The dude's got, like, a gazillion universes he's juggling, all with planets weighted down with beings that moan about their plight, and plead, and threaten, and go through all sorts of dramatics to get his attention. You know what the message is to them all? *God helps those who help themselves.*"

146

Which meant it was up to me to sort this out. I probably had less than two days to be part of this world, and in that time I needed to stop Calie from stealing a body and snuffing the previous resident *and* find the human or humans who had killed twenty nonhumans over the past two decades.

Suddenly, life within a Raven story sounded like a piece of cake.

Satan took himself and the patio equipment off in a flashy smoke-bomb cloud of illusion. Entertaining himself again, no doubt.

Stealing one of my tricks of the trade, too, which irked me, because it illustrated how damn helpless I was in this world. Other than that brief moment when I'd *seen* into the past and identified that Pavan Banerjee had been nailed to that convenience store exterior wall with railroad spikes, not a glimmer of the magic I possessed in the books had come through that open door from the world of fiction after me. Which meant that while I was not human, I was stuck being as powerless as a human.

Samael hadn't given me much, other than further problems, but he'd left me with the only piece of advice that I could follow up on: *God helps those who help themselves.* All I needed to figure out now was how to give myself a leg up on all the investigations.

There was still that lunch date with Delia, but as she was the second oldest witch in the coven, I now wondered whether she was living in a stolen body, too. If so, there would be no help there.

I needed to get off the estate. Logic dictated I grab a change of clothes to keep in the trunk—disasters and cleanups should be taken as future givens—thus, a quick swing by my room was needed. Other than that, chances were that I wouldn't be back on the grounds until it was All Hallows.

The trip back across the lawn, the nip up and then down the stairs, and I was back in the Mustang within fifteen minutes. Rather than make a flashy retreat, I drove down the drive at a pace that was so sedate, squirrels nearly bounded by me faster.

I headed for the Botellos' place.

Where I'd been met with hostility by Pavan Banerjee's widow and Rolph Lund's older brother and boxing scam buddies, the late

147

zombie's family welcomed me with open arms, still buoyed by the joy and goodwill engendered by their recent trip across the southern border for their daughter's wedding.

"Tio Xavier? Ah, he was the pride of the family. A great fighter of the bulls, a matador, did you know?"

I'd read the fan sites. I knew.

"We were sad when he died and yet happy that he chose to remain here in Detroit rather than be shipped home for his burial," Paolo Botello, his nephew, said as we settled into a crowded, very colorful parlor. Posters of Botello were everywhere, the largest showing him taking a stance before a really ticked-off bull, his short jacket dazzling with embroidery that continued down the outer leg of his short, gold trousers. His scarlet cloak swirled behind him, teasing and tempting a bull with picadors' lances embedded in its sides.

"Tio looked magnificent in his coffin, for he wore his best clothing. Like that," Paolo said, pointing to the mega poster. Rather than be a replica, it showed slight signs of weathering, meaning it had probably graced the exterior wall of the arena where Xavier had faced down a line of doomed Ferdinands.

"It was so convenient when he returned," his wife Pilar added. "We thought we'd only be visiting him on the Day of the Dead, but when he turned up on our doorstep a month after the funeral to be with us for our son's birthday, we were thrilled to have him with us longer."

"He was well loved and a legend in your country," I said. "That is probably why he continued to live beyond his death."

Paolo's head bobbed. It was balding, with a few long, suspiciously dark lanks combed over the now-empty pasture that receded from his forehead. His wife was as plump as he was but had let nature have its way with her once-dark hair. The gray streaks were generous and swept back into a sedate knot at her nape.

"Yes, that is what *tio* thought, too," Paolo said. "He found it both amazing and sad, because while he could spend more time with us, he was no longer what he would have wished to be. If his followers had seen what their adoration had done to him, he was sure they would weep."

That or run screaming in terror.

"Can you tell me about the time leading to his second death?" I asked. "Were graves in the cemetery being disturbed or desecrated before or after it? If you'd seen him recently, had he mentioned anything strange happening in the area?"

They looked at each other, then turned back to me.

"Do you mean other than the comings and goings of the vampires who live in the mausoleums? *Tio* didn't come out during the day much. He didn't want to frighten anyone. Said it was easier to keep to the shadows at night. Once the sun set, it was usually only the vampires and their servants, or spirits that never strayed far from their own graves, that were out."

"And did he have any confrontations with any of the vampires' servants?" I could imagine a Renfield like Hammer, or one of his men, deciding to accost a lone zombie. Even if Xavier Botello was the only zombie in the cemetery, duded up in the *traje de luces*, the suit of lights he'd worn in the arena, he would have stood out.

"Some," the Botellos admitted. "The younger ones would jeer at him, tell him to just crumble away like the inferior being they considered him. Once some of them rushed him, but *tio* merely used his cape and the moves that had kept him ahead of the bull's horns to best them. I remember him laughing about the confrontation, since the result was that one of them tumbled into a recently dug grave and another gave himself a concussion against a firmly planted tombstone."

It sounded a lot like my confrontations with the theophylaktos team.

"Did that occur just prior to his final death?"

The couple exchanged a look again, both their brows wrinkling in thought.

"It is difficult to remember," Paolo said. "The horror of what was done to *tio* makes it difficult to recall how much time had passed."

"If only we'd kept a diary of his visits and his stories, but for the most part what he talked about we'd all heard many times before," Pilar added. "It didn't seem noteworthy."

"Still, I don't think it was more than a few weeks before," Paolo said. "More than a month, but less than two, perhaps."

This time it was Pilar who nodded. "*Si*, I think you are right."

"One last question, then, and I'll stop stirring up sad memories for you and be on my way," I said.

"Few of our memories of Tio Xavier are sad," Paolo insisted. "It is nice to talk about him to someone."

I took that for politeness rather than complete truth, for they were a very pleasant couple.

"What is your question, Señor Farrell?" Pilar pressed.

"Would you happen to know the names of the vampires living in the cemetery, or of any of their minions?"

Sadly, they didn't. That meant I would be prowling around graves, looking for evidence of frequent comings and goings. Not my choice of venues, but as I lacked minions, it was a simple case of "If you want something done right, do it yourself." I'd been following that rule for twenty volumes already. I should feel right at home.

The St. Romaric Cemetery wasn't the most prepossessing burial ground. This was one of the older sections of the city. The families who built the aboveground mausoleums had moved away long ago. The standing stones of the graves around the bone houses were tipsy, the names on them nearly weathered away by the elements.

A dilapidated wooden board bolted to the rusted gate advertised that there were still lots available, but as the part of the sign that supplied a telephone number was missing its last four digits, getting hold of whatever office now handled things was going to be difficult. Regular maintenance of the lawns appeared to be continuing, probably because there was the option for new burials in the section still in use. Chances were that a church had once stood near the burying grounds, but it was nearly as long gone as anyone's memory of St. Romaric himself now, demolished so well there wasn't a remnant of wall nor a dip in the turf to indicate where a basement had once been. Towering old trees left a blanket of dead or dying leaves on the ground.

The gate was wedged open thanks to drooping hinges and a buckled cement path. I roamed through the more ancient sections, acting like a tourist with a history-gathering bent.

It didn't take long to find where the leaves were trampled, crushed, and knocked aside by visitors outside the largest of the mausoleums. Some of the marks indicated a scuffle might have occurred—the unwilling victim at a late-night supper, no doubt. The names and dates on the mausoleum in question showed that it hadn't acquired a new occupant in over a hundred years, which seemed to further prove I'd found at least one vamp's daytime digs.

Doubted it was of any vampire I'd had the displeasure of meeting in the past few days though.

I decided simply knowing where to find this vamp, and where its Renfields would be hanging about, was sufficient and went in search of Xavier Botello's gravesite. It was perhaps sixty feet away, which meant he'd have run into the gang from the mausoleum frequently. Even though he was no longer in residence, unless the family had managed to gather some of the ashes that would have been left when the fiery torch he'd become had gone out, the grave was well manicured. Someone had removed earlier accumulations of leaves and bracketed the headstone with twin pots of coppery mums.

But the distance between Botello's grave and the vampire's lair was close enough. The blood minions rocketed to the number one spot on my suspect list. I'd need to return when they began to gather. Maybe swing by and pick up Beelz first, see if he'd like to do the Great Dane impression again.

There weren't many graves showing fall offerings like Botello's, but then it wasn't a bunch of flowers that caught my eye as I was turning back toward the entrance gate. It was the ridged posture of a woman dressed in dull, washed-out colors. She looked a walking shadow in a plot that featured a host of less solid shadows. Well, less solid if you didn't count the granite tombstones. A soft breeze was stirring the trees, setting them whispering. Leaves danced across the potholed drive that meandered through the cemetery.

I ducked down, crouching behind the tallest standing tombstone in the vicinity, which happened to be decked with the weather-worn form of a two-foot-tall angel. It offered excellent cover as I spied on Farha Banerjee.

I hadn't even considered whether she had managed to find anything of her husband to bury and would thus have a grave to visit. But then, this could also be the sort of monument raised by sailors' and fishermen's families for those lost at sea. An empty grave, but a place to honor and mourn the lost beloved.

Farha had brought no flowers. She hadn't bothered to clear away the coverlet of dead leaves or the dried remains of a vine that crept over one corner of Pavan's tombstone. She simply stood unmoving, solemn, and as gray as one of the granite statues that graced the older section of the cemetery. She finally moved five minutes later, raising her arm to check her watch. Then, as grim as she'd been at the grave, she turned and strode quickly down the drive and out the front gate, turning left. I'd need the map in my glove compartment to verify the direction, but I guessed she was returning to work after an early lunchtime visit.

The fact that Pavan's grave was near Xavier's made me wonder whether Drow Stowe had become part of the local vampire's pinochle group despite having been turned by Yves of the One Detroit Center club. He'd obviously needed some assistance to hold Pavan in place for those spikes to be hammered in. Perhaps the boys who hung out here had been more than happy to get in good with another vampire. Double the chance of being taken into the exclusive membership rather than remain a go-fer. It could have been a damn good ploy on Stowe's part.

The question remained, though: Why had Stowe gone to the trouble of turning Banerjee, a man who, according to his wife and good friend, didn't want to be a vampire, if all he intended to do was then murder him with the combined whammy of a stake to the heart and the glory of the rising sun? It simply didn't make sense.

Why was I even considering it?

That answer was easy. I'd been led to it.

Hell! What an idiot!

Of course, being back to square one on Pavan Banerjee's murder meant I had another line of investigation to follow.

Since St. Romaric's church had long vanished, and the telephone number as well, where were the records kept?

Lacking the contact number or the name of a neighborhood association that might act as the property's caregiver, I did the next best thing. I headed for the nearest convenience store and asked if there was a local police station or government office nearby. Turned out that, thanks to the city's financial problems, there were neither. There was a local undertaker, though. I headed to the Fontaine Funeral Home for information.

"A list of those interred at St. Romaric's?" the secretary who greeted me echoed back when I asked. "I don't think I've heard that there is one. We have records of burials arranged through us, but that's all. The Archdiocese of Detroit still owns the property, but the available lots aren't on sanctified land. That area was always a potter's field. The diocese probably has records of plot sales and any historical documents that were removed before the church was torn down, but I don't know what else they might have."

Whatever they did have would take longer to get hold of than I had left on my ticking investigative clock.

"I'm researching unsolved murder cases, and recently"—like within the past thirty minutes—"came across the fact that two of the victims were buried not far from each other in the cemetery. All I'd like to know is whether that's an anomaly or something that is worth following up on," I said.

"Murder cases? Are you with the police, or writing a book?" she asked.

I smiled. "You got it right the second time. People never get tired of reading about true crime."

She shivered. "Gruesome topic, though."

"But if what I uncover can lead the police to making an arrest or two, I'll have aided in taking a dangerous person off the streets," I said.

"Detroit could do with that," she agreed, and turned to her computer. "What are the names of your victims? I'll see if we were involved in their final resting arrangements and whether they were buried at St. Romaric's."

Oddly enough, Rolph Lund, Tado Gallo, Amélie Lumumba, and Jamyang Yontentsang turned up in her search.

"What's even weirder," I told Deer Woman not long after I left the funeral home, "is that none of these people lived within spitting distance of St. Romaric's, other than Xavier Botello's family. The funeral home staff suggested the other burials were a result of their aggressive advertising campaign. They have made a practice of suggesting plots where they are available in older cemeteries like St. Romaric's, hoping to bring attention to the sites as historical areas. Plus, the lots are cheaper, because St. Romaric's is a fairly forgotten sort of place. But it's still weird that all the victims' names I had her look for were buried within a stone's throw of each other in the same cemetery."

"Beyond weird," she agreed, leaning into the open window of the passenger door rather than climb in the car. "Though how does that help in narrowing in on the murderer? It could indeed be the advertising and the fact that the burial ground is conveniently near the funeral home. I remember someone mentioned they'd seen ads on the sides of buses and along the highway for the funeral home. It's probably why we contacted them when Tado was murdered. I'm sure we went with their suggestion of the local plot simply because it wasn't consecrated ground. While it doesn't bother some of us, it does other nonhumans."

I felt I was jumping at anything that came up. That ticking clock in my head was making a hell of a racket now. Time was running out, and I felt I was nowhere near solving even one of the murders, much less finding a connection between six murders or twenty. One other than my fictional self, that is.

But I had to. It might not be the assignment that Calista brought me into this world to do, but it had become very important to me since then. Was it because I'd killed the fictional versions of these people in the books and needed to atone, or was it simply that I needed to prove it wasn't Calie's plotting that had allowed me to track murderers in the books but my own ability?

Samael had said I had qualities Calista lacked. I wanted one of them to be the validation of my investigative abilities.

"I know it's early, but have you heard back from First Nations about Woodrow Stowe?" I asked her.

Doe shook her head. "Not yet. Perhaps I'll hear something tonight. Will you be by later?"

"Yeah, to see if Kit is interested in another tagalong as backup, so the vamp I need to interview doesn't do me in first," I said.

She smirked. "I heard you held your own rather well last time."

"I hit one vampire with a chair and he fell over laughing," I insisted. "And I had some help at the end, even in dealing with Hammer and his boys. If Samael hadn't shown up to smite the not-so-good reverend, who knows how it might have gone?"

Her eyes widened. "Satan got involved in the fight?"

"Just amusing himself," I said. "Still..."

"Raven." She drawled my alias. "You're not human. You're not nonhuman. How the hell can someone kill you if none of us can figure out if you are even a living being?"

"Good point," I allowed, "but why take chances?"

There was still time before the appointment with Delia, tracking down professors at the college, and talking to the Albino Wookiee's agent. I swung by my office to take another gander at the files of all the victims. There had to be something in them that I'd missed. Or I hoped there was. Deer Woman's team had been very thorough and efficient. Now if only I could be so.

Other than the day I'd leased the office, I hadn't been there during regular office hours. It was strange to find the parking lot nearly packed with vehicles and people coming and going on a regular basis. Stranger still to realize they were all human.

Not that I had anything in common with any of them. I was still among the unclassified type of walking, talking, breathing beings. Maybe I was a new type of golem, a sentient one with free will. The fact that I disagreed with Calie's life choices and had no intention of being involved in sacrificing someone in the pursuit of her longevity showed that, right? All I had to do was keep that little fact from Calie and her coven mates.

I'd met the perky receptionist twice now, but her name escaped me. As her desk lacked a name placard and her fantasy-inspiring chest lacked a name tag or ID badge, I was at a disadvantage. She looked up from the bottom desk drawer, one hand on the handles of her purse.

"Hi!" she said. "Did they tell you that by tenant vote the building is usually closed for lunch? If there is anything you need me to do"— her voice took on an edge—"it will have to wait until I'm back."

"Which will be...?" I queried as she rushed around the counter and into the aisle.

She pointed to the sign on the counter in front of me. *Back at 1 p.m.,* it read. The expression on her face told me what she thought of my mental faculties. They weren't getting high marks, but hey, I was a bit distracted by all the possibilities clamoring for notice in my noggin.

155

"In an hour," Miss Lackaname said, putting undue emphasis on the announcement. "If you leave, be sure to lock the outer door. Welcome to the building, Mr. Farrell."

And with a rapid staccato of ridiculously high heels and some delightfully perky hip action that had her skirt swishing around shapely thighs, she was gone. Other office residents queued up in the hall, blocking access to my office.

While waiting for the line to vanish, I gazed out the broad window in reception that faced the parking lot, amazed there weren't any fender benders with all the vehicles backing and maneuvering on the pavement outside. Just the thought of lunch made me hungry, but I'd be having a slightly more leisurely, though business-related, lunch with Delia in two hours. I could probably survive. And in the event I was wrong about that, when the opportunity arrived, I headed down the hall to where a snack machine waited to tempt me with rows of things that P. T. would abhor. There was enough change in my pockets to collect a mini-feast of munchies.

My office was one of the few that fronted on the reception desk. Probably because it was a single room rather than one of the mini-suites, which the directory board on the wall told me were home to a handful of small businesses. On either side of my nearly cubicle-sized office were an architect specializing in GREEN (yes, it was all in caps) residential buildings and a math tutor who had hours posted on the door for remedial algebra, geometry, precalculus, and not-so-precalculus lessons. It was doubtful there were things we'd have in common... unless they socialized with Sukis or their human counterparts, of course.

There still wasn't an official brass plate on my door, just the page the realtor had printed off and taped up. I should give him one of my business cards, see if he couldn't jazz the pseudo nameplate up a bit. Probably should wait to see if I was still around to view it, though. I had a little more than 24 hours before Calista would steal some unsuspecting soul's body. Considering I wasn't going to be cooperative, but also didn't know how to stop her, there was a pretty good chance it would be back to fictionland for me when dawn arrived on November 1. Since she'd be in the replacement body, Calie would no doubt sit down at her laptop and kill me off in Book 21, to show me who was boss.

Let's just say I was distracted, what with juggling the bags of variously flavored chips, pretzels, and cookies, plus a can of pop, while fishing the door key from my pocket, my mind running in circles screaming with frustration over *all* the cases on my to-be-solved list. Otherwise I might have noticed I'd had a visitor. Instead, the scratch marks on the lock only registered as I turned the key and the door crept open a quarter inch on its own. Enough to make the faint click that had not been there on my previous visits.

Abandoning my snacks, I turned around and dove at nearly light speed behind the unmanned, not-as-solid-as-I-would-have-liked reception desk. I had barely rolled into a fetal position, my arms up to protect my head, when the door of my office exploded. Okay, it was the entire office. The blast took large sections of the architect's and the tutor's niches with it, and it blew out part of the floor of the suite above. The wide reception area window that overlooked the parking lot shattered, shards flying out to decorate the landscape shrubs.

Returning to fictionland didn't sound like such a bad idea anymore. At least there, I had some magical abilities to keep me—

Oh hell! I'd felt the pulse of the explosion but hadn't been injured by it because there was a shimmer to the air around me that I knew like the back of my hand. Well, my hand in the pages of a book, anyway. Somehow, I'd subconsciously thrown up a protective magic-infused shield.

There was no time to rejoice over it though. The moment I recognized it, the damn thing crumbled, leaving me coated in debris.

The paramedics gave me a going over and patched up the latest injuries. They weren't bad thanks to that temporary invisible cocoon. Mostly cuts from glass and ceiling tile shards that rained down once it vanished. There was enough insulation and wallboard dust coating me that it looked like a giant dust bunny had detonated in my arms.

When I couldn't stop coughing, one of the medics handed me a bottle of water. She was an attractive, early-thirtysomething brunette. Unfortunately, she wasn't the one picking through my hair for shrapnel. A baby-faced, chubby guy from forensics had decided to be overly thorough in collecting evidence.

Detective Chad Durkin, the late-thirtysomething plainclothes cop stuck with investigating the explosion, merely looked weary.

"You don't have a license as a private investigator, Mr. Farrell, yet your business card says you're an investigator," Durkin rumbled, notebook at the ready. Probably shouldn't have handed him one, but it was the only thing I had on me that said I belonged in the building without supervision.

"Because I'm not," I said. "I am a researcher. All investigations are paper trail stuff. Information gathered for writers, for fiction projects. My aunt's the author of The Raven Tales series."

He didn't look impressed or interested.

"You are engaged in collecting information for her, then?"

Ah, tripped up by my own instigation of the Calista Amberson Replacement Search. Saying yes wouldn't work. All he had to do was hit the internet to find out Calista Amberson wasn't writing the next book. That duty was being turned over to a yet-unnamed writer. Only the covey of witches and a rebellious Raven would ever know it was still Calie pounding the keys.

"Honestly, no. She's ill and retiring. Her health is why I moved to Detroit, but I've been considering writing a book of my own. I haven't been in town long enough to line up clients, so I'm my only client right now." Sounded feasible, right?

"What exactly are you researching?" he asked.

Well, that was tricky. I mean, I'd barely settled into the office, and some being had blown it up already. Some being who might be the sort of creature Durkin and the rest of the police force thought was overstimulated historical peasant boogeyman hooey.

"Something I thought was tame, detective, believe me. Just skimming through cold cases for something that would sound promising. Most of the information was gathered from sources easily available on the internet."

"Does that mean you think you inadvertently spooked someone into attempting to kill you?"

He wasn't buying my story, but honestly, in his place, I wouldn't have either.

I shrugged. "Totally clueless."

"We'll be combing through the remains of your office," Durkin said. "If anything strikes us, I'll be in touch."

I heard the silent order not to leave town. Not that I wanted to. Still, knowing remnants of the map I'd pinned to the wall, and marked with the kill sites, and the file copies Deer Woman had given me could both come to light among the debris was worrisome. If my new laptop had survived there would be cookies to send them to various sites I'd pulled up.

What the police would make of these things, I'd no idea. The Otherworlders' deaths hadn't been investigated by humans. For the most part, very few humans knew other species of higher intelligence shared the planet with them. It seemed doubtful there were many uniformed law types who were part of witches' covens in their off hours, although Calie's group did have a cop among its members. The fact that she was one of Calie's crew made me suspect her, since my nonhuman clients thought Calie was involved in the murders.

"You about finished pawing through Farrell's wavy locks?" Detective Durkin demanded of the forensic tech.

"Think so, sir," the pudgy guy said.

Durkin waved him off, and me as well.

"Keep your phone handy in case I have further questions, Farrell," he said, turning to a uniformed officer to add, "The receptionist get back from her lunch yet?"

I wished I had a chance to ask Miss Nameless a few questions myself. Let's face it, my office door had faced her desk. If anyone had seen anything, it would have been her. There wasn't a chance in hell that she'd be exchanging information with me, though. The police would warn her not to, no doubt. Plus, she was probably out of a job now that the building was sorta condemned—at least turned into a no-touchy-touchy crime scene.

There was zilch time left to devote to my near-demise—if said demise was even possible without a delete key being involved. I'd already called Delia to push lunch back until the police released me from the scene. My time was running out, and the attempt on my life severely cut into what remained of it. The explosion had destroyed everything I'd already gathered or made a note about, or at least made it impossible for me to access any of the information. I wasn't back to step one, but I was running on memory alone now.

I called Delia. She told me Calie was relieved that the attempt to blow me up hadn't been successful. The explosion made the news, complete with video of me sitting in the back of the ambulance. Calie was also furious with both of us about the find-a-replacement campaign.

As I already knew that, and doubted Calista's sincerity about my health, I suggested we cancel lunch and continue with what we were both doing, to rile her more.

Because the parking lot had been crowded when I arrived, the Mustang was parked far from the explosion site and hadn't suffered at all. Wished briefly that I could say the same about myself. To believe that the office had been destroyed because I was getting close to something didn't sit well with me. I mean, what exactly did I have in the way of evidence? *Nil, neitt, nix, nada, rien* about summed it up. I hadn't even moved very far ahead on suppositions!

No one was in danger of me turning fictional vigilante on them. Therefore, why plant a booby trap on my office door? Just in case I hadn't left my alternate persona's justice-dispersing ways behind in the books?

Pondering that needed to take a back seat to other things on my to-do list. Once settled in the luxurious seat of the Mustang, I headed for the nearest ATM. Newly restocked with funds, I headed to a pharmacy for stuff to sting the heck out of my new cuts, then found a motel to grab a shower in. I signed in as Jeb Smith and paid in cash. The guy at the check-in counter wanted to know if I was expecting a guest to share it, short-term, with me.

"I should be so lucky," I told him and snagged the key.

Once freshly groomed and wearing the clothes I'd grabbed before leaving Calie's estate, I headed for the campus to track down Amélie Lumumba's professors.

Late afternoon on campus is apparently a lousy time to find faculty members. Those who don't have afternoon classes or committee meetings have hightailed it, even those with lab facilities. Fortunately, Amélie had progressed to the point in her studies where it only took one secretary in the Pharmacology Department to supply information on the professors she'd had.

"Such a dear girl, and extremely focused," the secretary said. "We were all stunned to hear she'd had a seizure and drowned in her bathtub."

That wasn't exactly what had occurred, but it was a much more comforting story than the true one. She'd been sealed in an old claw-foot tub, the bottom and drain sealed with well-set concrete. Clearly a premeditated act. Water had been added, but so had salt. As a freshwater being, the biskimi had died trapped in a saline environment. Her killer had gone beyond murdering her, though. They'd poured enough salt in to pickle her. If the abandoned warehouse where the crime was committed hadn't been the safe house where a pack of werewolves met to lock themselves up during the nights of the full moon, she might not have been found until the building was demolished or some curious homeless person managed to pry up the bolted-down steel door that covered the tub. They would have been in for a shock because Amélie had reverted to her natural form.

I was quite relieved that in the twentieth book, I hadn't been nearly as cruel in dispatching the evil biskimi Calie invented. I went for quick demise with a dash of the dramatic, not slow torture. Didn't think that I'd changed when it came to theories of demon dispatching in realityland, either. They were more likely to do for me on this side of the line, unless some more frickin' magic caught up with me.

That fret had to take a back burner. There was data to collect, information to wheedle.

The Pharmacology Department's secretary helped track down the lone faculty member who hadn't escaped campus for the day. He was grading project papers in his office, she said, and gave me directions.

From the groggy sound of the voice that bade me enter when I knocked, Dr. Charles Quafelle was grabbing a few winks rather than dealing with student compositions. He looked a bit rumpled, but that might have been his normal state of haberdasherial éclat. His tie was loosened, his shirtsleeves rolled up, and a cockscomb of extremely fine, blah-brown hair stood up at the crown of his head. A soot-gray houndstooth sport coat and a creased white lab coat were tossed aside on a chair laden with books and yet more papers.

"Amélie." He sighed her name sadly when I introduced it. "Such a brilliant young woman."

She'd probably been far older than he, but I couldn't say for sure. All I knew about her was what appeared on the internet and in Doe's files. Her real age had not appeared in any of the data.

"What can I tell you about her?" Quafelle paused. "Admittedly, not much, but then I doubt many could. She was a very focused student, and I got the impression others thought her standoffish because she frequently declined invitations to join them and wasn't interested in the university's sporting events. Her family was from the Congo, but her English was flawless."

"She had family in Africa yet, then?" I knew she didn't. Oh, sure, there were other biskimis, but not family as Quafelle understood it. Plus, she wasn't buried in the Congo but in the St. Romaric Cemetery where the other Otherworlders were interred.

Quafelle smiled softly. "Yes. She was a scholarship student and lived quite frugally. Of course, I'm judging this by the fact that she brought food from home rather than dashing off to the student union or local fast food restaurants as others do, and her wardrobe was limited to jeans and long sleeved T-shirts. I remember her being teased for always wearing socks with her flip-flops. I never saw her in any other footwear, not even in the dead of winter. She also wore gloves of some kind year-round.

"Her death was quite sudden. We had no idea she suffered from any sort of brain-related problems. Pneumonia would have been my guess, since she was never dressed for Michigan winters, but the coroner's report clearly pointed to a different conclusion."

Except there hadn't been an official report of any kind. A vamp might have done a mass hypnotism on those the biskimi had associated with, to make them think they'd seen reports or even attended a memorial service for her. Any of it was feasible, for the Otherworlders were experts at cleaning up evidence of their true natures.

"If we'd known, we could have helped her," the professor said sadly. "Research is a very large part of what the medical school does, Mr. Farrell."

I couldn't exactly ask him if she'd had enemies who might have wanted to do her in. I did the next best thing. "Was there any rivalry between Miss Lumumba and any other student?"

"Rivalry? Not that I ever noticed. Her research was only in the beginning stages. There were years yet to go for results to be seen. We usually steer students toward projects that will ensure them jobs, but in her spare time Amélie always returned to her pet project. It had something to do with a skin complaint commonly seen in the area where her family lived but little known in the rest of the world. Amélie jokingly termed it 'biski crud,' apparently combining a tribal word with an English one."

162

I thanked him for his time.

This biskimi hadn't been a danger to anyone. She'd been on her way to possibly preventing her sisters from passing on a nasty skin disease. The fact that she'd always worn gloves and long sleeves and kept her legs and feet from exposure indicated that she wasn't taking chances with the people she encountered while working on the problem. The flip-flops, though... well, maybe beings that swim in their natural habitats feel weighted down by other sorts of footgear. I couldn't ask her. Not even with a Ouija board.

Based on the victims on my list, Otherworlders were adapting to the modern world. They were changing, finding ways to survive that didn't bring attention to themselves in a communications-mad world. Weres in populated areas locked themselves up during the full moon. Vampires had willing hosts they rarely turned. Trolls were running bars or rackets, and zombies only visited loving family members. Beings that would have difficulty hiding their true selves found ways to blend in and be part of things, and creatures that engendered diseases decided to find cures or preventive measures to stop the cycle.

They had tuned down the violence because they didn't want to be like humans, the cruelest, most vicious creations to walk the world. At least in Otherworlder eyes.

Yeah, the nonhumans were changing, but the humans were apparently just as screwed up as they'd been at the start. Samael certainly hadn't a kind word to say about the first three of them, Adam, Eve, and Lilith. And Sam was the freaking Devil. You'd think he would understand them, wouldn't you?

I was burning daylight and getting nowhere, at a pace that would land me a premier spot in the hamster wheel derby. Should I try to get another copy of the files from Doe? Probably not. I knew what I needed to know from them. I'd narrowed in on six victims and, while I had more information on some than on others, I could work with it.

Before I left campus, though, I revisited the Pharmacology Department's secretary to see if she still had Amélie's address in the files. It took some compliment-heavy wheedling, but I got the address.

Before I could head off to reclaim Kit or Beelz for the second of my vampiric visits, this one in the now infamous cemetery, there was a booking agent to see.

The day had been one of highs and lows. Losing my office to a bomb did not count as a high. An adrenalin boost, definitely, particularly with that surprise magical defense system materializing around me, but I was now out a place to hide from Calista. And I had a lot of unused business cards with a nonexistent address on them. I think there was something in the lease agreement about "do major damage to the property and you're out on your ass." Or words to that effect. It didn't matter that I hadn't personally set the bomb. I tripped it. *Mea culpa, mea culpa.*

When I had time to spare, the bit of magic that secretly followed me from fictionland could be sorted out. And hopefully harnessed, if I got to stay in this world. Right now, the clock was ticking on the investigation. Detective Durkin wouldn't let me near the remnants of the office anyway.

Sager and Mischo Talent was located on the sixth floor of a building with an elevator that I judged to be a death trap. I took the stairs. Smartly at first, then at a wheezing snail's pace for the final few steps to the door.

The office was a smidgen larger than mine had been and featured one large folding metal table with an uncomfortable-looking folding metal chair on either side. Said chairs were occupied by scruffy guys who could have been mirror images of each other but for the wild fair hair of the one and the beaten-up fedora pushed back over heavily salted bushy dark hair on the other. If they were the two guys featured on the poster propped up as a makeshift screen at the window, then they had only begun booking talent when the bottom fell out of the big top market. It didn't take white greasepaint and overdrawn lips on a phiz to spot a clown. They both sported natural red bulb noses, the result of twin bottles of cheap whiskey at their elbows.

"Ah, a live one!" the guy lacking the hat said as I stood gasping in the doorway. The panel hadn't been closed, and the act of knocking had let it swing wide.

Hat Man pushed to his feet and hastily emptied a third folding chair for me to perch on. "Welcome to Sager and Mischo Talent, where you get the best booking in the Motor City," he said. "Let me guess what you're looking for. A magician for a kid's birthday party."

I was willing to play along. "Nope."

"Don't be ridiculous, Mike. This is a best man if I ever saw one. He needs entertainment for a bachelor party. The only question is do we have male or female strippers."

"Neither."

"Fiftieth anniversary celebration?"

"Graduation party?"

"Bar mitzvah?"

"Community theatre production?"

I leaned back, arms crossed, and waited for them to run down. It took another five minutes, and by then, they were really reaching for ideas. When they reached speechless, I cleared my throat.

"Jamyang Yontentsang."

Sager looked at Mischo, or else it was Mischo looking at Sager.

"What language is he speaking?"

"Albino Wookiee," I clarified for them.

Wild Hair Guy slapped his hand flat down on the tabletop. Papers jumped. As did both liquor bottles. "Damn, I haven't thought about that dude in a long time. He head for Hollywood, Mike?"

Mike shook his head and looked solemn. Apparently, he had a better memory for clients. "He died, Louie."

"Geez, you're right. Damn, but I miss that guy. Not much on conversation, but pleasant as hell."

Mike leaned back in his chair. "Why are you asking questions about Yang Sang?"

"Yang Sang?" I bleated.

"Yeah, he agreed to shorten it because no one could say..." he waved at me.

"Jamyang Yontentsang," I supplied.

"Yeah. Made sense to shorten it, *capisce*?"

"So, what are you here about then?" Louie demanded. "You not looking for talent, we don't got much time to give you."

I leaned forward, bracing my forearms on my thighs.

"I'm investigating his murder," I said.

They both reared back. Mike had been reaching for his whiskey bottle, but that halted his hand in midair.

"His what?"

"Murder."

"Never heard that he was murdered."

"Really?" I wasn't entirely acting. I was surprised. "What would you call it when a nine-foot-tall guy covered in shaggy fur is bound hand and foot and then dropped into a steam room with the temperature cranked up?"

Mike's hand on the bottle was a bit shaky, but it let him make a connection to his mouth.

"Jeezus," he muttered.

"Nobody told us," Louie whispered. "We heard he got hit by a snowplow skidding on ice."

"Murdered," Mike repeated, his voice alone telling me he was having difficulty taking it in. "And you're lookin' inta it?"

"Trying," I admitted. "Considering the true details of Yontentsang's demise were covered up, this isn't the easiest job I've taken on."

"Who the hell are you, anyway?" Mike demanded.

I flicked one of the business cards at him. The phone number belonged to my cell even if the office had gone up in smoke.

"B. Farrell. Why does that sound familiar?" Mike asked Louie.

Louie took the card from him, then turned a frown my way. "What's the *B* stand for?"

I cleared my throat. "Er, Bram."

Louie tapped the card against his brow, apparently knocking thoughts loose. I knew he'd made the connection when his eyes widened and he sat up straighter in his chair.

"The Raven?" he demanded. "You mean, you're real?"

"Well, I'm not exactl—" I began.

"The guy in the books that local dame writes?"

"My aunt—"

Louie reached across the table and punched Mike on the arm.

"You know," he told his associate. "Bubbles was crazy about those books. She talked about 'em all the time."

"Bubbles was crazy, period," Mike said. "She believed there were vampires in the shadows and that every pooch howling at the moon was a werewolf."

"Yeah," Louie agreed. "But this guy"—he jerked a thumb my way—"kills them sorts of things."

Both leveled narrowed eyes at me.

"You sure *you* ain't the one what done Yangy in?" Louie snarled. "Seems ya know a damn lot about it."

"I'M NOT THAT GUY!" Okay, yeah, I shouted it, but it was true. I wasn't that guy any longer. "He's fiction. Made up. A story. Do I look like I'm fiction?"

As difficult as it may seem, they managed to shrink away from me in the tiny office.

"Sorry," I said. "Yeah, I've got the same name as a character in a book, but he's an investigator too, and never kills anything that doesn't deserve it. Jamyang Yontentsang didn't deserve to be cooked to death. His killer needs to be found and punished."

"You're gonna kill 'em?" Mike asked.

"No, I'm not going to—"

"Somebody should," Louie said. "The law don't follow through on stuff like this. You find the perp. If ya don't got the stomach ta do 'em yourself, you call this number."

He hen-scratched a series of numbers on the back of my card and handed it back to me.

"Tell 'em it's for us."

After that, they shared what photo op shots they still had of Jamyang in their files and reminisced about him. None of which was helpful to my cause.

As I left the building, I found that I hadn't needed that magician's flash paper starter I'd borrowed to use at Renaissance Man's office. All it took was acute irritation with a couple of old clowns, and I could still set fire to something simply by holding it. The business card with the hit man's phone number on it was already smoldering.

Like I really needed the police to find that sort of information on me, if they pulled me in for more questioning on the office bombing. Flicking the card into the air, I watched it vanish in a mini but impressive looking pillar of flame, then ground the remains that floated to the pavement into fine powder with my shoe.

The only stop on my list now was that interview with a new batch of vampires at the mausoleum in the nearly forgotten cemetery. I needed to pick up Kit and my miraculously transforming hellhound first, though.

167

Couldn't help wondering if any of my other fictional magic tricks would show up if I needed them later on. Would have been handy to know how to evoke them at will rather than inadvertently, too. Real handy!

Since I'd missed lunch, even that pre-lunch of munchies, thanks to the bombing, food sounded like a sensible stop. I couldn't depend on Kit's adrenaline shot kisses to get me through things or any late developing magic. I needed fuel.

Then again, eating would give me an opportunity to chew over things, mentally stirring them up to see what might float to the top or sink to the bottom of the info pot. I was closer to the Sukis' corner than I was to Calie's estate. I pulled over to the curb and gave Kit a call.

Her cell rang and rang and rang, but there was no answer. I redialed, thinking I'd fed in the wrong number, and got the same response a second time. Maybe she was otherwise engaged. You know, siphoning off a few months of some dude's life while making him think he was getting one hell of a bargain on a joyride. It wasn't exactly a process that could be interrupted by a nonpaying partner who had no discernable life force to share.

As a substitute, I called Doe.

She didn't answer with a greeting, but with a bitch. "No, Raven, I haven't heard back from First Nations yet."

Must have recognized my number. I hadn't heard that being psychic was one of her abilities, in any incarnation.

"Damn," I said. "But that wasn't why I called. I was trying to get hold of Kit, but she isn't answering her cell. Any idea when she went off with her current client?"

"Let me check with Neko," she said.

I heard a murmured conversation, but no recognizable words came through.

Then Doe was back, an edge of concern in her voice.

"The last either of us saw Kitsune was around two." According to the car's clock, it was nearly eight, which meant Kit had been incommunicado for six hours. "Of course, it's been very slow here today. Maybe she decided to return home."

If she had, I would have expected her to catch my call, though.

"Does she do that often?" I asked, trying to sound casual rather than worried.

Doe was slow to answer. "No, not usually. But then, she doesn't usually take a day off, and she did to back you up yesterday. I assumed she'd joined you again."

"Perhaps she's just in the shower," I suggested.

"That must be it," she said.

Each of us obviously making attempts to blanket the other's niggling fear that something had happened to Kit. I didn't know whether Doe had heard about events at my office earlier, but I wasn't about to bring them up.

"I'll go grab something to eat and give her a call then," I said but as the purr of Neko's voice thrummed in the background, I'm not sure Doe heard me.

"Raven? Are you on the way to this neighborhood, or nearby? If so, Neko wants to know if she can bum a ride home. Her place is on the way to Kit's."

I was five minutes away and gentleman enough to accede to the request. Before I pulled back out into traffic, though, I called Kit again.

No answer.

Neko went all slinky cat without transforming from doxie mode when she slid into the shotgun seat of the Mustang.

"Ooh, this is so comfortable, I could curl up right here and never budge," she purred and stretched luxuriously. A lesser man would have broken out in a cold sweat from the feline musk rolling off her. I flipped the fan on full and vented the essence out into the unsuspecting Detroit night.

"Beelzie has a similar reaction, only of the canine variety," I admitted. "At least he circled his own tail several times and gave a definite huff of contentment upon settling in."

"I can tell," Neko said. "There's a mix of hellhound and fox scent lingering. But you"—she twisted in the seat, placing one pseudo human knee nearly where my hand would fall on the gear shift between the seats—"you still don't have a distinctive scent, Raven."

169

Careful to avoid physical contact, I put the car in gear and pulled away from the curb. "Not of paper or ink?"

"There was a hint of that the day we met, but it's dissipated since then."

I didn't know if I was relieved or needed to worry. For all I knew, Calie was busy chanting me back into the book world right that minute.

"Which way should I go?" I asked. "Doe just said you lived between here and Kit's place."

"I haven't been around long enough to profit from what we do like Kit and Doe have," Neko said. "My neighborhood isn't as upscale, and my apartment is just a single room. Far smaller than Kit's condo."

She sounded apologetic.

"At least you don't live with your mother," I said, trying for flippancy. "Of course, Calista doesn't like me to call her that, even if she did give me life of a sort. You should see the skimpy TV I'm stuck with."

Best not to mention the Clydesdale-sized shower.

Neko grinned, her slightly curving lips giving her face a very feline cast.

"Poor Raven," she murmured. "Cursed to live on an estate."

One with a wooded area haunted by the Devil and littered with his theophylaktosian accessories, of course.

"There are downsides," I insisted. "Though you'd probably enjoy the cook's meals. She serves a lot of fish and chicken."

Then again, if Neko turned up in cat form, she'd probably get stuck with the same sort of specially formulated pet chow that was forced on the mighty Beelz.

"Sounds delicious," the bakeneko agreed, then told me to turn left at the next intersection.

It wasn't long before I began recognizing the terrain. The pavement was bathed in deep shadows, since the sun had snuggled down beyond the western horizon. The gloom under old-growth trees spread ahead of us. People who'd been out in yards earlier, dealing with fallen leaves, had headed indoors to warmly lit rooms and the glowing screens of televisions and computers. A breeze swirled leaves from the gathered piles here and there, plastering some against fences or sending them skittering across the roadway.

170

We passed the Fontaine Funeral Home, which I'd visited not long ago. Apparently, a showing was in progress that evening, as cars lined the street on either side and shadows passed or paused at windows, their owners' outlines partly smudged by the sheer fabric draping the glass and partly contrasted against the muted lights inside.

It felt like we were crawling through the neighborhood, but the speed limit was regulated to the otherwise residential nature of the area.

Neko said something. I think she was explaining what she liked about this neck of the city, how peaceful it was, or how well established. I'll admit, I wasn't really listening. The fact that I kept being directed back to this neighborhood was spooky. Even Amélie, the biskimi exchange student, had lived within its borders.

To all appearances, it was an area managing to hang on by its fingernails. The homes were a mix of late Victorian mini-mansions, many of which had been converted into apartments, and single-family twenties bungalows. Yards were small but for the most part well kept. There wasn't much evidence of children on the properties, so I figured the residents were older, their offspring moved on to other parts of the city or away from Detroit entirely. Some of the homes were decorated for the season with pots of mums, pumpkins, and gourds arranged on porches. Streetlamps spotlighted some and left others barely glimpsed ghost-like shades. Although we were bare hours from All Hallows, there wasn't a carved jack-o'-lantern in sight.

Of course, I wasn't really looking for them. My eyes were trained on the headlights closing quickly on us from the rear.

I had a bad feeling about those lights. A *really* bad feeling.

With the funeral home's guests' vehicles lining the narrow street and massive tree trunks flanking the sidewalks, there was nowhere to pull over. Whoever was in the driver's seat, they weren't being law-abiding and traveling at a pedestrian-conscious speed. The gap between us was vanishing rapidly.

From the corner of my eye, I spotted the narrow entrance to an alleyway and hastily swerved over into it.

As did the vehicle behind me.

It was a monster compared to my sleek Ravenmobile, and it smacked into the rear of the Mustang like a battering ram, shoving us into a power pole and toward reconfiguration as an accordion.

171

I heard Neko scream. Heard the crunch and grinding of fenders and paint jobs rubbing each other the wrong way. The airbags deployed as the Mustang hit the metal post and dented it. The demon vehicle backed away just enough to get powered up for another plow into us, sending me lurching against the side window. Skull met safety glass. I saw stars that had nothing to do with the heavens above. Then the driver's door was yanked open and something short, solid, and nasty hammered into the side of my head. Those stars became entire galaxies, swirling around me, making it impossible to see clearly.

I heard something slash near my ear and wondered whether I'd feel cool steel sink into my flesh next. Instead, a hand gripped my arm and yanked me free of the car. I hit the pavement hard, expecting a further attack. Instead, the gurgle of liquid from a container and the scent of gasoline had me attempting to scramble to my feet.

A foot tripped me up. A hand gave me a far from gentle shove that sent my head into something solid and unforgiving. Crumpling to the ground was the extent of my capabilities. There was the whooshing sound of traveling flame, then the heat of Hell licking at me.

I managed to hold one hand up to shield my eyes from the conflagration I knew was inevitable. Amazingly, I saw two shadowy forms reenter the vehicle that had turned my car into a pile of debris. One of them tossed a package into the wreckage. Then the truck maneuvered around my prone form and sped away. I could see what they'd left behind, though.

Neko was spread-eagled on the hood of the Mustang, her face turned to the night sky. She wasn't capable of seeing the stars any longer. Her throat was cut and she'd been gutted.

Flames licked at the remains of both my car and the bakeneko. My brain was attempting to retreat to fictionland, where Calie would remove me from danger with a handful of hastily typed words. It wasn't going to happen this time. Ye Olde Raven was going to be a cooked goose and go into whatever realm catered to my type, still clueless about the monsters killing the fairly peaceable nonhumans of

Detroit. If Calie was successful in her quest for a new form, when she opened a new file for Book 21, I wondered whether Neko would end up reconfigured as a vicious creature for me to terminate. In a way, simply by her association with me in the real world, I was the one who'd gotten her murdered.

But they hadn't tried to kill me, the pseudo human. The attackers pulled me to relative safety, yet they'd done just the opposite with Neko. Had they thought the shape-changer with me was Kit?

Kit. Who was missing. I doubted that was a coincidence.

Even to my battered noggin, killing Neko didn't make sense. Whoever was in the villainous vehicle had come prepared to take out an Otherworlder, take them out quickly. If they had already kidnapped Kit, there was no reason to expect I'd be tooling about with a nonhuman. Kit was the only Suki who had been at my side for trips away from the corner worked by the trio of life-sucking ladies.

That meant Neko's killers couldn't tell one nonhuman doxie from another. It also meant they had competition, and the competition might well have Kit. Hopefully she hadn't met a similar fate at different hands.

My mind was racing, but my body was barely capable of crawling away from further danger.

"Jeezus!" a man's voice said nearby. It sounded more like a prayer.

"Give me your arm," he instructed, draping one of mine over his shoulder when I managed to stir to something resembling life. He physically lifted me, getting me back on my feet to stumble with his help further away from the Mustang. We'd barely taken shelter behind another vehicle when the Mustang went to Valhalla in a glorious explosion. Scorched vehicle parts rained from the heavens. Windows in the nearest parked cars added shards of glass, scattering them along the sidelines. My Good Samaritan pushed me to the ground, sheltering me with his own body. He flinched when the hail of pulverized glass grazed us both.

People were pouring from the nearest buildings and from the funeral home. I glanced to where Neko's form had been, but the hood had blown free and now rocked on its back in the middle of the road. In the gutter was the crumpled, burnt body of a housecat. In death, Neko had reverted to her natural form. The SPCA would be upset to

173

find an eviscerated, roasted feline, but at least the police when they arrived wouldn't be asking awkward questions about a mutilated woman sprawled across my front bumper.

I needed to call Doe, tell her that... tell her what? That I was sorry I'd gotten Neko killed? That sounded so...

So, what? Inhumane? Considering the Otherworlders believed humans were the most vicious beings on the planet, my being responsible for Neko's death made me more human.

I was guilty. It was my fault.

I just hoped there wouldn't be another nonhuman death laid at my door. I had to find Kit, but where to start?

I must have groaned, because the guy who dragged me to safety yelled to the gathering of spectators, "Any of you a doctor or nurse?"

"No, I'm fine," I insisted.

Of course, no one paid any attention to me. Maybe I shouldn't have attempted to get to my feet since doing so involved swaying and nearly tipping over on my face. With a hand on the glass-scoured bumper of my hiding place, I managed to make it upright.

In the nearest yard, the owner was out spraying down his house with a hose to keep it from catching fire should the situation go from horrific to further hell. In the distance, I could hear sirens. More than one, and drawing ever nearer.

"Here," a woman said, pressing a handful of tissues into my hand. "Hold this against that wound on your temple."

I was wounded?

Must have looked at her blankly, for she took the fluffy mass from my hand and pressed it against my head herself. Hurt like Hades!

"Head wounds tend to bleed a lot," she said. "You might have a concussion, too. How many fingers am I holding up?"

"Two," I hazarded. In truth, there were two solid ones and two fuzzy friends standing behind them. Maybe it was an aura. Maybe I was hallucinating.

Whether she approved of my guess or not, she smiled faintly, obviously attempting to soothe or humor me.

"The paramedics will be here shortly. You'll be in good hands with them."

Of that, I wasn't so sure.

She took my hand and guided it to take control of the temporary wound blotter. The moment she looked away, I took the tissues off my head. They were damp and dark with something viscous and sticky. Was it red ink as I feared?

I needed to get on Kit's trail, spread the word among the nonhumans about the vehicle Neko's killers had driven. Prove I was still investigator enough on this side of the line to solve the cold cases; prove I was more than just a beef fancier and smartass. Passing police and paramedic inspection for the second time in eight hours was going to slow me down.

I stared at the pseudo ink blotter. It wasn't soaked with anything that constituted a printed page. The blotch was thickening and looked nearly black with a hint of crimson in the light afforded by my still-burning car.

Blood. Real blood. I stared at it dumbfoundedly. Oh, yeah, that would get the medics worked up. And leave me kicking my heels as the sands trickled down to that deadline.

The evening evolved into quite a colorful night. With the firefighting vehicles, the ambulance, and a brace of police cars all with their flashing lights rotating out of sync, it was like being in a dance club where the temperature was cool, damp, and a bit nippy rather than warmed by the heat of dancing bodies. Having a bar morph into existence would have been nice. I could really have used a couple fingers of Evan Williams. Heck, an entire hand's width worth of it. Even though I didn't mention it, the paramedics warned me not to drink alcohol and attempted one last time to get me to agree to go to the hospital for a proper scan of my brain. Fearing it would be empty—it certainly felt like all that inhabited my skull was pain—or consist of piles of crumbled paper and a parcel of Calie's old clue and plot notes, I refused treatment.

A patrolman had taken my statement, but it was the one I overheard a resident give that was of more interest.

"Was sitting on my porch enjoying the evening," the man being questioned said. "Always something to see on nights when there's a viewing down at Fontaine's. The Mustang was crawling down the street, very law-abiding, sticking to the speed limit. That big monster of a pickup had his pedal to the floor. I could see the Mustang's driver looking for a place to pull over out of the way, but what with the viewing and folks home for the night, there were no gaps at the curb 'cept for the alley. Thought he'd escaped an accident when he pulled into it, but that damned truck barreled right for him. Not for the alley, mind you, but for the Mustang. It's a miracle anyone made it out of the Mustang alive.

"Thought at first there were two people but must have been mistaken. My eyesight isn't that great at night for small details. Sure as hell no one walked away unscathed from that crash but the two who caused it, and they came prepared with cans of gasoline to finish the job. Surprised they pulled the driver free. Gangland warning to him, I'll bet. Just like on TV."

Silently I gave him a lunar blessing. At least the chance of me going to jail that night had been halved.

When the paramedics slapped the final bandage in place over an abrasion, the first face I saw was that of Detective Durkin. The odds on my chances of being arrested began to creep up.

The fire department had won the battle of the flaming Mustang, but it needed to cool off before any pieces could be removed from the scene. Durkin was leaning against the hood of a police car, his hands shoved into his trouser pockets, his buttoned suit jacket bunched up around his wrists, as he watched the firefighters do their thing.

"Bring any marshmallows?" I asked, ambling toward him.

"Ford briquettes give them a funny taste," he said. "Fire department is going to find evidence of a bomb, you know. Cars burn but only explode with help. That means this is your second bombing of the day, Farrell. You still maintain your *research* is harmless stuff?"

I matched his stance, enjoying the feel of cool bumper as compared to the heat that still radiated from the Mustang. Wasn't the least surprised the attackers had brought more than just extra gas. Why I'd been dragged free, though...

"Yep, sticking to my story. Mostly because you wouldn't believe me if I told you the truth."

"Try me."

I'd be bound for the loony bin once I spilled, but if I didn't spill, he could probably drag me in for neighborhood endangerment. The

176

power pole didn't look too good, and a garage and the nearest parked cars had all suffered both explosion and fire damage. Add in the disaster at my office earlier, and finding reasons to move me into the city hoosegow would be no problem for him.

I dropped my voice to a level only someone standing next to me would hear, although to be honest, there was enough going on around us that being overheard was unlikely. Still, this wasn't exactly going to be the sort of conversation that needed to be shared with the populace.

"You ever read one of my aunt's books?"

"Nope." He didn't even sound apologetic about it.

"What kind of loyal Detroit son are you?"

He grinned slightly. "I'm from Buffalo."

I snorted. "Like that excuses you. You heard what sort of characters are in The Raven Tales?"

"Ones that people dress up like at this time of year?"

"Ones that exist year-round. Outside of All Hallows' Eve parties," I said.

"Vampires, werewolves, witches?"

"Zombies, trolls, elves, demons, devils, ghosts, goblins," I added when it seemed he had too short a list. "All real. My aunt learned of real murders among the Otherworld community and incorporated them into the Raven books. They're all cold cases, some twenty years old. Until today."

"Until today?"

I gestured toward the remains of the toasted Ravenmobile. "Number twenty-one."

"You mean the car, or the cat at curbside?"

"Her name was Neko. She was a bakeneko from Japan. A cat who'd learned to shape-shift into human form to seduce humans. She lived in the neighborhood. Worked a corner a few miles away with a couple succubi. I was giving her a ride home. The supernatural community will want her body for burial. If you can keep it from being discarded or turned over to whatever department usually handles roadkill, it would be appreciated."

Durkin stared ahead, but I don't think he was watching the gear-laden men of the fire department as they circled the car, occasionally blasting something with foam to prevent a flare-up. The scent of

177

gasoline was still strong, though I doubt there was a drop of my car's lifeblood left to drip dangerously into the street.

"Hmm," I said when Durkin didn't comment on Neko's pedigree or my request. "I thought you'd be calling the guys in the white jackets by now, to cart me away."

"Might yet," he said. "You have a dead banshee on that list of characters?"

I did.

"In *Raven Takes The Reins*, Book 13, my fictional doppelgänger was hunting Mag Heffernan, a banshee. Eight or nine years ago, here in Detroit, a banshee named—"

"Cliodhna O'Dubháin," Durkin supplied. Mag's real life counterpart's name.

I stared at him. Maybe my mouth hung open as well.

"My great-great-hell of a lot of greats-grandmother," he said. "Once, she appeared to escort the family members who died during the Great Famine away. After that, she turned up to continue to warn of deaths for the family that remained, all of whom had emigrated to America. She was the harbinger that helped everyone prepare for a wake. Used to scare the hell out of me when I was a kid."

"Until someone found a way to kill a spirit being."

"She was family, not evil."

"In the book, Mag Heffernan was the ultimate hag. The only thing Calista lifted was the way Cliodhna died," I assured him. "Mother O'Dubháin's is on the list of Otherworlder murders I was assigned to solve."

"By your aunt?"

I choked off a laugh. "Hardly. She's one nasty witch. And I mean that literally. No, it was the nonhuman community that set me on this course, because human law enforcement hadn't investigated any of the deaths."

"Not *hadn't*," he corrected. "Couldn't. No budget to investigate suspicious crimes involving creatures ninety-nine-point-nine percent of the populace think are just fairy tales."

I couldn't argue with that. I was the only one who was totally fictional.

"That mean your appearance here tonight isn't entirely luck of the draw?" I asked.

Durkin chuckled. "You were at the center of a bit of excitement earlier today, Farrell. I googled you when I got back to my desk. You don't exist other than as a fictional character. No tax records, no school history, no parking tickets."

"You going to give me a parking ticket now? My car does appear to be in a no-parking zone." The sign was darkened from having been licked by flames. The mangled remains of the Mustang were blocking the entrance to the alley, too.

"Do I need to show you my driver's license? Bank card? I'm afraid the car insurance is in yon roasted glove compartment, and I didn't have the car long enough to get the paperwork to arrange for more than the dealer's temporary plate placard."

"Oh, I found the bank account and the insurance rider," Durkin said. Both so new that if they'd merely been on paper, the ink wouldn't have dried. "If you've got a driver's license, it's not a kosher one."

I didn't offer to show it to him again. It wasn't in the least bit kosher.

"What happens now?" I asked.

"I'm hoping you'll help me," Durkin said. "Missing persons. We've got three of them currently and only one lead."

"And I can help you in what way? Are they Otherworlders?"

Durkin shook his head. "Purebred humans, but the only lead I've got... well, he's not a bit human. A ghoul, name of Solomon Prisk. As he isn't at home to visitors or answering his phone, you'll probably have better luck running him to ground."

It wasn't like I was able to refuse. Besides, maybe the ghoul knew something about the cases I was determined to solve.

"Okay. And our next move?"

"I give you a ride down to the station, and you tell me and two other cops everything you know about these deaths you're investigating and what really led up to someone attempting to kill you twice today."

"And these two other cops are going to believe me?" I demanded. It seemed highly unlikely.

"Probably," Durkin said dryly. "One's a vampire who works vice, and the other is a werewolf assigned to SWAT. Of course, as far as anyone knows, they're as human as you or me."

Well, as *him*, at least.

Day Five, October 31 - Deadline Day

Considering I'd entered the real world sometime after midnight, what might well be my final day on this side of the fiction line arrived while I was still within Durkin's aura. I could nearly hear the seconds ticking down to my personal—extremely possible—end of days.

Before Durkin and I left the scene of Neko's quick but horrific death, he had his men slip the bakeneko's burnt body into a construction-weight black plastic bag and placed it in the trunk of his car.

I called Doe to give her the bad news. Didn't mention that I was about to be grilled by the only three cops in Detroit who knew there were Otherworld beings. Apparently, the nonhumans themselves didn't know these three existed. Well, there was Calie's witch cop who, for all I knew, only wrote up parking violations, but it seemed my clients were clueless when it came to Calie's coven.

Doe still hadn't heard back from First Nations, but she now had other priorities to deal with regarding Neko's death. The Fontaine Funeral Home would no doubt be arranging for another plot in the St. Romaric Cemetery soon.

I also called Kit's number again. Still no answer. Considering Durkin had mentioned missing persons, I couldn't help wondering if the ghoul who might or might not be involved had expanded his business to include Sukis. That it even crossed my mind was the sort of sign to engender panic, which meant finding her needed to be pushed aside temporarily. Panic wasn't part of my book persona, therefore, I channeled my old self. Weirdly possible to do, but then when had my *life* been anything other than weird?

En route to the police station, Durkin swung by the corner where Doe waited to receive all that remained of Neko. Then, because my stomach was growling, he headed for a pizza parlor for a to-go order.

I'll spare you the boring details of the interrogation. Information sharing session. Whatever you want to call it. Turned out I knew more than Durkin and his two cohorts did, but that was because none of them were as connected to the Otherworld residents of Detroit as I already was.

Even though the entire interview was conducted at the police station, no recording or record of it was made. As a cover, the SWAT werewolf had brought a deck of cards. We played poker, betting matchsticks the vamp supplied, while I talked and they took mental notes.

In the end, all three admitted that they were limited in what aid could be given, even if the ghoul turned out to be the one making humans go missing. Covert identities, impossible workloads, and budget restrictions tied their hands as much as the inability to keep Otherworlders imprisoned did. The idea was that once Solomon Prisk was shown—not *proved,* but *shown*—to be guilty, I had their unofficial consent to visit Raven-style justice on him.

Should I survive my own assignment long enough to uncover the perp and have enough evidence to convict, the police would be glad to step in and make the official arrest—assuming the arrestee was human. If the guilty party turned out to be an Otherworlder, they weren't going to be any help at all. There were no facilities set up to hold or control a paranormal, demon, or legendary being, and there were no laws regarding nonhumans on the books. It looked like I'd inadvertently picked up a long-term, nonpaying job, if I managed to stay on this plane rather than being jettisoned back to the fictional one.

We wasted a hell of a lot of time and came up with nothing. I might have lost a car, but I came away from the session with the cops richer by 127 matchsticks.

A half hour before dawn, the cops left. I strolled off to find a donut shop and waited for a more decent hour to call Burt for a ride. I also called Kit's number again. Still no answer.

When the cab finally collected me and we returned to the estate, Burt settled into the controlled chaos of P. T.'s kitchen to enjoy a cup of her specially blended coffee while I headed to my room for a shower and change of clothes. For a guy who'd shopped just a few days before, I was running out of undamaged duds. The one undestroyed set of clean clothes remaining would see me through whatever the night brought, I figured, and so I dropped my current torn, singed, glass-glittered, bloodstained rags into the trash. Nothing was going to remove the smell of gasoline from them.

Beelz followed me into the shower. I filled him in on what had gone down the night before, about how Kit was missing.

"Think you remember her scent well enough to follow it to find her?" I asked as I toweled off.

He shook water from his coat. I toweled off again, taking that for a no.

"If we broke into her place and got you something she wore to refresh your schnoz?"

He gave me that canine shrug, not looking very confident.

"Was afraid of that," I admitted.

Which meant either we made the attempt anyway, or I needed to find someplace where I could rehash everything I knew over again without being disturbed. That wasn't about to happen at Calie's place. P. T. was deep in pots and pans, preparing for Calista's All Hallows Feast. One that she had no idea would morph into Calie's transformation ceremony, but then she wouldn't be hanging around when that happened. She'd be far from the estate, in her own home.

Other than finding Kit, my other worry was that Calie had found a body to steal.

Only one person was likely to know.

"How's the Amberson replacement search going?" I asked when Delia answered the phone.

"We're swamped with wannabes," she said.

"Wannabe Calistas or wannabe *New York Times* bestsellers?" The third book of The Raven Tales had made the top of the list, an achievement all subsequent titles had matched.

"They think it's the same thing," Delia admitted.

"And if Calie has her way, it damn well will be," I growled. "They just won't be themselves any longer."

Delia sighed. "Then you know what's going to happen tonight."

"Know what I'd like to stop happening tonight, is more like it." Short of kidnapping the chosen one, I'd no idea what would stop it, though. "Has Calie contacted any of these eager sacrifices?"

"She wants nothing to do with them. Thinks this is unnecessary hoopla that you and I cooked up, though she admits it will work well publicity-wise for a new name to appear on the next book."

"She's already worked out a plot?" I demanded. If she had, it meant there was a dead Otherworld being that she knew about that Doe and the others didn't. Calie had always used a murder that was a done deal—or so I'd thought. Still vacillating on whether that bucket had a hole in it or toted its allotted load.

"Not that she's mentioned," Delia said. "You haven't had any vibes?"

When had I had a chance to even think about a forthcoming adventure, when I was neck deep in one right now?

Then it hit me what that meant.

"Hell, Hades, and every other version of perdition that exists! Damn it, Delia! I'm living a damn adventure. How did she manage that?"

"You mean everything we're doing is fictional? That can't be so, Bram. The rest of us are real."

Or maybe they only *thought* they were. Let's face it, until shortly before I crossed over, I'd no concept of being a made-up person, even if I hobnobbed with other fictional characters in my off hours.

I groaned out loud. My head could explode later. I needed to sort through what I already knew. Had to treat it like it was all real. It was what I'd always done in a book. It was what I needed to do now, since I just might still be *in* a book.

"What's the schedule like here tonight?" I asked.

"Reception with an open bar at six, followed by a buffet dinner at eight. There will be guests who aren't coven members at both. Calista plans to plead exhaustion before midnight if the nonmembers haven't shuffled out the door by then. The coven will slip away to the meadow after changing into ceremonial robes."

I let out a whoosh of air. "Thank goodness. I was afraid they'd all be naked."

"Oh, everyone will be sky-clad for the ceremony itself, Bram. It's simply too cool out at that time of night to stand around in the altogether prior to it at this season."

Considering what would happen, I wasn't looking forward to standing around in the moonlight with a covey of naked babes.

"If Calie doesn't contact one of the folks who are clamoring for a chance to write a Raven tale, how would she go about finding her victim?" I asked.

"There is a list of requirements for vessels," Delia said, emphasizing the last word. I couldn't help wondering if the requirements were her own as well. "The subject has to be an adult, anywhere from eighteen to early thirties. The chosen is either an orphan with little to no family or someone estranged from their family. Usually, Calie has shopped around for candidates. Befriended the sort of girls that fit the requirements, then honed them into willing sacrifices."

She sounded too knowledgeable on the process for my comfort. Like she'd witnessed the process in action more than once in the past.

"Delia," I said, dropping my voice to what I hoped was the sort of tone that would lure a confession from her. "Exactly how old are you?"

There was a pregnant pause at her end of the line. Then the words burst forth.

"Too old," she said. "You're right in guessing I've aided Calista in the past and that she has aided me in finding a new form and transferring into it. It was easier prior to the explosion of technology. There were plenty of girls who craved death, usually ones who lost a sweetheart in a war and didn't want to live with that loss. They believed in witchcraft back then, Bram. *Our* version of it, which lacks the devil worship others practiced. We are Earth magic-based, dedicated to Luna's calming influence."

Considering how Luna's pull on the planet affected the seas, the weres, and humans' more violent tendencies, I didn't see her influence as calming.

"And today?" I prompted.

"The world has changed. It was already getting difficult to take on a new persona in the nineteenth century. Governments were instigating more and more identifying paperwork on people, and the newly reorganized police agencies began following up on reports of missing persons. All of it made acquisition of new forms more difficult. I was ready to forfeit further existence the last time but couldn't resist the lure of living another life when one offered itself," Delia admitted.

"But the original Calista Westbury wasn't given that choice, was she?"

"Calie told you about that?" Delia sounded stunned.

184

"Why does everyone keep forgetting I'm an investigator? I looked at the facts. Back when she was Lovidia Smarts, Calie made sure her next body's resident was primed to leave. Or thought she was. When the Nazi hunters began closing in on her, she jumped early, didn't she?"

Delia gasped. "You figured that connection out?"

Duh. Ferreting out data and tracking evil was in my fictional DNA.

"She always was impatient to begin anew." Delia's sigh was nearly answer enough. "It's amazing that she's stayed in this form for this long. Part of the reason for that is you, Bram."

"Me!"

"She liked spinning tales, and you were always very real to her. Her hero. The sort of man she fancied."

"*The what?*" I demanded.

But it all came together now. I'd known Calie was lying. She'd brought me into the real world to be her new form's paramour. Except I wasn't the same character she'd created.

It took several deep breaths to calm down, to shake the abhorrent idea from the forefront of my mind. There was a case to solve—more than one. Those who had known and liked, or loved, Pavan Banerjee, Xavier Botello, Rolph Lund, Tado Gallo, Jamyang Yontentsang, Amélie Lumumba, or Neko were depending on me to work a miracle. It was what I did in volume after volume. Why should they doubt that I wouldn't pull it off in the end?

And the end was fast approaching. When Calie had her new body, there was every chance that she'd erase me entirely and write herself a new and more accommodating hero to morph onto this plane. She was experienced, now that she'd pulled off the process successfully with me.

"I know Calie," I told Delia. "She's going to have backup plans. If the first thing she plotted out doesn't work, she'll take another road. What will it be?"

She thought for a moment, then said, "The coven. She'll choose one of the younger members."

"Who's most likely to be the chosen one?"

"Honestly, I don't know, Bram. She hasn't shown any favor toward any of them. If she'd always planned to take over one of them, she would have. That's got to be her last option, and frankly, she seems fairly sure that everything is in motion to her liking right now. You're the only one she's unhappy with, and even that will fade."

I wasn't sure it would. Since I was hoping I'd find a way to stop Calie, there were miracles I needed to pull out of my hat that night.

"It's wrong, Delia. You've already admitted that the world has changed, and finding new and willing receptacles isn't as possible any longer. Even though the new forms come complete with the required paper trail, it's still evil."

"Perhaps not ethical," she bartered, "but not evil. Nothing given by Luna is ever evil."

I wasn't as sure about that. After all, I was a moon-born being, and I had some very evil moments in my fictional past.

Maybe even in my real-life future.

When I rejoined him in the kitchen, Burt was sufficiently caffeinated to stay awake for a week.

"Mmm," I said as the scents in the room hit me. "What's that arresting aroma? Your perfume, pet?" I inhaled deeply near P.T's ear.

She ducked away and told me what was cooking. I lost my appetite immediately. Shall we leave it at this? No livestock were being harmed in the preparation of comestibles for the evening.

"Your aunt asked that you be reminded to dress properly for the cocktail party tonight," P. T. said, returning to the stove to stir whatever the good-smelling but creepy-sounding ingredients were.

"You mean like in a suit? I don't own a suit."

P. T. smiled over her shoulder at me. "She knows that. You'll have to go shopping. I'll bet Burt knows a good place to get fast service for what you need."

"Just any old suit, right?" I hedged.

"Something dark, but she'd prefer a tuxedo."

"A tuxedo."

P. T. turned to where Burt was seated.

"Do you hear an echo in here?" she asked.

Burt chuckled. "We talkin' member of the wedding party or prom night duds?"

"George Clooney movie premiere type," she answered.

I did not have time for this. Also knew I wasn't going to get out of acquiring a tuxedo. "Daylight's burning," I said. "You ready to get this chore off the list, pal?"

Burt signaled his readiness by getting to his feet.

"Beelz?" I asked the dog, who was reclining on his well-stuffed dog bed, out from underfoot. He lifted his snout and barked. By the time Burt and I made it to the exit, he was already out the dachshund hatch and waiting at the cab's rear door.

"A tuxedo," I groaned as we headed down the drive. "I'll look as dapper as you do," I told Beelzie, turning to glance into the back, where the hellhound reclined sphinxlike on the banquette seat. He curled his lip at the mere idea.

"We've got a hell of a schedule today. Let's scratch the damn suit off the list first."

Burt nodded. "There's likely to be some alterations needed, so that's a good idea. Where else will we be headed? The car dealership again?"

"Let's let the insurance pay off the last one first," I suggested.

If I ceased to exist, I wondered who would get the cash. The newly named and newly housed Calie, reclaiming what had once been hers anyway? Probably. Her coven sister—either the insurance one or the lawyer—would keep it in the estate's account.

"Otherwise, I'm giving you an option on what comes next. I've got some really nasty neighborhoods to visit. If you'd rather not be along for the ride, drop Beelz and me at a car rental place."

Burt took a turn smoothly, heading us toward town.

"How nasty?" he asked.

I spilled, holding back only one fact: that the victims had all been Otherworld beings. I dropped the real reason we were revisiting kill sites though.

"Kit's missing. I think someone kidnapped her to keep me from investigating one or all of the old cases."

He didn't glance over at me, not once, but his lips thinned as his jaw lifted slightly.

"If someone has kidnapped Ms. Kit, I'd like to help, even if it's merely to serve as your driver," he said.

"Done. That means we spend as little time as possible on the tux, then head for Kit's place and burgle the joint. Beelz needs something with her scent on it to help him sniff around."

187

"You mean we're breaking in? You got experience in that sort of thing?"

With magic being an unreliable resource right now, my method was going to be more the firm kick to the lock method, if Kit didn't have a key hidden somewhere on the landing outside her door.

"Maybe," I vacillated.

Burt did glance over at me this time, a grin curving his mouth and putting a sparkle in his eye. "Then it's good that, in another life, I had a very intimate relationship with quite a few locks."

"Sounds kinda kinky," I said.

"Nah, but profitable? Very," he confessed.

I probably looked more like a movie extra than Clooney once I'd been measured, the tux chalked up for minute adjustments, and a collection of overtly colored cummerbunds rejected. With time of the essence, it was good that a selection of highly polished black shoes was available for one-stop shopping. Both Burt and the salesman had sided against me wearing my twentieth century boots, my black running shoes having been jettisoned with the rest of the gasoline- and smoke-scented clothing. Bet they wouldn't have favored my wearing those, either.

After paying a hefty service charge for the necessary rush job on the alterations, we were back on the road in a half hour.

It took Burt less than thirty seconds to trip the lock on Kit's condo. While he admired the view and drooled a bit over the size of her flat-screen, as I had not long ago, I ripped the pillowcase off on her side of the bed, scooped up the towels she and Beelz had nested in together and the blouse she'd worn when playing Ms. Fox-Jones, and shoved them all into a bag I found in the closet. The collection should give Beelz enough solid whiffs to work with, I figured. I'd certainly gotten nostalgic as her scent had wafted to me while I swept them all up.

We were back in the cab and headed for the Grab It Quik, the site of Pavan Banerjee's death, within a few minutes.

The memory of my now-destroyed map with the death sites pinpointed was all I had to go on, but as the only far-flung site was Rolph Lund's bridge—and he hadn't died at the crumbling span but dropped dead in town—travel time between locations was minimal, though trailing Beelzie as he sniffed was time-consuming.

Kit's kidnappers had to be involved in the murders. Why kidnap her, other than to distract me from them? Searching the nineteen kill sites within Detroit, there was an outside chance we'd find her.

We didn't. Her cell went to voicemail when I tried it again.

I touched bases with Doe. She'd arranged Neko's funeral for the next day. She hadn't heard back yet from First Nations. And she hadn't heard from Kit either.

"Listen," I cautioned her as I leaned back against the bumper of the cab while Burt hustled in to the haberdasher to retrieve my unwanted evening wear. "Calista's planning catastrophic things tonight. There's a chance that I'll be totally erased from the real world by the end of the evening. She's not happy with me, and I'm ticked off with her. If I'm not around to finish the job you gave me, get hold of Detective Chad Durkin at the Detroit PD. There might be something he can do to help."

"A police detective! Why would he be sympathetic where the death of an Otherworld being is involved?" she demanded, sounding just shy of enraged that I'd shared information with a human.

"Because he was related to our dead banshee, Doe. He also works with two officers who *are* paranormals. If you don't know about them, it's because they're good at keeping a low profile. What I'm trying to say is that the nonhuman community isn't alone. Not saying you'll get a heck of a lot of aid, because the department is shorthanded and overworked, but I'm not your last resort."

She wasn't listening, not ready to trust beyond the community she knew.

"You'll be around to finish the job, Raven," Deer Woman insisted. "Calista isn't about to send you back. She's had a plan for you all along."

"Yeah," I agreed, "but the guy who stepped out of the series isn't the one she was expecting, Doe."

Plus, we weren't dealing with a witch with a normal life cycle. We were dealing with a truly ancient being who didn't like to take no for an answer.

Besides, witches aren't Otherworld beings. They are humans who use magic. That equated to vicious in Doe's eyes. Maybe even in mine!

"I'm just giving you a heads-up *in case* something fatal happens to me tonight."

"Duly noted, though I don't believe anything will happen," Doe said. "While you deal with the coven, I'll shake First Nations' trees again."

I didn't envy First Nations. When Deer Woman wanted something, she was an even more dangerous woman than she had been as a forest spirit luring young warriors to their deaths.

"Thanks," I said. "I'll be in touch if I'm still alive later on."

"You'll be here," she insisted.

Before she could cut the connection, I stopped her. "Hey, you wouldn't happen to know a ghoul named Solomon Prisk, would you?"

"Why?"

"Just a name that's come up lately," I said. She didn't need to know why.

"In connection with the twenty? Sounds like you're making progress, Raven."

I wished I had her confidence in that regard.

When I got back to the estate, P.T. had turned the kitchen and a mountain of prepared food over to servers from a catering service and skedaddled. Burt dropped Beelz and me off at the rear door and darted back down the drive.

With the tux and bagged accoutrements slung over my shoulder, I slipped in the back door and headed for the servants' staircase rather than run the chance of coming face to face with Calie before she had her civility mask in place for guests. Beelzie scanned the kitchen, taking in the number of foreign legs in the room, and opted to follow me. To make his trip swifter, I swept him up under my free arm and took the stairs two at a time.

He chose to enjoy the Clydesdale shower stall with me, no doubt wishing to rid himself of the scents and garbage we'd encountered during our unsuccessful scouring of the kill sites. I know that was what I was attempting to do. If I could wash the horrific pictures of what Kit might be enduring from my mind as well, that would have been super. Also callous, though, and truly unworthy of the man I wanted to be.

"If something happens to me tonight, could you keep looking for Kit and rescue her if it's at all possible? Do your Great Dane imitation or something, huh?" I asked the hellhound.

He yipped, which I took for an affirmative.

"Don't want to tell you what to do, but considering what Calie's planning tonight, I'd suggest you hightail it from this joint. But if I survive past moonset, it's steak for you, pal."

The Mighty B's tail did a rapid staccato at the promise.

Then, while I put on the penguin suit and ran my hands through my hair rather than a comb—which I didn't own anyway—he burrowed beneath the pillows on the bed to recoup his strength. Looking very un-Ravenish, I headed downstairs.

Calista was going for *grande dame*, draped in sequined black from neck to toe, her long hair styled in a *Town and Country*-perfect crown of twisted Medusa coils. An ornate, antique-looking, heavily jeweled necklace was clasped at her throat, and her age-marked hands sparkled with a tasteful assortment of diamond-encrusted rings. A makeup artist had done the next best thing to photoshopping her, softening her sharp features. In her gracefully held pose, there was no sign of the woman who was dying of advanced cancer. She'd made sure that where she awaited the supplicants that evening put her center stage. The receiving line already twisted out the door into the encroaching twilight.

She'd been on the watch for me, much to my chagrin, and regally gestured that I heel at her side rather than snag a glass of bubbly from a cruising waiter.

"Bram, dear," she cooed, "I'd like you to meet..." and she trotted out some name that barely finished pouring into my sieve-quality ear before it dripped out the other.

Some were startled to find my name was the same as the character in The Raven Tales. Others chuckled and pumped my hand, saying things like "The mysterious nephew. So you exist after all!"

Very hard to keep the glib comebacks locked down, believe me. Delia took pity on my plight, securing a tumbler of Evan Williams to smooth over the torturous but required mingling with Calie's guests. They came from political offices, from the fields of medicine, the arts, and big business. Hangers-on, every one of them, although there were a number who were introduced as presidents, vice presidents, CEOs, and judges. A few entertainment celebrities showed up as well, gushing about Calie's thoughtful contributions to their pet charities. The paparazzi followed them in. A few selfies were taken with Calista.

Working on my second dose of bourbon, I managed to duck out of the crush around my creator. But then I had my own horde, doggedly cutting off any attempt I made to slip away. Calie had apparently assigned the coven members to keep me in sight at all times. The younger ones took that as a green light to get cozy, linking arms with me and fluttering their eyelashes. The giveaway was that they laughed at anything I said that might pass for droll. But when I gazed back and murmured, "Has Calie approached you about your future within the coven?" they found reasons to signal the next jailor in line.

Oddly enough, the new arrival always brought a fresh tumbler of exquisite bourbon with her. Beyond keeping me busy, it seemed the job entailed getting me sloshed. But then, an intoxicated Raven would be much less likely to put a hitch in the plan later that night. Whenever possible, I employed the illusionist's art of distraction so I could commit connoisseurial crimes, pouring Evan Williams into the handiest potted plants rather than down the offerings personally.

When the chance to slip away materialized, I grabbed it, quickly stepping out one of the opened terrace doors and disappearing around the nearest shrubbery.

Doe wasn't surprised to get another call from me.

"Anything?" I demanded.

"Not on Kit; not on Drow Stowe," she said, ringing off before I could ask anything else. Not that I had a further question, but being on the phone did have the magic effect of keeping some people at a distance. The minute the cell was back in my pocket, the next coven member launched from those drifting toward the tent where the buffet awaited.

I ducked around another hedge and ran smack into Samael.

Reeling back on my heels, I snarled at him. "What? No 'laktos dudes running point tonight?"

"They would have taken the penguin look a bit too closely to heart. It is Halloween," he said before casually sipping from the glass of champagne in his right hand. He looked far more turned out for the Oscars than I did.

"I suppose you're here to officiate later on."

"Just coming to observe the proceedings. It's always interesting to discover what new face my daughter will be wearing," he murmured. "The girls worship Luna, not me."

"Must be very disappointing for you," I sniped.

The Devil chuckled. "Refreshing, really. My followers have some very strange ideas when it comes to ceremonies and my appearance. Rather trite and unimaginative, really."

He sounded bored.

"Bottom line, though?" he added. "I'll turn up anywhere there are going to be naked, intoxicated babes."

A regular guy, isn't he? And, yes, I'm being facetious.

"You wouldn't happen to know where my girlfriend is or who has her, would you?" Worth a shot, I figured.

"Ah, you have me confused with the other guy," Samael said. "I'm not the omniscient one. Your kitsune has gone missing? It does happen to demons occasionally."

If he was hoping to get a rise out of me over the reminder of what Kit was, he didn't know me at all.

"Aren't we all demons, just at different points on the scale?" I asked.

He laughed, his handsome face creasing in honest lines of amusement.

"Damn, but I wish I could claim you as one of my own, Bram. Sadly, you don't have the necessary qualifications."

"Such as having more substance than wood pulp and inkblots?"

"You said it, I didn't," he said and then added, "I think I'll mingle a bit and see if there are any souls in the crowd who are teetering over bad decisions."

So saying, he cocked his left arm out. A stunning starlet type materialized next to him, a platinum blonde in a body-skimming dress that made me think of sinning with mermaids. Of course, that could have been because it was a watery, bleached seaweed shade. I wished for an entirely new batch of paint chips, to identify the color more precisely, as her tailfin sashayed away from me.

Then another coven minx closed in, tumbler in hand, and I was dragged into the buffet tent on the south lawn. Lot of seafood and plant trimmings. I might have starved to death if I'd had any appetite. I'd lost it, though. A glance at the darkening sky had shown it to be cloudless. Probably because I was a creature of the moon, I could feel Luna's pull as she began her climb from the horizon into the heavens. The hours were spinning away from me while the questions remained unanswered.

A small jazz combo was supplying background music. A few women swayed to the music, but for the most part the band was ignored. As was I, temporarily, which meant my mind kicked back into investigation mode. Or maybe it was merely Raven mode.

Which of the women cruising the buffet and hitting the open bar would wake up in Calista's cancer-colonized body, I wondered? Would it be possible to stop the spirit jump, or would I have to stand by impotently while a young woman's life was stolen?

And if I did manage a miracle and stop Calie, would I cease to exist in much the same manner as I'd been born, sheathed in moonlight?

Everything depended upon me surviving the night. While I'd given Doe a fallback option with Detective Durkin and asked Beelz to find Kit, I didn't want either of them casting those other lots. I was The Raven, the guy who solved mysteries, who visited justice on those deserving its harshest decisions. I wanted to stay in this world and do the same job, though perhaps no longer in the same manner.

Would the Fates, or any other godlings in the many pantheons that had found favor over time, feel inclined to grant the necessary miracles to a man who was a figment of imagination?

The only answer I came up with was the one Samael had given me before the situation had amped up with bombings, murders, and kidnappings: *God helps those who help themselves.*

So be it, I decided. I tossed off the E. W. in my glass, for a dollop of courage. When the opportunity presented, I stole out of the tent.

The sound of vehicles leaving the estate had grown nonexistent when the first of the witches arrived in the meadow-that-should-not-exist. She started, nearly spilling the pitcher of whatever, when she found me lying on one of the two stone tables that had been erected by unknown minions earlier in the day. I'd loosened my tie, unbuttoned my collar, stacked my feet heel to toe, and linked my hands behind my neck while I stared at the stars above.

The moon was inching toward her apex. Luna was still 2 percent away from officially reaching 100 percent luminosity, but that wouldn't matter to Calie as much as the date did. Besides, it was only a handful of hours until the 100 percent mark would be met. Full luminosity would merely seal the deal.

Right now, it was peaceful as... well, not Hell, nor any location that had ever been used in a Raven tale. The only sounds were those the breeze caused, denuded branches scratching against each other as they stirred.

"Damn spooky place, isn't it?" I drawled. And it was, at night, with those long, narrow branches reaching from the shadows, the rustling of the drying brush, and the skittering of desiccated leaves hustling along like feral creatures, all seeming to move away—or attempt to—from the magic-induced glade.

I'd prowled the entire area and found nothing. No theophylaktos minions, no witch familiars, no guards of any sort. Yet I had the feeling that something was there, unseen and waiting. Something I'd encountered before; something that attempted to reach out to me, though whether with ill intent or not, I hadn't been able to decide. Perhaps it was the ghosts of every one of the fictional nonhumans I'd destroyed in the books. Perhaps it was Neko's spirit.

The witchy neophyte carefully set the jug she carried on a flat-topped rock and fussed over clearing a few newly fallen leaves from the surface.

"We wondered where you'd disappeared to," she said.

Probably Calie had vented some baleful displeasure at the group for losing track of me.

"Not one of my earthly powers," I said. "Calie is probably saving some hocus-pocus aside to poof me back out of existence for being a bad boy in giving you all the slip."

"She didn't seem overly worried," the young witch said. Her voice was soft and wary, though whether of me or the events yet to play out was a toss-up. She was a comely little thing, brunette, blue-eyed, shapely but not in full bloom as Delia and the other cougar-age sisters were. When the light breeze teased her dark, cowled robe open, a long expanse of bare leg showed. I wondered if she would find herself in a diseased, elderly body by dawn.

"Liar," I accused, sitting up and swinging my legs over the side of the altar. "I know Calista slightly better than that."

A rustle in the trees announced the next arrivals. Two of them carried deep crimson silk panels. The third had a tray with loaves of bread and what looked like a well-herbed bowl of olive oil.

"Leftovers?" I asked. "Kinda paltry fare. Let's order pizza. Someone can go raid Calie's wine cellar or go on a beer run."

I reached for my phone as though planning to make the call.

And found my hand wouldn't move once it made it to the tuxedo jacket's inner pocket.

"Get him off the altar," Calista ordered, striding into sight. She had one hand outstretched, apparently the one that had thrown whatever spell held me frozen in place.

It took three of them to shift me, and they staggered as they dragged me outside the soon-to-be-enchanted circle. I was lucky the ground was cushioned by the pile of leaves Samael had raked up the other day, for the women dropped me unceremoniously, then stood huffing and puffing from the exertion.

Calie ghosted across the newly manicured meadow to stand over me, the silvery robe she wore seeming to flicker with both shadow and light as the breeze stirred its long folds.

"Comfy, dearest?" she purred. "The spell will wear off eventually, but it is best if you don't get in our way right now."

I thought a scathing comment at her, since speech was impossible while in the grip of whatever she'd tossed at me.

"Your presence isn't really required this evening, Bram, but I do like to include you in things. My hope is that you'll understand better what I do and why I do it. However, trusting you to merely be an observer, not an actor in events, is an entirely different thing," Calie said. "Stopping me is exactly what you would do in one of The Raven adventures, isn't it? That can't be allowed. I have a surprise for you, though. A pleasant one, I trust."

She called to one of the older witches on the opposite side of the glade. The woman nodded, extended her arms, closed her eyes, and tilted her head back as she chanted something I couldn't make out. A further dramatic movement with her hand, and a patch of previous shadow was ripped away to reveal Kit gagged, bound hand and foot, and curled in a fetal position at the foot of an ancient tree trunk.

A tree trunk I'd walked past several times without sensing her presence.

196

She was awake but immobilized. They'd probably put a controlling curse on her, too, preventing her from reverting to her fox form to escape.

"I believe you've been searching for her," Calie murmured. "Rather frantically, in fact. Such an endearing trait, dear, but not one that I wrote into your makeup. It makes you predictable and thus weak. But I'll deal with correcting that another day. Tonight, I have other priorities, as you very well know. The demon has other uses that will suit my plans."

Other uses? By all the gods! She was going to transfer into Kit's form!

As though the thought marched across my brow as an advert, Calie read my mind.

"Don't be ridiculous," she snapped. "I wouldn't inhabit a filthy fox form. She's here as a deterrent to any heroics you might attempt. I won't hesitate to dispose of her if necessary."

I made a growling noise, the only thing I was capable of while under the spell's restraints.

That's when Samael strolled into the clearing with his mermaidish companion. Calie spun to greet him, only to stop short when she saw the woman on his arm.

"You brought a *date* to my rebirth?" she demanded, coolly.

Her arctic tone would have frozen a lesser being on the spot. Sam gave her a wide smile and let the woman at his side dissipate.

"Daughter," he greeted. "Which spirit shift is this one? I've lost count over the years."

I doubted that, but she didn't supply an answer to the question, either.

"It's always an honor to have you attend, Father," Calie said. I noticed that she didn't attempt to hug him, kiss his cheek, or even take his arm, but kept her distance. Apparently, only I was stupid enough to rub shoulders with the Devil over beers or cider.

He looked over the crop of witches, all of whom had frozen in place, without the aid of a spell, upon his arrival.

"You're missing someone," he said.

"Those escorting the vessel," she explained.

But Sam shook his head slightly. "No, I passed them. You're still missing someone. Your lieutenant, isn't it?"

Calie laughed softly. A bit forced, I thought, but a laugh all the same.

"Military titles, Father? We don't use them."

He simply looked at her, waiting for an answer.

She turned away rather than face him. "All right, yes, the second oldest of us is indeed absent."

"At such an auspicious occasion?"

"There was a difference of opinion," Calista said. "She wavered."

I did a quick check of the robed women around the clearing. Delia was missing.

"Did you kill her?" Samael asked casually.

Calie scoffed at the suggestion. "You'd know if I had."

"Perhaps," he agreed, but that left room for doubt, didn't it? "I see your creation has also run himself into your inflexible will."

They both stared down at helpless little me.

"A temporary disappointment, that's all," she assured him. "It will be corrected."

"And the other?" he asked, lifting his chin to indicate where Kit lay curled in her bonds on the opposite side of the clearing. Two witches had taken up guard positions. Considering they were standing a yard away to either side of her, it seemed the chore wasn't one they felt comfortable fulfilling.

"A surety for Bram's cooperation."

Samael chuckled. "Parenthood is so difficult, isn't it, daughter? No matter what they are given, children simply choose to go their own way."

Calie's lips thinned in anger. "Bram is not my child."

"Isn't he?" He nudged my prone form with the toe of one impossibly black shoe, the sheen on it seeming to reflect the moon far above. "Hear that, junior? Call me *gramps* again and I'll toast you."

Then he laughed, snapped his fingers, and the paralysis that held me was gone.

I took a deep breath and pushed upright, dusting bits of dried leaf dandruff from the tux.

"Like that would stop me," I snarled.

The Devil smirked. "See, daughter? He takes after you."

Calie made a noise of distaste and moved away to supervise the draping of the stone altars with the glistening, bloodred cloth. I made a move in Kit's direction, but Samael's hand on my shoulder yanked me back to the sidelines. Felt like something molten emanated from his mitt to work its way through the layers of my clothing and scour whatever ran through my veins. The moment he released me, the sensation cooled, dissipating so fast I nearly thought it had been overactive imagination at work. Only the hint of a pilot light remained.

"Patience, kid," he growled quietly. "You were configured to be a predator, not the prey. Act the part. Trust to those who have your back."

"Like you?" I demanded, incredulous.

"Hell, no. Look more closely."

I'd been in the meadow long enough for my eyes to adjust to the shadows. The only light was that supplied by Luna as she moved into position above us. Behind Kit, a smaller shadow was moving, one whose demon red eyes flashed my way as it worked. Beelz had found his way to our favorite succubus and was worrying away at her bonds with his teeth. As I watched, he yanked back and fell into the brush as the rope broke. The witch guards glanced back at the sound Beelz's stumble made, but with his head turned aside, the glow of his eyes wasn't apparent. Seeing Kit still frozen in place, the guards faced forward once more.

The moment they did so, I heard Sam quietly snap his fingers, freeing Kit from the immobility spell. A heartbeat later, both Kit's guards staggered on their feet. She'd pulled enough life force from both to bemuse them and probably have a quick mini-meal herself.

With neither guard the wiser, Kit hastily rubbed at her wrists, then put her hands back behind herself, looking the picture of meek captivity once more. Beelz nosed forward and worked on the rope around her ankles.

Before I could take a relieved breath, Sam turned to where the path from the estate trailed into the meadow.

"I think the main attraction is about to begin," he said. His hand closed on my arm, his grip like iron, a strong reminder to stay where I was.

"Predator, not prey," he counseled.

It wasn't an easy motivational slogan for me to follow at the best of times on this side of the fiction line, but the surge of fury that flared up when a mesmerized young woman in a robe that matched

Calie's was lead into the circle by four dark-robed figures allowed my core predator to break free of the cage I'd unconsciously built for it.

The woman in shimmering silver was P. T.

"*NO!*" The shout escaped my throat of its own accord, sounding harsh and strangled. Sam's arm blocked me from lurching forward. I shook him off but stayed where I was. Acting too soon wouldn't be doing P. T. any favors.

If it was a favor I could pull off, that is.

Calista ignored my objection and moved to stand beside the rock where the ceremonial comestibles waited.

P. T. was unnaturally complacent, no doubt bemused by one of Calie's spells, her actions not her own. She was led to where Calista waited, the witches on either side supporting their unwilling draft pick as she swayed on her feet.

I spared a quick glance at Kit just as she slipped into fox form and followed Beelz deeper into the woods, her guards none the wiser. Now there was only one female to rescue, though how in Hades it could be accomplished was beyond me.

Calista raised a hand and caressed P. T.'s cheek, brushed back a flyaway strand of her blonde hair.

"Philomena Theora," the old witch greeted. "Twice blessed in naming by your parents, be twice blessed in answering the Goddess's call."

P. T. didn't answer. But while her body was not hers to command, her eyes were alive with confusion, fear, and a hint of anger. Rather than focus on Calie or the women on either side, her gaze darted around the area. With each face she recognized, the fear grew. It was laced with despair when she found me.

"The great cats are patient killers," Samael said, his voice pitched to reach my ears alone.

Patience was a freakin' virtue. What the hell did he know about it?

"It takes patience to lure a soul from the light," he said, this time straight into my mind. "A thought created me, in the Beginning. A thought created you, Raven. We are alike in that."

The hell we were! I was fictional.

I glanced aside at Samael, but his face was set in a smirk that could have meant anything.

He thought me fair game for torturing with multiple possibilities of what reality really was, did he? The fact that I had two types of reality already to confuse me must be generating enough silent chuckles to make me a damn irresistible entertainment feature. It wasn't like there was much on TV worth watching. He'd already corrupted that.

While I ruminated, events moved ahead in the meadow.

Calie removed her rings and necklace, setting them aside on the stone filling the role of side table. No doubt the ceremony would be considered at an end when she reclaimed them to deck out her latest vessel in familiar gems. Now, she waited while one of her minions poured a chalice of a mystery elixir and presented it to her. Nodding her thanks, Calie took the cup in both hands, hands that resembled darkly veined claws next to those of the young acolyte.

Calista took a healthy slug of whatever the chalice held, then wrapped P. T.'s elegant fingers around the bowl. The witch on P. T.'s left guided the rim to the younger woman's lips and forced the liquid in. A shared piece of dipped bread followed. Although chances were that P. T. had created the bread from a recipe Calista supplied, she didn't appear to enjoy the torn bit shoved into her mouth or the spell the witch on her right seemed to cast to force her to chew and swallow.

When the brief ceremony was complete, Calie smiled with mock fondness on P. T. "Under the Goddess's goodness, I thank thee, Philomena Theora, for the gift of this body."

P. T.'s eyes were frantic with terror, though she still couldn't have known what was about to occur. Her gaze swept the twin cloth-covered altars. The realization that a sacrifice was about to be made, and that she was it, caused her legs to buckle despite the controlling spell, leaving her sagging in the arms of the two witch attendants.

"Our Sister comes," Calista announced, her face turned to where Luna climbed above the treetops, allowing moonlight to inch across the floor of the meadow.

In unison, the coven members let the robes slide from their shoulders to form pools of shadow at their sandaled feet. Two stepped forward to take Calista's garment, sparing her the trouble of shrugging it free. As her silvery robe was ghosted away, P. T.'s was removed in a mirror-like movement.

Next to me, Samael made a sound of appreciation followed by one of regret. No doubt in the ancient past, an orgy had been included in the process, but we were the only two males in attendance. A fallen angel and a paper cutout.

He was a silent watcher. I couldn't be, though.

"How is the spirit jump accomplished?" I snarled, attempting to disguise just how impotent I was feeling as the ceremony progressed.

"In much the way I suppose you were born," he said, mind to mind rather than aloud.

I'd been poofed into existence through Calie's chanting at a crowd of ancient lunar goddesses fueled up by a thunderstorm. Chanting might begin at any moment, but the power generated by a storm was missing; the sky was free of clouds. Did that mean there was enough juice to be channeled to Calie through the gathered witches to substitute for Mother Nature at her violent best? Delia had expected my creator to use the group to manifest me. Separately, the coven members weren't powerful, but when joined by a single purpose and molded by my creator's will? I wasn't placing any bets on that outcome not being beneficial this time.

Calista was escorted by her acolytes to the raised stone slab on the right and helped to recline upon it. Her body still not under her own control, P. T. was soon in a like pose, hands crossed on her breast. Then the members of the coven stepped back into the shadows beneath the trees and began to chant in a language that had no modern counterpart.

P. T.'s eyes were wild; Calista smiled faintly, obviously satisfied that things were playing out as she had planned.

And I was an idiot indeed. I knew the identity of the final element: moonlight. Those shadows of goddesses had turned up at my so-called birth, but they had followed the streaming blue-white light as it struck me that first night. I remembered what it felt like getting whammied with the ability to see colors, to actually hear the fury of the storm and taste the rain as it blew into the room on scent-laden gusts of wind. I'd been taken unaware, unknowingly yanked across the barrier between imagination and reality. *Life* had exploded into being in a Big Bang instant.

It wasn't new life that would be formed tonight, though. Tonight was about stealing a life.

The chanting, the sip from a ceremonial cup, the sharing of bread, even the spell that robbed P. T. of motor skills—it was all stage dressing. Luna was the trigger, the alchemic ingredient, whether the congress of lesser manifestations of the Goddess was called upon or not.

And how could one man, real or not, stop the moon?

The apex had nearly been reached in Luna's arching stroll across the heavens. The silvery blue-white stream of power-infused light would soon blanket the meadow. It was already growing nearer to the twin altars.

Moments later, the life-changing glow glided over Calie's form.

She arched as though in response to the abrupt pull of an invisible bond, then collapsed back on the unforgiving stone, her body obviously cast off. Even I could see a disruption in the moon's light that resembled a disembodied form, a figure created of fog, a wisp of smoke, rather like the faint images taken by the multitude of goddesses that had whammied me. It flowed with the viscosity of cream spilled across a table, inching ever nearer P. T.'s magically constrained form.

The lunar light reached the base of the second altar. Inched up it.

I couldn't breathe and felt as trapped as I had when in Calista's confining spell. Samael was holding his breath as well, though he was thoroughly into the proceedings. The spirit within the beam appeared to be preparing to dive into the new vessel. Time was running out.

Without realizing I'd done so, I tore from Samael's grip. Leaped forward, breaking into the circle of witches, putting myself between the moonlight and P. T. Threw myself across her to block the spirit's entry, hoping like hell that my familiar magical shield would materialize to protect us.

When Luna's light struck my back, I knew the force field had failed to form. I bucked as searing pain urged me to abandon the heroics. This was nothing like the sensations that had accompanied my "birth." This was pain from the Inquisition level of Hell.

Stupidly stubborn, I held the position. My hands gripped the edges of the altar slab, my tuxedoed form pressed intimately, protectively over P. T.'s sky-clad one.

The meadow lit up as if paparazzi cameras had flashed in unison to record the moment when I assumed the part of a lightning rod for a demonstration in a witchy physics class. At least it felt like Zeus had entered the fray by jamming a bolt of pure energy into my spine.

This is it, I told myself. I'd become the stepped leader for negatively charged electrons to kiss the positively charged meadow, and paper boys like me just weren't meant to be conductors of such power. There was the sound of thunder in my ears. My hair felt like it was sizzling in sync with ions freshly stripped from the atmosphere. Any moment now, I'd drift away in a smattering of singed pages.

In my mind I heard a roar, one that could only be Calista's, it was filled with so much fury and frustration. It battered at me. But I was already flaming, thanks to the fireworks. The pain certainly bore that out. Still, idiot hero to the end, I resisted the urge to lift my head, a hand, anything that would give the transforming light—and Calista—a crack through which her ancient Lilin spirit could enter P. T.

Then, the pain was gone as quickly as it had begun.

The breeze was cool as it wafted through the meadow, teased my tumbling hair. The silence was only temporary. When it was broken, it wasn't by a human voice but by the hoot of an owl in the distance.

Moonlight now filled the glen, but it was a complacent, nurturing glow. It felt as though Luna was smiling fondly rather than lending her power to the prehistoric spirit who had made a bargain with the Goddess, somewhere just outside the gates of Eden, eons ago.

"Bram?" P. T.'s voice whispered, the constraining spell now vanquished.

Was it P. T., or was it Calista in the latest vessel, though?

"What's The Raven's favorite meal?" I asked her.

"The Raven?" Confusion swirled in her eyes. "In the books?"

The meager negative shake of her head seemed to indicate she was clueless, but Calie could have been playing the game.

"What's *my* favorite meal?" I countered. A more telling question. I hoped.

"What?" Either she was honestly puzzled or a well-practiced actor.

She tried to push me away, but the heroics I'd indulged in kept her trapped.

"What's my favorite meal?" I repeated calmly.

"Could you get off me?" she asked. "I can't breathe."

"Not until you answer."

"Bram." It was a wheedle, not an answer, though.

"What is it?"

She sighed, abandoning the battle.

"Beef," P. T. said. "T-bone, flank steak, rib roast, Salisbury, filet mignon, or ground and pressed into patties that are no doubt fried and served with oil-drenched strips of potato." It was the same disgusted tone she'd used in the kitchen when dealing with my lack of appreciation for her masterpieces. "The sandwich probably has bacon on it, too."

I kissed P. T. Long, hard, and with a silent, mental bow of thanks to the Goddess for sparing her. Calie had lost. Still, it wasn't until I was totally satisfied that Calista wasn't sharing P. T.'s delightful form that I rolled off and swept up one of the discarded robes to cover her chilled flesh.

Somewhere along the way, probably after I'd thrown myself into the sacrificial circle, disrupting the transference, the coven members had swooned to the ground. The meadow was littered with naked babes.

Samael had disappeared. But Beelz was back, his tail going at quickstep pace. He looked up adoringly at P. T. as I lifted her off the altar and set her back on her feet.

She held the robe protectively against her breasts.

"What happened?" she asked, gazing at what looked like the aftermath of one hell of a sorority party.

I went for the most basic answer. "Calista Westbury Amberson moved on to her reward."

If Samael had scooped up Calie's disembodied soul when it became available—and I figured there was a very good chance that he had—that reward wasn't going to be the one others would expect.

"She..." Her voice cut off. I knew she'd caught sight of the hull that had once housed my creator.

"Committed suicide rather than endure the cancer," I said. "Do you remember any of what happened?"

Her blank expression answered that question.

"I think my aunt put something in whatever the girls were drinking, to ensure that no one tried to stop her," I said. The unconscious coven members certainly made the lie believable.

"But I'm an employee, not a friend. What am I doing here? And why were we all naked?"

"No idea," I claimed. "Beelzie and I were just out for an after-banquet stroll and stumbled across you."

Yep, big lie, but one she wouldn't catch me on. Not if she couldn't remember being in Calista's witchy grasp.

"How about he and I escort you back to the house?"

205

P. T. nodded acceptance. "Would you cover your aunt's friends with their robes while I put this one on?"

"Sure you feel up to it? You probably had some of those potent shooters they were downing. You're looking a bit tipsy yet. Unless that's a result of my thoughtful mouth-to-mouth resuscitation."

"I can manage," she insisted, conveniently choosing to ignore the hasty, flippant explanation I'd offered for being pressed against her intimately when the constricting spell broke. I wondered whether she would eventually remember anything of what had taken place.

Chances were she'd never tell me if she did. Would probably hightail it from the estate as quickly as possible and find a shrink to convince her she'd had a very vivid nightmare.

Beelz plunked his rump down at P. T.'s side, assigning himself guard duty as I moved away to fulfill her request. Before I tossed a single ceremonial robe over any unconscious witch, though, I swept up Calie's rings and necklace. There was a trickle of power when I touched them, but it was temporary, dissipating the moment I dropped them in my pocket. For all I knew, I'd need to pawn them when the bank account ran dry. Miracles had happened, after all. I'd stopped Calista and I was still here!

November 1, Day One 2.0

While P. T. hid her lovely form from sight beneath far too much fabric, I worked my way around the circle of collapsed witches, giving them a modicum of modesty with one hand while using the other to place a 911 call, alerting the paramedics that I'd found a party gone wrong on the Amberson estate. Also that my aunt was dead, probably of natural causes or exposure. I'd let them figure it out.

Then I called Doe, while I was still out of P. T.'s hearing, to tell her Kit was free and safe.

"The last I saw her," I said, "she was in fox form and scampering off into the woods with Beelzie but he's still here. If you haven't heard from her yet, it's probably because she was weak and needed to waylay a few losers for a snack."

"I'll give her a call, though she probably doesn't have her cell with her if she reverted to animal form," Doe said.

"Could be they took it from her. I'll check," I promised.

"I knew you'd find Kit and survive Calista's plans," Doe said.

"Ha! You're just glad you don't have to resort to Durkin," I countered.

"You don't give yourself enough credit, Raven. You'll be back on the job we gave you tomorrow?"

It already was tomorrow. Midnight was long past. It was November 1, the first day of the life I'd really doubted I'd get a chance to live. Whether it was adrenaline or the fact that sleep still wasn't something written into my daily schedule, I knew I'd be on the job as soon as Calista's debacle was swept under the prized Oushak rug.

By the time the naked babes were covered and P. T. had stumbled through the bracken back to the house (I'd had good reason to have my arm around her waist), the now familiar sound of distant sirens was tainting the quiet of the night. I lowered P. T. to the entrance steps and slipped inside to check on Delia. She was lying on the living room floor, obviously having rolled off the sofa, but she was conscious and showing no sign of having been bewitched into statue state. She was trussed up like a pig ready to have a starring role at the neighborhood luau, though.

She looked really relieved to see me.

"Calista?" she asked once the gag was removed.

"Not newly vesselized, if that's what you're asking. I'm afraid I got in the way."

Delia sighed in thanksgiving.

"If only I'd realized earlier," she said as I worked at the cord around her wrists. "She didn't hire P. T. because she wanted a change of diet. She knew the girl's name."

"Philomena Theora? It's a mouthful, but..." I began.

"Bram! The Raven is supposed to catch nuances! Haven't you noticed something about all of our first names? Calista, Neva, Lovidia, Delia? And P. T.'s parents gave her *two* of the same form: Philomena Theora."

"They all end with an *a* and sound vaguely Mediterranean," I said, bemused that I'd missed the link. Yeah, she was right. I was an idiot. I should have realized that. I was The Raven—or I'd thought I was. Maybe I wasn't such a hotshot investigator after all.

The final knot at Delia's wrists gave way.

"I'm not even sure I knew what P. T.'s real name was before tonight," she continued. She bent to work on the bonds at her ankles. "Is she okay?"

"A bit woozy from the spell they put on her, but otherwise probably just chilled from being sky-clad. I hope there is a doctor among the group, because there are going to be a lot of chest colds."

Delia apparently had experience escaping bonds, for she was out of the ties at her ankles in nothing flat.

"Sounds like visitors have arrived," she said.

"Paramedics. I told them I feared Calista had drugged her friends, then died, possibly of exposure."

"I can work with that," she said. "Go give P. T. moral support. I'll gather the necessary people together tomorrow afternoon to sort out any further details. If it's all right, we'll meet here, where we know we won't be overheard or interrupted.

"Once things quiet down, Bram, try to get some sleep. You're going to need it."

If only she knew how curious I was about sleep, and whether I'd ever get to enjoy any, she wouldn't have said that. The fact was, I didn't have time for sleep, even if it was ready to make time for me.

P. T. was already in the hands of the first paramedic team to arrive. She didn't need me, but the medics did, to lead them to the wasted witches and my creator's empty shell.

The morgue wagon was the last to leave, pulling out as Luna slipped below the western horizon and the sun glinted on the eastern one. Doe had called to let me know Kit had made it home and to remind me about Neko's funeral. She and Kit would be the only attendees from the Otherworld community. The bakeneko hadn't made friends beyond the two of them. Despite what she did to survive, Neko had been skittish around others. Humans would have called it shyness. She'd been too feral to trust others easily, even if she'd wanted to fit in as one of the Sukis.

I promised to be there. I was responsible for the lovely, lonely cat's death, after all.

Beelz and I had the entire mansion to ourselves now, and it seemed strange. He was snoring away on his bed in the kitchen, though. I made sure his water bowl was filled and headed for the shower.

The tuxedo wasn't looking its best any longer, but I suppose I wasn't either. Yesterday's jeans and T-shirt would have to suffice. At least no one had attempted to blow me up for thirty-six hours. My once pristine Diesel Wieter jacket had a few burns and tears now, but that simply made it interesting. I lacked a car to leave the estate to find replacement items, anyway.

For that matter, the house lacked anything resembling decent breakfast fixings. I wasn't starving enough to fall back on buffet leftovers. I'd already seen the selection. Hadn't wanted it last night, much less in the light of day.

As it was after eight, I put in a call to Burt. By the time he'd arrived, Beelz was awake. I checked the locks on doors and windows before we headed out. Did a quick check of the office, and found Kit's phone in the topmost drawer of Calista's desk. Next to it sat a pad of paper where Calie had made notes for the next story in the Raven series. Apparently, the evil perpetrator my alter ego would have sent to Hell would have been a succubus.

Which was wrong. So wrong.

Not that Calie had been planning to work in a nasty Otherworlder death or that she had been considering plot options. Not even that she'd made these notes. She had, after all, thought she'd be sitting down at this desk in P. T.'s form today.

No, it was that she wasn't using a crime that had already been committed.

Yeah, I'd considered the idea that she had been instrumental in the deaths I'd been investigating, but kept coming back to the same question: Why bother? She didn't *need* to use a real crime, it was just convenient to do so. Neither she nor any of the other coven members had a reason—a motive—for killing any of the victims. But someone, somewhere, did. *Who* was the question; well, that and *why*. Would the answer be found when I tracked down Durkin's ghoul?

For twenty books, Calie had taken whispers about deaths among the nonhumans and turned them to her own uses. These notes were nothing more than ideas she'd have to work with, lacking a previous death to use. Kit wasn't dead, and though Neko was, she hadn't been a succubus. The bakeneko had been born a cat. Demonization came later.

I needed to identify another thing all the cases had in common. A person the victims might all have known or interacted with.

I didn't realize I'd settled into the desk chair to think until Burt leaned on the horn to remind me he and Beelz had the motor running and the meter ticking away.

Rather than leave Calie's notes where they might be found and taken by one of the witches—I had no idea who might have keys to the mansion—I tore the sheet from the pad and folded it away in a front pocket. Kit's phone left the house with me, too.

"Where to, boss?" Burt asked when I slipped into the shotgun position next to him.

"Breakfast, Target, then a florist," I said. "If you're available to be at my beck and call for a few days, I'll skip the car rental agency, but if you've got better places to be..."

Seems he didn't. We peeled out.

They were beginning to recognize me at the restaurant. "What would you like with your bacon today?" the waitress asked. "Besides the side of sausage to go, that is."

I was going to need all the energy I could get. "Something that will soak up a hell of a lot of syrup," I said. She brought me a clone of the Leaning Tower of Pancakes I'd enjoyed days before, and a full pot of coffee—the nice strong caffeinated type.

To ward off scurvy, I had a glass of orange juice, too. Never can be too careful, right?

"Since a funeral home isn't on the list today, I take it your aunt had preplanned her final services?" Burt said, stirring three packets of pink stuff and two half-shots of cream into his decaffeinated cuppa joe.

"Ah..." My mind was a blank. "No idea, but then I'm fairly new on the scene. Her friends probably know. How'd you know she headed to the big bookstore in the sky?"

Or, in Calie's case, the hot seat in Daddy Dearest's lowest circle of Hell.

"It was on the morning news. Didn't you see it?"

I'd talked a lot about the barely twenty-four-inch screen of the set in my room, had slavered over Kit's giant wall-mounted version, but I'd yet to actually turn a television on. Not in any of the twenty Raven Tales, not in reality. I had caught those few minutes of a sports show at the bar with Samael, but that was the extent of my viewing history.

"Nope. There was too much going on last night. The fact that her passing would be breaking news in Detroit went right over my head."

Burt made a noise that sounded a lot like Beelz when he found my activities odd. Odd by whose standards, though? "Well, you did mention the florist."

I had. "I've another funeral to attend this afternoon. One of Kit's coworkers. Beelz found Kit, by the way. She was practically under our noses."

"She all right?"

"Far as I know." Didn't sound too lover-like, did it? "She needed rest, so I didn't pester her."

Instead, I pestered her while we were on the road to restocking my closet.

"Hey," I said when she answered her home phone. Brilliant conversationalist, that's me. "You suffering any aftereffects from your adventure?"

"Other than a desire to suck down a dozen football players' life lights? I'll be fine once the hunger is appeased," she said, making me very glad I hadn't a speakerphone feature. Burt didn't need any hints about her true nature.

"You rescue the sacrificial victim?" Kit asked.

"Amazingly, yes."

Kit chuckled. "Don't sound so surprised. You're The Raven, after all."

I wished people would stop telling me that.

Wished I knew what the heck I was now.

"I found your cell, and Burt's back on duty today," I said. "You need us to pick you or Doe up before we head to St. Romaric's?"

"We'll meet you there. Doe's giving her First Nations contact hell. Hopefully we'll know more about Drow Stowe when we see you. Anything else you need?"

"For you to have pigged out at lunch?" I suggested.

"Not sure whether you've become a real boy, but don't want to tempt me if you have, huh?"

"I'd rather tempt you in other ways."

She gave her delightful, short, foxlike bark of laughter, then told me to give her love to Beelzie and cut the connection as Burt pulled the cab into the Target parking lot.

My purchases were meager; I was quickly denuding their shelves of my size and color preference, apparently. Could be we'd need to swing by Walmart on the way home to give their shelves the locust treatment, too. In bright daylight, the Diesel Wieter looked a bit like a reject from a charity shop. Considering I didn't know whether I'd have access to Calie's bank account to restock my own, replacing it would have to wait. Frugality needed to reign. The Raven had frequently scrimped between cases. This version of me could, too.

Of course, if there were to be any further cases, I needed to solve the pesky one Doe had given me first. Durkin's, too.

I fished the sheet with Calie's story notes from my jeans pocket and smoothed it down on my knee, blank side up.

"You got a pencil or pen?" I asked Burt.

"The things you expect me to supply," he grumbled, then indicated that I should rifle the glove compartment. Buried in the back, I found a short pencil that looked like it had begun life noting down golf scores. While I wasn't playing a course, the pencil alone supplied a handicap, since it was in desperate need of sharpening. I made do.

There were many similarities tying the murders of the various Otherworlders together.

Number one was me, at least the *me* that was featured in The Raven Tales, where I tracked down and meted out vigilante justice to a being of the same genus, though not personal history or crime.

Number two was that they had all lived in, or worked in or close to, the boundaries of the same neighborhood. They might all have met the same local merchants, neighbors, trash collectors, mail carriers, or other assorted persons.

Number three was that their friends and relatives had all contacted the Fontaine Funeral Home and arranged for burial in the nearly forgotten St. Romaric Cemetery.

Number four was that, of the nonhuman deaths I'd been asking about, only Rolph Lund had not been a quiet, gentle soul. But then, Rolph was a troll, and quiet and gentle were foreign elements to the makeup of the species. He had been killed while out for a night of fun, dancing with women susceptible to his brand of charm. They might have considered him a really sweet guy. I didn't know. I hadn't stumbled across any of his possible girlfriends to talk to. For what it was worth, I was going to give Rolph the benefit of a lot of doubts and say he fit the profile.

Which left the question wide open of why each of these beings had been killed and of the identity of their killer or killers.

And yet...

No, it was gone. That tantalizing link that I hadn't nailed down. Damn.

While I cogitated, Burt had wound his way to the florist I'd patronized a few days earlier in picking up posies for P. T.

Before climbing out of the car, I turned to glance back at Beelz. Rather than lounging across the entire seat, he was on his haunches next to the driver's side rear door, nose raised to catch every scent that wafted in through Burt's rolled-down window.

"You want your name on the card?" I asked.

The hellhound bared his teeth. A deep growl rolled from his chest.

"No, huh?" Well, Neko had been a cat. He was a fox-loving hound. "Be right back."

"Take your time," Burt urged. Well, the meter *was* running.

The scents in the shop were a bombardment to someone still fairly new to this world. Some of them were perfumy, probably the flowers, but others were of damp, of soil, of some sort of treatment that wasn't Mother Nature's idea of fertilizer.

It also smelled of females. One of whom ghosted into the shop proper from a back room before the bell at the door had resumed its rest.

"Mr. Farrell, isn't it?" she asked.

Remembered my credit card. No, wait, I'd paid cash that day, hadn't I? She'd culled it from the card I'd scribbled out? This was not a time to have a memory breakdown. And if I was having one, was it the result of too many things on my mind or a sign that with Calie gone I was deteriorating on this plane?

"How can we help you today? Still in the doghouse with that special lady?"

For all I knew, I probably was, but considering I had no idea of where P. T. lived, I couldn't request a delivery to apologize for seeing her naked when I saved her life.

"No, today it's a funeral, I'm afraid. I need something special. Something that doesn't look like it would drape a horse's neck after a high-stakes race. Something appropriate to the dearly departed. You wouldn't happen to have any catnip plants, would you?"

She didn't bat an eye. "An extreme cat fancier, were they?"

More of a cat that men took a fancy to, I thought, but I agreed aloud that such was the case.

"We don't have catnip, but I'm sure we can find or create something to fit the requirements," she assured me. "When and where is the showing?"

"No showing, and the burial is this afternoon at two."

She chewed on a corner of her bottom lip. "That's very short notice. Do you want a live plant that the family can take home with them?"

"Seasonal and capable of surviving a few nights out of doors," I said. "We can fall back on a pot of mums, if necessary."

"And look like you stopped at the supermarket or garden section of a hardware store? I think not. If you'll trust me, I'll put something together and call you when it's ready. Would that suit?" She tilted her head to one side, waiting for my answer.

I fished in my pocket for a business card with my cell phone number prominently displayed.

"It would suit very well," I said, and handed the card over. "Here's the number. The cemetery isn't far from here. Won't need the flowers until, say, thirty minutes before the service."

"A suitable tribute will be ready well before then. Thank you for using our service again, Mr. Farrell," she said and whisked herself into the back room.

I let myself out. That was how many business cards gone of the original 250? Barely a dent in the box. I'd have to obliterate the dead office address and start distributing more. So far, the flower shop had one, and I'd handed others out to Durkin and to the Albino Wookiee's agents. That one I remembered clearly, since I'd managed to set it on fire with a thought. Otherwise, I'd given them to Pavan Banerjee's minister friend, the guy at the Grab It Quik—who'd probably put it in file thirteen—Farha Banerjee's employer, and Farha herself. In fact, I rather thought I'd given Farha two of them, since she'd looked more prepared to shred the first one than save it.

Whoever wired my office to blow up had had one of those cards. The cards were the only way anyone knew where to find me when I wasn't holed up at Calie's well-secured estate. I hadn't been holed up there or at the office very often, either.

Ergo, the list of possible perpetrators who had it in for me personally narrowed down significantly. If I hadn't been distracted with Calie's demands and a total of twenty cold cases clambering for solutions, I would have made the connection before.

At least I hoped I would have. Raven, after all.

That's when the muse link in my brain rang a bell and pointed out something else I'd missed.

An awful lot of my business cards had gone to people connected to Pavan Banerjee.

I walked over to the cab, placed my hands on the roof, and smacked my head against it a couple times.

"Feel better now, or should I book an appointment with the body shop in anticipation of more dents?" Burt asked as I slid back into the shotgun seat.

"Remains to be seen," I said, as my cell phone rang.

"I've got some bad news," Doe said, not bothering with a greeting.

"Bad news in what way?" I hedged.

"I heard back from First Nations. It took them a while to track down someone who remembered Woodrow Stowe, because he was never an official member of any of the tribes."

"Does that mean he wasn't a Native American at all? Was he pretend Canadian, too?"

"He had trace blood to a tribal family where the last member died over twenty years ago," Doe explained. "Oddly enough, Stowe was accused of murdering his possible relative and took off never to be seen again."

So much for that trail, but perhaps it wasn't entirely dead.

"Was there any mention made that he was interested in... umm..." I stumbled for something that wouldn't insult her or freak Burt out, since he could hear my end of the conversation. I settled for something so bland it was embarrassing. "Er... unusual things?"

Doe accepted the classification. "Other than tribal ones?" she asked.

Every tribe had a Deer Woman spirit or another of similar ilk in its pantheon. She was probably the closest demon type to European ones, but there were skinwalkers, wendigos, and others who were unique to the New World.

"Oddly enough, I asked that question of the contact myself," she said. "The answer was yes. He was fixated on them, particularly the Skadegamutc, although it is a creature of the Wabanaki, who lived in modern-day New England, not in the Northwest Territories."

I'd nearly forgotten about that nasty bugger. If any North American paranormal deserved to be taken down by The Raven, it was the Skadegamutc. When human, it was an evil sorcerer. Not exactly a school crossing guard sort of guy. But once the sorcerer died the shit really hit the communal barbecue pit, because the Skadegamutc rose at night to feast on the flesh of the living. Considered a ghost-witch, it can only be killed with fire.

Might sound a lot like a zombie, just one with a better human background, but the Skadegamutc was probably the closest Drow Stowe could come to finding a vampire of local origin. The European model was far more prolific. There were a limited number of evil sorcerers to morph into nasty creatures of the night. But European-style vampires? Ah, those were the prolific boys and girls of the para world.

"Stowe drifts into the tribe claiming kinship to someone, kills them for some reason, and takes off, landing in Detroit, where he finds the one thing on his Christmas list," I summarized for myself. "And after achieving it, he rethinks things and kills again, then disappears."

"Completely disappears," Doe agreed, "which I find odd, considering he doesn't appear to have been intelligent enough to pull that off. Becoming a vampire doesn't make a person more clever. In fact, I would have expected him to be staked within a short time, based on his human past."

I totally agreed with that.

"There's only one way I know of disappearing without a trace," I said.

"Getting murdered and buried," Doe said. "It helps when there isn't anyone interested enough to ask questions."

"Stowe isn't on the list, and he didn't surface as a model for a character in any of Calie's books. We're asking questions twenty years too late." Geez, I was really beginning to hate when that happened. "I wonder if he had a record with the police department before he was turned."

"Maybe you should ask your new pig friend," she suggested.

"Durkin's not a pig. I haven't spotted a single gravy stain on his tie yet. But I'll give him a call."

Reminding me once more about Neko's funeral—like I'd forget it!—Doe rang off. She'd fulfilled her promise to harangue First Nations. It was time for me to earn my fictional reputation for solving puzzles now.

"Where to next?" Burt asked.

I'd no idea. "Find a park so Beelz can shake a leg. Hopefully I'll come up with something by the time he's ready to roll again."

So, while Burt wove a mysterious path through the streets, I fished out Durkin's cell number. He barked his name, rather than a greeting, when he answered. I barked back.

"Farrell. Any intel on what caused the explosion at the office?"

"Intel? What kind of shows are you watching on the tube? And it's police business, not something for a vigilante to poke his nose into," he said.

"It was my hide that was scheduled for recycling," I insisted. "Plus, we both know I'm saving the taxpayers money here by freeing you up to concentrate on more mundane crimes. I think it's related to what I'm working on."

He sighed, looking for—and falling far short of—Academy notice for his performance in a supporting character role. "Okay, yeah, we have a few leads. It was a small device and homemade, but by someone who knew what they were doing. We even got a partial print but haven't been able to identify it yet."

"It's not in the system?"

"It could be in the system and not surfacing yet," he snarled. "What part of budget cuts do you not understand? You civilians always think things roll along as quickly in real life as they do in a cop show."

Sad that fiction is far more efficient, isn't it?

"And if I could narrow your search down, what would it be worth to you?" I asked.

"Don't bargain with me, Farrell. If you know something..."

I didn't, but there was a glimmer of an idea that I doubted originated with Calie's now out-of-work muse, though he had been helpful in giving me a nudge. I owed him a six-pack from the microbrewery of his choice. His shadowy form gave me a high five and ducked back into the annex office he kept in my mind. He returned to what looked suspiciously like a game of Angry Birds.

"On the off chance that he's still around, run Woodrow, a.k.a. Drow, Stowe through the system. He might be Canadian, but I won't swear to it. Also see if there is a Timothy Halston among any military records. Look specifically for any bomb disposal training," I said. "And then see if there are any prints on record for Farha Banerjee, who emigrated from India in the late 1980s or early 1990s. I don't know whether she ever became a citizen, has a green card, or is in the country illegally. Both Halston and Banerjee are in their mid to late fifties, but I'm guessing."

"And why didn't you mention them when we talked before?" Durkin demanded.

"Because it didn't occur to me that two of them were anything other than victims before."

"I'll put someone on it," he promised. "I suppose you want to know the results?"

"Damn right," I growled. "I also want to know if you found the vehicle that played demolition derby with me the other night."

Durkin grunted. "Yeah. It was abandoned a couple blocks away. Stolen and wiped clean of prints. You think the same perps were involved in both attempts, don't you?"

"Perps!" I repeated. "Now who's been watching too much television?"

Then I rang off. His final question didn't really require an answer.

Burt had brought a newspaper along to read while he waited for me. Yeah, I know. Really old school of him, right? He was content to study the sports page while Beelz and I communed with nature. I found a sturdy tree to stretch out beneath, my back to the trunk, and the demon mutt reconsidered marking it as his own, though I could see there was regret in his eyes. He really liked the tree.

"It makes sense, doesn't it?" I demanded of him. "Only Farha and Halston knew where the office was, and there were two people in that ramming machine. I saw Farha at the cemetery and while I thought she didn't see me, I was probably wrong. I was driving the Mustang, which means she could have hung around to see what sort of transportation I was using. All they had to do was wait for me to show up at the Sukis' corner to see Kit. Because they didn't know one sexy demon from another, they thought Neko was our favorite fox. All they had to do then was follow us until an opportunity to do some damage presented itself. That sound feasible to you?"

Beelz rolled over in the grass, exposing his undercarriage to all and sundry, and did the dachshund version of a contortionist act, enjoying the feel of the grass against his back. I took it for a yes.

"Okay, then. We're in agreement. Halston and Farha also knew where the office was. That means they've tried to kill me twice and haven't succeeded yet. Or that was the plan, and at least one of them has begun to lose or rethink that hating feeling. Why do I say that?"

Completing his wiggling, Beelz righted himself and checked out various body parts that he felt needed attention.

"Dude!" I groaned. "We're in public!"

In apparent apology, he attempted to lick my hand. I moved it away quickly. "Don't. I know where that tongue's been. Let's get back to the case at hand, hmm? Two attempts, but on the second one, I got coshed and then pulled to relative safety, while the other hijacker did the opposite for Neko. I can see Halston not wanting to kill me, if it's even possible, short of feeding millions of copies of Raven books into a shredder. He's been a man of the cloth for decades. But if he's also the dude who rigged the office... well, maybe he was detached from that because it was unlikely that anyone but me would be there late at night. The car thing was different. He had to deal with me in the flesh. Or whatever."

Beelz yawned and rested his head on my crossed ankles.

"All of this gives us a possible means and opportunity but zilch on motive. I mean, I've been attempting to solve Pavan's murder. Has Farha been prickly over that because it wasn't only Pavan who died that night, but Drow Stowe, too? Stowe could have killed Pavan, and while he was distracted doing that, Farha or Halston might have had an opportunity to stake Drow. A vamp normally could easily overcome a human, even more than one human, hence something had to give them the advantage. And if it played out that way, the reason they are trying to stop the investigation is that they fear retribution by other vampires."

The hellhound turned his red eyes my way and murmured something that sounded like a question. I got the gist of his comment.

"You're right," I said. "Even if all that is on the nose, it doesn't explain the deaths of all the other nonhumans. Damn."

Beelz and I sighed in unison. What was I missing?

A few minutes later, Burt strolled across the leaf-coated carpet of green.

"It's after one," he announced.

Beelz hopped to his feet. My own journey upright lagged behind him a bit.

"Time to head back to the florist, then on to St. Romaric's. You think there's time to swing by a drive-thru window on the way?"

"More than enough," Burt said. Moments later, we were back on the road.

The florist called just as the food was being handed out to us. Beelz had a double patty, hold the bun and condiments. Burt and I went for doubles with all the condiments, plus cheese and bacon. If I was in the act of fading away, I was going to go out with a satisfied smile on my face.

Doe and Kit were already at the cemetery, waiting for us at the entry gate. I nearly didn't recognize Deer Woman. I'd only seen her decked out in Suki trawling duds. Today she resembled a back-to-nature hippy, with a suede-fringed buckskin jacket and a white open-collared shirt shoved into black denim jeans. She still wore the tall boots that hid the hooves she had in place of feet. Her hair lacked the pastel streaks and was hooked behind ears featuring quail feather earrings.

Kit wore dark jeans too, but the rest of her outfit was shades of rust, from the tall oxblood riding boots to the burnt orange scoop necked tee and matching corduroy jacket. Her hair was in the familiar, swaying, fox-toned ponytail.

Neither of the Sukis had added makeup to enhance their seductive pseudo human faces, but the occasion was a solemn one. I understood.

As I always wore black, I looked funereal to begin with. So did Beelz, who hopped out of the cab on my heels.

"What lovely flowers," Kit murmured, drawing near to nearly dip her nose into one of the blossoms as she inhaled deeply. "I think Neko would approve of them."

Doe was carrying a cat-sized wooden box of simple construction. She handed it to Kit and bent down to give Beelzie's coat a rub. He didn't look appreciative, but then Kit was his favorite.

"No new vehicle, Raven?" she asked.

"Waiting for the insurance to pay out, though whether they'll immediately cancel my policy or not is a bit of a mystery." Always a chance I'd never get insurance to cover me again. I had called to report a vehicle immolation within thirty hours of picking the car up at the dealership, after all.

"Fortunately," I added, "it looks like finding the two responsible for killing Neko and my car is well on its way to happening. And there's a good chance they are the ones responsible for the deaths of the other Otherworlders on your list. But that's something to deal with after Neko's burial."

"It is good news, though," Doe said, standing up again and taking the bakeneko's remains back from Kit. She'd always been the alpha doxie of the three. I supposed she felt responsible for their lost member. I certainly did, even though Neko's death had been inadvertent—wrong place, wrong time.

"Why don't we all share an early dinner afterward?" Doe suggested. "Toast Neko's memory? And then you can tell us all about what you've discovered. We'll see that you get home. My car is just over there."

She gestured to where a very nice, late model Jeep Wrangler Sahara, dune-colored, with black removable back cover and tires that clearly said *off road* rather than *city driving*, was parked. Being a Suki paid well, if Kit's condo and Doe's car were good indications.

I bent down to the cab's window.

"You're off duty, pal," I said to Burt. "The ladies will get Beelz and me where we need to be after this."

Personally, I was hoping Kit would invite us back to her place.

He saluted. "Just give me a call when you need. I'll swing by the estate and drop off the stuff you bought. There's a couple nice bushes near the rear door to hide it all behind."

I returned his salute and promised to buy breakfast the following morning. As usual.

Once he pulled off, the four of us slipped past the battered gate onto the St. Romaric's property. Neko's plot was toward the back, which wasn't surprising, as most of the other Otherworlders were buried in that quarter. Since that section was situated behind several ancient mausoleums, we were soon hidden from the road, not that there was a lot of traffic along it in any case, but the sounds of the city gave way to those of nature at the grave site. It was a peaceful area which seemed appropriate for a Japanese demon, particularly when what had happened to Neko was taken into consideration.

I was sure Durkin would soon have enough evidence to arrest, if not convict, Farha Banerjee and Timothy Halston for attempted murder (mine) and destruction of property. With luck, Durkin's werewolf and vamp associates could be included in the interrogation and scare one or the other of the humans into a confession on the other deaths, too. Halston would fold. Farha, fueled by grief and revenge as well as fear, might take longer, but the end would be the same.

Though why either of them had declared war on the nonhuman community was puzzling. That they had homed in on the less violent members made sense: Mere humans had little chance against a turned beast, a demon being, or any of the legendary types. They were all powerful predators, particularly when riled. And yet it still didn't seem logically possible for humans to overpower and butcher any nonhuman without the help of magic. I'd interviewed plenty of humans on this case, but other than Rolph Lund's brother and sister and the vampires, the Sukis were the only other magic wielders I'd talked to.

Nearby was the Smart Car of excavation equipment. With barely enough room for a single operator within the cab, one side carried a long-armed claw to dig a grave while the other had the broad scoop to push soil back in place over the dearly departed. A groundskeeper lounged against the cab, earbuds in, head bobbing as he texted on his cell. Just leaning against the machine, whiling away the time until he had to finish his job.

Despite the size of the box holding Neko, which probably looked like a poor man's cremation urn, the standard six-by-six-by-three hole had been dug. We all stopped short of the edge. Beelz went right up to the drop-off and stuck his nose over the side, checking it out.

Doe set the box on the ground. Idly, I wondered how it was going to be lowered to the floor of the pit. Kit looked into the distance, past the waiting backhoe, to where a small copse of trees had managed to survive residential expansion in the more prosperous past.

"Do we each say a few words, or does each species have its own traditions?" I asked.

"I've no idea," Deer Woman said.

And then she kicked the box into the grave.

I was still startled over that action when she gave me a push that sent me lurching forward, floral tribute still in hand, to tumble into the hole after Neko. My landing on the box caused the thin wood to buckle and sent a spike of pain driving into my knee. The flowers didn't hold up well, either.

Beelz instantly morphed into Great Dane form, but Kit was ready for the transformation. She encased him and the waiting workman in a time bubble, holding them in stasis while she and Doe still moved freely.

That didn't bode well for me, did it?

It kicked the last part of the puzzle into place though. I was a sap. No, that wasn't the puzzle piece, just the element that kept me from solving the damn mystery in the first place. Calie had figured it out, though, and been preparing to begin writing the story before the *demons* were dispatched in the real world, preferably by me. Such high standards she'd had for her paper creation. But I'd flubbed it.

There is one truth I should have remembered. Demons lie, and they do it damn well.

Where had I gotten all the information on murders of the twenty Otherworld beings? Not from The Raven Tales. From Doe, who *was* a demon.

Who could overpower a magic or power-pumped nonhuman? Another magic or power-pumped nonhuman, particularly one that was, yeah, *a demon*. One like Kit, with time-warping capabilities, would have no trouble freeze-framing a victim for easy dispatching.

And what if these demons were succubi? Or more succinctly, *my* friendly neighborhood succubi?

Sap pretty well sums things up, doesn't it? And I'd soon be a dead sap.

Attempting to ignore the throbbing pain in my knee, I used the perfect ninety-degree angle of the grave wall to push back to my feet.

"Surprised, Raven?" Doe smirked. "Not as surprised as we are over how easy you are to best."

Next to her, Kit chuckled. "I quite enjoyed testing your abilities," she said. "Finding you were more focused on whether you were human or not, or had a future, was very amusing."

Realizing my mouth was hanging open in disbelief, I snapped it shut.

"I can't believe it was all a sham," I said.

The smile she gave me held none of its previous warmth. "What part of a succubus's nature do you not understand, Raven? It's what I do to survive. I deceive, I seduce. I kill."

Doe exchanged a grin with Kit. "We particularly enjoy the kill part."

And they weren't choosy on who they killed, either, I'll bet.

Anyone brave enough to be standing near could have heard my jaw clench.

Note to self should I survive: *Don't believe everything anyone tells you this side of the line.* Calie had lied to me, and so had Deer Woman and the kitsune. All three of them had led me on: Calie in making me believe she wasn't long for this world and needed another writer to continue the series, the Sukis in conning me into believing modern Otherworlders were cutting back on the nastier of their legendary habits. They'd pandered to my need to prove there was still Ravenness in me, too.

Bram Farrell, perfect sucker.

"Farha Banerjee and Halston are innocent of the deaths of the nonhumans, aren't they?" I said.

"Oh, not entirely," Kit answered. "They did kill Drow Stowe for turning Pavan Banerjee, and then slaughtered Neko for some reason. Doe and I simply decided to do further cleansing of the community, removing those who were embarrassments, traitors to their true natures."

It wasn't easy to carry on a conversation when there was every chance that the excavation toy would be refilling the grave with me still in it. Particularly with the pit nearly as deep as I was tall. The two Sukis loomed over me, my time-trapped hellhound just feet away from them. I wondered if, when they released him, he'd dig me back up. If there would be anything left worth resurrecting.

"Otherworlders who don't measure up to your standards deserve death?" I demanded, staring up at them.

"Yes," Doe said baldly. "Oh, we kept Neko clueless about our hobby. She was weak. The fact that Stowe's killers managed such a swift kill on him shows that he was, too. Predators thin out the weak members of species. Neko's death is simply a weeding of her race's defective members. If it had been Kit in the car, neither of the humans would have survived the attempt to kill her."

That I could believe. I'd seen her in action against Hammer's boys, in the ring at Binky's, and up against a vampire, after all.

"Unfortunately, your witch mother interfered, thinking that having me in her control would keep you in line," Kit added.

"She still managed to capture you and keep you prisoner," I pointed out. Even sounded proud of Calie's accomplishment when I said it, too. It was a hell of a thing to pull off now that I knew Kit's killer teeth hadn't been drawn.

"Yes, she tricked me, sending in hormone-happy humans as a distraction. Because I didn't scent any magic on them, the spell she cast took me by surprise. I wanted to suck the souls out of everyone in that glade, but Samael was watching, and he'd been the one to lift the curse that held me."

225

Damned if I wasn't beginning to like the Devil himself more by the minute. Now, if he'd just show up to kick some Suki butt...

It wasn't going to happen. If I survived, it was going to have to be through my own talents. Of which there were few, in the real world.

"Not exactly a good way to keep a low profile," I said. "And even if you are killing some of your marks, you don't kill all of them, which seems to indicate stealth is still important to you. If so, why wind me up to investigate twenty deaths? Sooner or later I'd have found evidence of your involvement."

You'd have thought I'd become an A-list standup comedian, the way they laughed.

"What evidence, Raven? Those deaths all happened long ago, and there were no questions asked at the time, not even by the humans these subpar creatures walked among. They deserved to die for abandoning their true natures."

"Even Tado Gallo?" I asked. "He was one of your own kind."

"Who fancied himself in love with a human and planned to marry her," Doe answered, disgust clear in her voice.

"Then why kill me?"

"Because while you are far from your fictional self, The Raven never lets go of a case until it is solved. That part of you hasn't changed. It wouldn't take evidence on old crimes to pin things on us. Humans are handicapped against us, but the Otherworld community can be vicious when riled. If the deaths Calista borrowed for your adventures couldn't be proved, you would simply find new crimes to pin on us, even if the deaths were those of useless humans."

Deer Woman was right about that. I was worse than a terrier in a ratting pit. Calie had crafted me that way. I doubted the rest of the nonhuman residents of Detroit would be keen to have their existence unveiled by an investigation of human kills, though.

"I'll be missed," I said.

"By a bunch of witches, most of whom you don't even know by name? By a cabdriver? By a DPD dick? If any of them begin asking too many questions, we'll supply the one-way ticket to Hell. Could be you'll already be there, keeping Calista company.

"Actually, we were going to let you bumble around a bit longer..."

Bumble!

"…but when you mentioned Sol Prisk, we knew it was time to eliminate you, too. Since you'll simply disappear, we won't even have to call him in to help us get rid of you."

"He's the one who staged the other deaths?"

"He knew how to kill Otherworlders. And these had to die, because they'd each seen us getting rid of human meals with his help."

Ah, a clichéd explanation by the killer. Calie would have loved it.

Kit grinned at the memory, then tossed her head. "I've got better things to do. Let's finish this, Doe."

Deer Woman nodded in agreement.

"It is time for a late lunch," she said, "and we know that Bram is only good for use as a napkin. Paper boys are very biodegradable, though. Good for the Earth."

That's what I was afraid of.

Kit strode over to the baby earthmover, pushed the time-frozen maintenance dude out of the way, and climbed into the cab. It coughed to life and rotated on oversized tires, unaffected by the freeze-frame bubble now that it had a driver wearing a spell-canceling amulet. She aimed the machine toward the pile of dirt waiting to be replaced in the grave.

Doe stepped back a few yards to be out of the way and waved the fox in for the kill. Even from the confines of the hole, I could see Kit's lips curved in anticipation of pleasure.

Obviously, I have lousy taste in my choice of paramours.

With both Sukis no longer hovering at the edge of the pit, I attempted to get a purchase to pull myself free. Ground crumbled away beneath my hands at the upper edge. The grave resisted having a toehold kicked into its wall.

If only I had something to stand on, to lift me into a better position.

When a set of three narrow steps formed at the opposite end of the grave from where Doe stood, you could have blown me over with a faint cough. Half a breath later, I was scrambling up them and hoisting myself over the lip of the grave. The steps melted away immediately. I didn't know if someone was helping me or if magic was once more working for me, but damn, was I ever grateful.

Deer Woman cried out a warning to Kit.

I spun and growled at the Native demon. "I don't like being lied to or used, Doe."

She sprang forward, hands morphing into vicious-looking hooves. In reflex, I went into fiction mode, swiftly raising my arm, hand upright as though to block her attack or stall her out with a flare of counter-magic. Maybe I'd be lucky and that invisible shield would morph into being.

It didn't. Instead, Doe flew backward, slamming against a large chunk of granite with a cherub reclining along the top. Not a real cherub, a stone one. A real one would have been majorly ticked off.

"Damn!" I murmured, impressed by the power I'd just wielded. It reminded me of the blast Calie had tossed to put me in my place.

There wasn't time to muse about it, though. Kit had the earthmover in gear and was barreling down on where I stood, still too close to the edge of the grave to feel safe.

"You're dead, Raven!" she screamed at me, and went full throttle.

I threw my hand out again but the weight of the mini digger was too much for my limited blast of whatever it was I was blasting. There was murder in Kit's eyes. I could read it there even at a distance.

Kit glanced back to where the maintenance guy had tumbled, and those long-lashed orbs narrowed in evil intent. She let the time bubble drop away, allowing her clear access to the power she craved. I could feel the pull she gave his life force. It was enough to buck his body.

"Not on my watch, babe," I growled and raised my hand again.

As though the words were a dare, she pulled on the hapless human once more.

I blasted her. The flame I'd managed to manifest when irked at the talent agents was amped up to blast furnace intensity by my fury. My flame hit the miniature construction vehicle, singeing the paint job and melting the tires. The edge of the shovel glowed red-gold, as though newly pulled from a forge.

Kit bailed out. Ran at me.

From the corner of my eye, I saw movement. Two movements. Deer Woman was back on her feet making a beeline toward me, determined to do some serious hoof damage.

228

But Beelz was free of the bubble, too. In Great Dane form, he was much quicker off the mark than a dachshund could ever be. He crashed into Kit, his jaws wide, his teeth ready to savage her.

I left him to his self-appointed job and barreled toward Deer Woman, tossing another blast of force to slow her down. She was changing into deer form, adding bulk and weight to run me down, trample me. I took her booted feet out from beneath her before they'd transformed and then added a pushing burst of air as she went by, sending her into the freshly dug pit. She finished morphing into a four-hooved creature as she fell.

The cry the succubus made was more animal than human. One of her front legs was angled unnaturally when she landed atop Neko's remains and my thoughtful posies. She'd probably broken bones in the fall. Unless she could return to human form, the deer was firmly trapped. There isn't much room for a full-grown slab of venison to maneuver in a measly six-by-six-by-three hole.

Beelz had finished with his chew toy and, as though he'd read my mind, dragged Kit's either dead or dying body to the grave and dropped it in. As she tumbled, the succubus's human form was replaced by that of a bloodied fox. It fell atop Deer Woman's crying, crippled animal form.

Leaving the hellhound to watch over the two demons, I checked the maintenance guy. His pulse was weak, but he was still alive. He'd feel weak but he'd recover. There were a couple things I needed to do before calling 911 for him, though.

First one was to do what The Raven was best known for: visiting justice on the well-deserving. I walked back to the graveside and funneled the heat of Hell into it, burning the Sukis' bodies to a crisp.

Damn. While I'd been doubting it for days, it turned out I still *was* The Raven, the vicious freakin' bane of reality-walking demons.

Beelz looked at me, his Great Dane head turned to indicate curiosity as the scent of sulfur and brimstone tainted the air of the forgotten churchyard.

"Yeah, weird, isn't it? In the books, I couldn't generate hellfire, but now I can. Think I inherited it from Calie when I got between her and a new vessel?"

The sound of a throat being cleared sent me spinning toward the nearest mausoleum, hand up to deliver one of my newfound magical searings. But the being leaning against the weathered stone did nothing more than smirk at me as he saluted and then vanished.

Well, I knew where the hellfire came from now. Apparently, Samael had given me a belated birthday present when he'd sent that spear of heat through my veins at Calie's leave-taking. He'd probably done it just for the amusement of seeing the stunned expression on my face upon recognizing its manifestation.

Beelz shrugged, indicating he didn't know what his boss was up to either. He didn't revert to wiener size until after I'd used the earthmover to totally fill the grave once more, though.

I called Durkin when the last bit of dirt had been pounded down over Doe, Kit, and Neko. The conversation was short, but he promised to deliver what I needed. When he arrived, he helped pour the gallons of holy water I'd requested over the repacked earth. He even added a touch of his own, burying a silver crucifix in the center of the dirt. Wasn't sure myself that it would do any good, but what the heck.

"I read one of your adventures," he said.

"You mean the stories Calista wrote about a guy with my name," I corrected.

He looked at the new grave. "No, I think The Raven is part of this world, not a fictional world. Just watch the vigilante stuff, huh, Farrell? Keep an eye out for Prisk, and keep me in the loop."

When he offered his hand, I shook it. Then I called 911 to take care of the maintenance guy.

I hotwired Doe's Jeep to leave the scene once the ambulance pulled away, taking the still-woozy gravedigger to the hospital to check him out more thoroughly. I'd claimed to be just a passing stranger who'd been walking the dog and enjoying the day when I'd stumbled onto the scene. Beelz pretended to be sleeping so his red eyes wouldn't draw the medics' attention.

Fortunately for us, the Jeep wasn't locked. The key, however, was buried where I had no intention of going to look for it. Between the hellfire, the holy water-soaked ground, and the cross, I just hoped all the bases were covered and that neither Deer Woman nor the kitsune would be troubling Detroit again. Oh, there would be other versions of them around, but the corner they worked was now open real estate for either human doxies or a new set of demon ones. I hoped it would be the former rather than the latter.

Instead of looking for a restaurant to recharge both Beelz and myself, I stopped at a supermarket and bought a couple steaks: one for me, one for him. There was a deli section, so I added potato salad as a vegetable.

There were quite a few vehicles parked along the drive at the estate when I got home, but the coven members gathered around the kitchen table chowing down on the leftovers of P. T.'s last culinary effort for Calie were not only happy to see me, one of them offered to broil the steak for me. Which, I figured, saved it from being burned to a crisp. My fictional self could only cook well-done demons. Well, perhaps my real-world self as well.

While Beelz and I ate, Delia, Neva, Zeta, and the rest filled me in on the funeral arrangements for Calista and how her absence would affect things financially.

"I was leery about the spirit shift thing," said the lawyer among them. Her name escapes me now, but of course it ended with an *a*. "Therefore, I made out two wills and insisted she sign both of them. One left everything to the then-unspecified woman she would become. She was to fill in the name when within the new vessel. The other was to go into effect if the shift wasn't successful. It left everything to you, as her nephew."

"Everything? What exactly does that cover?" I asked before popping another bite of steak into my mouth. It was done to perfection, by the way. I wondered whether the witch who'd fixed it would teach me her secret, for future use.

The lawyer had a list. She cleared a spot in the center of the table to plop it down, then went through it, ticking off each item with a pen as she read it off.

"The building and property of this estate, all furnishings and household goods and vehicles in the garages out back. The funds in all her bank accounts and stock portfolios. All book royalties for all twenty of the Raven books, plus rights to continue the series in whatever manner you wish. She'd already cashed out life insurance policies and banked the money. I'll push the probate through as quickly as possible, but you can begin deciding what to do with things in the meantime."

231

"And in that *meantime,* you won't run short of cash, Bram," Zeta, the banker, assured me. "I moved another hundred thousand from Calista's account into yours before the party yesterday."

"There might be a slight holdup on the insurance payoff on your car," Neva said, apology clear in her voice, "but as it wasn't your fault, as soon as the culprits are found and convicted, the check can be cut. In the meantime, why don't you drive one of Calie's cars?"

"Calie had cars? In the plural?" I was stunned. She'd never offered me a set of keys. I'd thought Burt or a limousine service were her ways to get places.

"Three, I believe," Neva said and looked to Delia for confirmation.

"At last count," my pseudo cousin said.

Earlier, Beelz had sniffed his way over every inch of Doe's Jeep and curled his lip at the thought of getting in, but the promise of food motivated him. He'd condescended, allowing me to hoist him into the shotgun position for the ride home. After the witches left, leaving half a dozen door keys for the mansion behind, Beelz led the way to the garages out back. I had a key to those, too; Delia rifled Calie's desk for a full set. The lock was shiny and new, though the door creaked a bit when I swung it open.

The view inside was breathtaking.

No wonder my creator hadn't appreciated the Mustang. She was sitting on a fortune in classic automobiles. I trailed my fingers along the lines of a 1909 Rolls-Royce Silver Ghost. Admired the workmanship of the 1935 Cadillac Town Cabriolet.

"This is the one we're taking," I told Beelz, and opened the door on the British Racing Green 1969 MGB Roadster for him. Fortunately for us, the tank was full.

I hadn't mentioned my suspicion to Durkin. He had enough on his plate, having brought Farha and Halston in for questioning. As expected, Halston caved about the two attempts on my life. Farha, Durkin told me as we distributed holy water, had gone into hysterics, insisting she had to return home.

The apartment over the dry cleaners was Beelz's and my destination once the sun set.

Luna was totally full yet complacent as she rose that night, causing only werewolves with consciences any problems. But as they'd probably locked themselves up tight, the city was relatively safe. Chances were there were more human predators drifting through the shadows than nonhuman ones, anyway. The Otherworld community was host to many species, but if they added up to 2 percent of the population in the Greater Detroit area, I would be damned surprised.

We were lucky to find a parking place on the street. Fortunately, the MG didn't take up a lot of space. I just hoped it would still be there, all in one piece, when we left. Still, an investigator has to take chances, and this, compared to what I'd been through the past few days, was a minor one.

There were no lights shining from within the tiny upstairs apartment, but I knocked on the door anyway. Polite to a fault, that's me. There was no answer. Not that I'd expected one.

"Farha's been arrested," I said to the door. "She won't be returning."

"And Timothy?" a voice asked through the panel. It was nuanced with a strong dash of outsourced help desk. English, but on the curry side.

"Also arrested."

The sound of locks turning broke the silence that followed. Then the door opened.

Life as a vampire hadn't been good for Pavan Banerjee. He might have been thin before his death. Now he was emaciated.

"Have you eaten?" I asked.

"Farha keeps a vial of blood in the refrigerator for me," he said. "But if she won't be returning, I don't think I'll avail myself of it tonight. You'll be safe, if you'd like to come in. It isn't everyone who arrives with a hellhound to guard them."

He gave the ghost of a smile, as though it was difficult to remember how to smile. Perhaps it was.

"Thank you," I said and stepped inside.

It was a poor place. A ten-by-ten front room crowded with a single bed, a table with an ancient television set, and a well-worn arm chair. Just past it was an even narrower galley kitchen.

Pavan gestured toward another room, farther back.

"They gave me the bedroom, and Farha sleeps out here. She and Timothy ensured that no light would enter my quarters. Between the two of them, they kept me supplied with enough blood to exist. Poor Timothy felt that what happened to me was his fault, and Farha refused to allow me to seek a second death. They didn't understand that my life was over once we three killed the beast who did this to me. I begged them to kill me again for five years before accepting that they would never agree." His smile ghosted into place again. "I believe I'll take the opportunity at hand, though. Would you remain to ensure that I'm successful, Mr. Farrell?"

"You know who I am?"

"Who else would you be? My sole entertainment has been reading. Calista Amberson's stories of your adventures were among my favorites. When I found the business card in my wife's pocket, I realized that The Raven was more than merely a fictional character."

"Sometimes I'm not sure," I confessed. "You can tell that I'm not exactly human, can't you?"

"You're not exactly nonhuman either," he said. "You need only wait until dawn. I'd like to die with the sun being one of the last sights I see. It's been so long."

"I'll stay," I promised.

And when the sun rose, Beelz and I stood in the parking lot of the park Pavan had chosen and watched his body be consumed by flame. He made no sound and even managed to smile for the few moments it took. I swept his ashes up afterward and drove to the river. Out of sight of any authorities who might frown on my actions, I released the remains of Pavan Banerjee into the morning breeze.

I had donuts and designer coffee when I pulled the Roadster to a stop in front of Calie's mansion an hour later. Delia was there ahead of me, sitting on the front steps, a leather briefcase at her feet.

"If I'd known you were coming I'd have..."

"Brought me a cappuccino?"

"Bought more donuts," I said. "What brings you out this early?"

"Unfinished business," she said.

I trusted her with the coffee to free up a hand to unlock the door, but I reclaimed it as she moved into the front hall. She didn't pause, but went straight to Calie's office, where she settled into the comfy chair behind the desk.

Beelz glanced into the room, then trundled off to his usual quarters in the kitchen. Nursing my coffee, I took the stance that was now second nature, shoulder propped against the doorframe, one knee slightly bent. The Raven totally at his ease.

"We need to sort out what to do with the Calista Amberson replacement search." Delia pulled two shiny, red-lacquered cases from her traveling office and pushed them across the surface of the desk toward me.

"Exterior hard drives," she said when I looked at them blankly. "Both filled with submissions from writers wanting to pick up The Raven Tales. Have you any idea how many writing samples and synopses there are?"

Only having a vague idea of how much data was stored on one, much less two, of those things, I hazarded a guess. "Enough for us to be considered a major publishing house?"

"Most likely," she said. "I've had to hire extra staff to read through things. I don't envy them the job. The samples I read were god-awful."

"You want me to read a bunch of god-awful pages, too?" I demanded.

Wished briefly that I'd written down all the things on my mental to-do list so that I could wave it at her. There had been a slew of them adding up. I had to figure out exactly what I could do in the magic department now that I'd produced a few awesome special effects; indulge in television and movie marathons; decide how best to begin disposing of Calista's embarrassingly large number of assets in Detroit, where there was a desperate need for asset sharing; track down the ghoul, Solomon Prisk, and maybe find Durkin's missing persons; find ways to use up the rest of my business cards without using them to light cigars... not that I was fond of cigars, but still...

"Not a very loving chore for a pseudo cousin, Delia," I griped.

"No," she said, and I swear the woman found a way to purr the damn word! She leaned back in the comfy boss chair and favored me with a Cheshire cat sort of smile. "I think *you* should write the next book."

"Me! I wouldn't have the slightest idea of how to spin a story."

"Tell the one you just lived," Delia suggested.

Doing so would probably get me out of reading a host of possibly asinine Raven Tale submissions, right?

Not surprising that I caved and wrote Book 21.

This is it.

Author's Note

About those first twenty books of The Raven Tales... er, they don't exist outside Bram's fictional world. He may give titles for them, but nope, sorry, not a one of them exists. What he calls Book 21 is actually the first Raven Tale, *this* book.

As they often promise at the end of superhero movies, Bram, his dachshundric hellhound, Delia, Burt, Ralph, Ruth, Samael, the theophylaktos dudes, Naomie, Detective Durkin—and Calie!—will return in future volumes of The Raven Tales.

J. B. Dane

About the Author

J.B. Dane is a recovering romance writer with over two dozen published titles under her belt. What she read while writing them was tales of mystery with comedy. If magic was added, it was icing on the cake.

When Bram Farrell walked into her office, she hired him on the spot. Fortunately, he's willing to share the bourbon with her as they kick otherworlders'... er... nether regions together.

Find the two of them with their feet on the desk at:
www.RomanceandMystery2.com/jb-dane.
Twitter @JBDaneWriter and Facebook @BethHendersonAuthor.